The Rainloft Academy

Maci Smithers

5ᵗʰ Corner Media LLC.

Perrysburg, Ohio

Contents

This book is dedicated to Sam, Bartlet and Arlo,
the best dogs in the world.

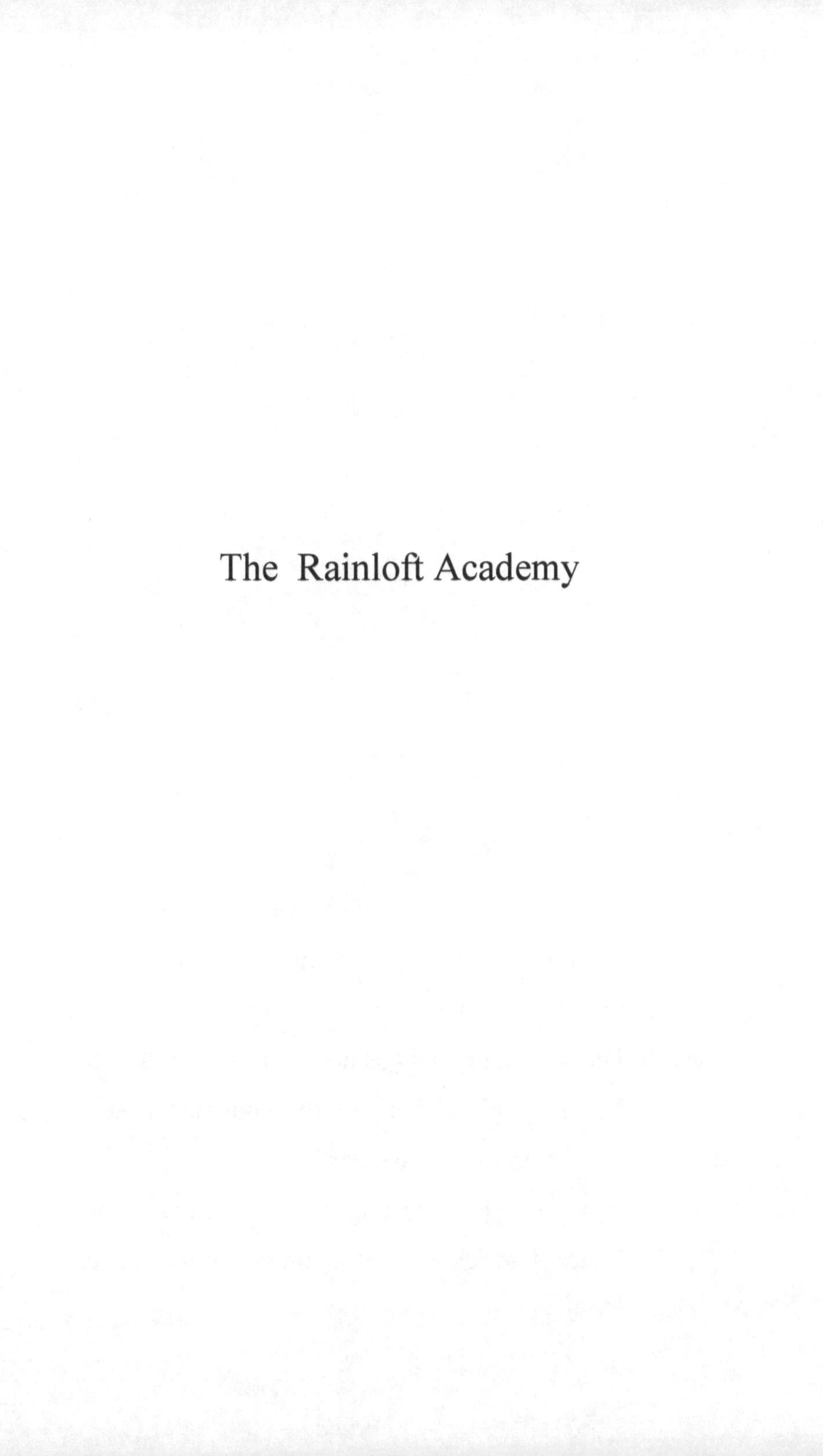

The Rainloft Academy

Prologue

I remember the day they came all too well.

It was a stormy Friday evening—thunder boomed and lightning flashed outside as my brother and I helped our dad prepare dinner. He was never the best chef in the family—Mom usually did all of the cooking. That is, before she went missing a year earlier.

Things were just starting to feel normal again. Mom's disappearance was hard on all three of us, especially Dad. He had to take on a second full-time job and provide for two stubborn ten-year-olds, all the while trying to cope with the loss of his wife.

Mom left a gaping hole in our family when she disappeared, and since, that hole had closed up a little. We all wished Mom would come back, but life without her had become our new normal. Although, what still bothered me was that even a year after she went missing, nobody knew where she had gone. In fact, to this day, that's still a mystery. It was like she vanished without a trace—one day she was there, and the next day she wasn't.

Anyway, a few seconds after I had started peeling the potatoes, the doorbell rang. "I'll get it!" my brother, Atlas, exclaimed, starting towards the front door with a tray of rolls in his hands. I didn't think much of it, at first, and continued preparing the mashed potatoes.

"Who could possibly have come over here in *this* weather?" Dad asked, setting a plate of chicken down at the dining room table.

When the front door creaked open and I heard the tray of rolls clatter to the ground, I knew something was wrong. I dropped the half-peeled potato I was holding and raced to my brother's side.

When I saw who was at the door, I froze. Standing there on my front porch, his black leather uniform dripping with rain was unmistakably a Rainloft Alumnus.

But he couldn't possibly have been there to take me away, I told myself. Only ninety-five kids in the entire world were chosen to go up to the Rainloft. There's no way I was one of them. Impossible.

"You must be June and Atlas," the man said in a gruff voice, unsmiling. "I need to speak with your father. Is he here?"

Without taking my eyes off the Alumnus, I pointed towards the kitchen with a trembling finger. *He's not here to take you to the Rainloft, June,* I told myself over and over again. *No way. No way, no way, no way.*

"Mr. Winters," the man looked past me and at my dad, who stood in the middle of the foyer, his eyes wide and his mouth agape. "I'm here to inform you that your children have been selected to attend the Rainloft Academy."

My mouth fell open. Everyone was dead silent for the longest time. "That's not possible," Dad said, forcing a chuckle. "Right?"

"I'm afraid it is, sir."

"*B-Both* of them?" Dad stammered, panic rising in his voice.

The Alumnus's mouth formed a thin line. "Yes, both of them," he said, impatience creeping into his tone. "The helicopter is parked out in the road."

I looked past the Alumnus. Through the rain, I could barely make out the shiny black helicopter just sitting there in the middle of the street. It was crazy to me how quiet those Rainloft choppers were—I hadn't even heard it land.

I had always wanted to ride in a helicopter, but the thought of getting in that one made me feel sick to my stomach. Once we took off, there was a chance that I might never touch the ground again. At least, not for the next eight years of my life.

"You have five minutes before we need to leave," the Alumnus said. "Gather your belongings, say your goodbyes, whatever you need to do. But don't even *think* about running."

At that, both Altas and I took off down the hall to our bedrooms. I scanned the room, thinking, *what should I take if I'm not going to be back for almost a decade?*

From what I had gathered about the Rainloft over the news, students had to wear uniforms and meals were provided. Since I wouldn't need to bring any of those, there was only one item that I could think of to take, and it was already on my wrist.

It was the last gift Mom gave me before she went missing. In fact, it was the day before her disappearance when she walked into my bedroom holding a silver bracelet with a pearl charm. The pearl is the birthstone for June, which is both the month I was born and my name. When she handed it to me, I was confused. Jewelry wasn't really my thing, and she knew that.

But when she vanished the next day, I put it on and haven't taken it off since. It was old and tarnished but it was the most important thing I owned, and the only thing worth taking up to the Rainloft.

I left my room at the same time as Atlas left his. He carried a small leather-bound journal, which was his version of my bracelet—the last gift Mom gave him before she vanished.

"I don't want to leave," he said.

"Neither do I," I sighed.

Dad snuck up on us and wrapped us both in the longest hug ever. When he finally pulled away, he kneeled down, looking us both in the eyes.

"I'm so sorry this happened," he said. His eyes were glossy, but I could tell he was trying to be strong for us. "I'm going to miss you two so much. The situation may not be ideal—that's for sure—but look at the bright side."

"There is no bright side," I mumbled, folding my arms and staring at the floor. "There's nothing fun about being trapped in a giant school-with-wings for eight years straight."

"But you'll get to become *superheroes*," said Dad. "You'll get super powerful and eventually become protectors of all of Lavon. Boy, what an honor that is— I'm actually kind of jealous."

Atlas smiled. I still wasn't satisfied. "Well, I don't want to be a superhero."

"We have to get going," the Alumnus interjected from the doorway, tapping his Rainloft-issued watch. It occurred to me that I would one day be in his position— knocking on some unlucky kid's door to tell them that they had to spend the rest of their life as a brainwashed superhuman… the thought alone made me shudder.

"I love you two so much," Dad told us. "Come visit me the second you graduate, okay?"

And then we were off. The Alumnus took our hands and we were halfway across the front lawn before I had a chance to realize what was happening. I bent my head and narrowed my eyes against the rain, the flooded lawn squelching under my feet with every step I took.

My mind swimming, I walked blindly through the storm, the Alumnus guiding me towards the helicopter. We came to a halt in front of it and its headlights flashed on, illuminating the entire neighborhood and nearly blinding me with their brightness.

The Alumnus pulled open the helicopter door. "Get in," he ordered.

I took one last look over my shoulder and through my blurred vision, I could see my dad standing on the front porch. My heart ached. I wanted nothing more than to go back into the warmth of my house and sit by the fireplace and laugh at my dad's awful jokes—like we did every Friday night.

But as I stood there, dripping, shivering in the rain, it occurred to me that things would never be the same again. Everything was about to change, and no matter how much I wanted to, there was no escaping that.

Everyone in the helicopter was silent for the entire ride. The Alumnus stared straight ahead, maintaining the same unwavering austerity all the way there. I kept my head turned toward the window, watching fat raindrops splatter on the glass and listening to the thunder bellowing furiously above us.

Despite the wild storm, the ride was shockingly smooth. Before ten minutes had passed, the Alumnus nodded toward the windshield and said gruffly, "We're here."

At first, I couldn't see anything but darkness. But when the lightning flashed in just the right way, it illuminated an enormous black silhouette more than double the size of a cruise ship floating in the distance. My heart rate picked up at the sight of the Rainloft Academy.

We touched down on a long deck extending from the side of the jet. In pictures, the Rainloft looked big enough, but in person, its size left me speechless.

The second I stepped out of the helicopter, the wind hit me like a smack to the face. It blew my hair in all directions and for a second I was afraid I would be blown away.

The Alumnus led Atlas and I up the landing deck and towards the school. When we reached the door and stepped inside to the dining hall, my jaw hit the floor.

From what I could see, it looked exactly like a normal school on the inside (just a lot fancier and a whole lot more boring). Five long tables with pristine gray tops stretched from one end of the room to the other, each labeled with a different colored banner hanging from the tall ceiling above. The words *Rainloft Academy* were printed in nondescript black letters across the far left wall, and an enormous black-and-white map was stretched across the wall on my right. If I hadn't just been brought up here in a helicopter, I never would have guessed that this place was hovering miles above the ground.

My footsteps echoed across the empty room as I followed the Alumnus out of the dining hall and down lots of winding hallways, all of which were just as deserted as the cafeteria. The low lighting made it feel like we were walking through a horror movie.

"Are we the only ones here?" I asked.

"No," the Alumnus replied as we turned a corner. "No students are permitted out of the dormitories past eight o'clock without a teacher's permission."

He stopped abruptly in the middle of the hallway. There was one door on the right and one on the left, each with a sign hanging up that read the word *Ready*.

"This is where I leave you," said the Alumnus. He gestured to the door on the left side of the corridor. "Atlas, you are to go into this room, and June—" he nodded toward the door on his right "—this one. Got it?" We nodded, and he set off back down the way we came.

Hesitantly, I knocked on my door. When it opened, a woman greeted me. Her bright red hair was pulled back in a tight bun and she wore yellow scrubs much like a doctor's.

"Ah, and you must be June. Please, come in," she said with a smile, stepping aside. The room reminded me a lot of a dentist's office—a big chair in the center of the room and a desk near the side. "You can go ahead and take a seat."

My thoughts raced as I crossed the room and took a seat in the big chair. *This can't be good,* I thought. *What are they going to do to me? How are they going to give me powers?*

I fidgeted with my bracelet as my eyes darted around the small room. It definitely seemed to be some sort of doctor's office—there were all sorts of different medical posters and charts littering the walls, including one in particular that caught my eye.

Type One: Telekinesis, Object Manipulation: Amethyst

Type Two: Mind Control, Mind Reading: Jade

Type Three: Time Travel: Topaz

Type Four: Teleportation: Tourmaline

Type Five: Power Mimicry: Aquamarine

In my ten-year-old brain, those words looked like a foreign language. "What's that chart?" I asked.

The woman smiled again. "Those are all of the different superpower types that we have here at the Rainloft," she replied cheerily. I knew she was trying to help calm me down, but her enthusiasm made me uneasy.

"Just relax," she told me. "Av—er, *Headmistress* Avalon will see you shortly."

And she left the room, leaving me trapped alone with my thoughts. Not for long, though, because the door swung open in a matter of seconds.

A different woman—Avalon?—walked in. She looked a lot different from the last one—she had cleanly cropped brown hair and wore a long, dark dress, but what I noticed first was the feathery black mask that covered most of her face. This woman looked like a masquerade member who had accidentally stumbled into this office.

"Hello, June," she said, shutting the door softly behind her. Her voice was warm and soft and reminded me of my mother's, but she looked like she meant business. "Welcome to the Rainloft."

And then I caught sight of the syringe in her hand. "What's that?" I panicked.

She chuckled. "Don't worry about it."

My fear grew as she stepped toward me. The syringe was filled with a shiny gold liquid the color of a sunflower. *What was she…? Did she plan to…?*

"Just relax," she said in her buttery-smooth tone. "This won't hurt a bit."

I didn't even feel the needle hit my skin. Within seconds, my vision began to grow dark and my thoughts became hazy.

"Relax," Avalon repeated as I dipped in and out of consciousness, "and I'll see you in a whole new world."

When I woke up, Avalon was gone. Instead, the red-haired doctor hovered over me as I resurfaced, blinking the blurriness from my eyes.

"How do you feel?" she asked.

"No different?" I shrugged, hoping that was the answer she was looking for.

She smiled, visibly relieved. "Well, June, you're officially a Type Three."

I stared at her blankly. "Huh?"

She kneeled down so that her eyes were level with mine. "You're a time traveler."

Chapter One

Ever since the first day I set foot on the Rainloft's grounds (approximately four years, three months and seventeen days ago, but who's keeping track?) I've been able to travel through time.

Is the Rainloft as bad as I thought it would be? Short answer, yes. But I've gotten used to it by now—the rigorous schedule and exhausting training sessions have become a way of life. I'd rather be on the ground, for sure, but I try not to think about that. There's nothing I can do about it, so why waste all my time dwelling on the impossible?

Anyways, allow me to bring this story back to the present day.

"Ugh, this food is *disgusting*," Thomas groans, wrinkling his nose at the cafeteria meatloaf on his plate.

"Agreed," says Fiona. She drops her fork and pushes away her tray of food. "Why is all of the food here so bad?"

"Not *all* of it is bad. Yesterday's spaghetti was *amazing*," Thomas smiles, licking his lips. "If only there were a way to get some of that."

Fiona grins mischievously. "Say, a way to *go back in time* and bring some back."

I keep my eyes on my book in a desperate attempt to avoid being dragged into Thomas's shenanigans again. I've allowed him to get me into trouble more times than I'd like to admit, and I'd rather not face Headmistress Avalon a third time this week.

"Yeah, but we'd have to go back *24 hours* to get a bowl of that pasta. I can barely manage fifteen minutes," Thomas sighs dramatically. "If only the *Most Promising Type Three* were sitting right across from us."

He and Fiona look at me expectantly. I *was* just awarded *Most Promising Type Three* by my Advancing Time Travel teacher, but that was because I had just barely managed to travel forty-five minutes into the past. There's no way any fourth-year Type Three could handle going back any further than that, let alone a full day.

"Leave me out of this, please," I tell them without looking up from my book. The dining hall is filled with students of all five different types, but I'm not allowed to leave the Type Three table. Believe me: if I could, I would move to a different table in a heartbeat—but different types aren't allowed to interact with one another, so I'm stuck sitting with all of the obnoxious Type Threes.

"Come onnnn," Fiona whines. "All you need to do is bring us a couple bowls of yesterday's spaghetti."

"In case you forgot, we're not allowed to travel outside of class," I remind her.

Thomas scoffs. "Who cares about the rules? That pasta would easily be worth a couple hours of detention."

"Pretty please?" Fiona says, giving me puppy-dog eyes.

I sigh, closing my book and standing up. "I said *no*. If you want to break the rules just for a bowl of spaghetti, go for it, but I'm going to class." I loop my leather messenger bag over my shoulder and start towards the exit of the dining hall, even though we still have five minutes left of lunch. "Oh, and good luck going back twenty-four hours."

I dump my tray in the garbage on my way out, fuming. Thomas and Fiona have been bugging me since the get-go—our first day here, they begged me to reverse time for them and make it so that none of us were ever selected for the Rainloft in the first place. As if they somehow forgot it was my first day too and that I had just as much experience with time travel as they did: zero. They've been conveniently forgetting that every day since. If we didn't have assigned seats in the dining hall, I wouldn't sit anywhere near them. In fact, I think I'd eat at the opposite end of the school from those two.

I try to forget about them as I head to Combat Skills—my least favorite class. So far I've learned nothing but the fact that time travel is absolutely useless in a fight. Type Ones can move and manipulate objects (and people) with nothing but a glance, which sounds incredibly helpful. Type Twos can mind-control enemies into doing their bidding—also very handy. What can a Type Three do? Flee from the fight by time traveling away from it? I repeat: absolutely useless.

I'm in the classroom and settled at my desk before the bell even rings. The Combat Skills classroom is enormous, much like the rest of the school. The architecture of the Rainloft Academy is all bold angles and big glass windows (you know, for in case we forget that we're hovering miles above the ground). The classrooms all look the same—bland gray walls and shiny white desks with extremely uncomfortable chairs. There isn't one square inch of carpet in the entire building—all of the floors are bright white tile. Stone statues and portraits of famous Alumni fill up all the blank spaces in the hallways.

Other students start filing into the room as I watch my teacher, Professor Stillman, write something on the whiteboard at the front of the class. When he moves out of the way, the words *Grandfather Paradox* are written across the board in his chicken-scratch handwriting.

Once all twenty Type Threes have taken their seats, Professor Stillman starts his lecture. "Today you're going to learn a new combat strategy," he begins, his voice echoing across the classroom. "This is easily the most valuable strategy a Type Three could use in a fight. Now, this technique is extremely difficult to execute, and most students aren't able to successfully pull it off until long after they've graduated."

The girl sitting next to me sighs. "Awesome," she mutters under her breath. *"Another* tactic that we can't use for another four years."

"This strategy often involves traveling many years into the past," Stillman continues. "Say you're battling a bank robber. The goal of this technique would be to travel back to a time before the robber commits the crime and eliminate them before they can rob the bank."

A kid sitting in the front row raises his hand. "You mean... *kill* the robber?"

"Precisely," says Professor Stillman. "When you travel into the present, you will enter an alternate reality in which the robber never existed. Therefore, the crime will never have happened. This creates what we call the grandfather paradox, but we'll talk more about that another day.

"Once again, this technique is very advanced and only experts can pull it off. I just thought I'd share it with you to show that Type Threes can most definitely be useful in combat. Any questions?"

"Professor Stillman," I hesitate, weighing whether or not it's worth it to critique his teaching. I decide *what have*

I got to lose? and continue. "What's the point in teaching us all of these combat tricks that we won't be able to use for years? I mean, what if we get into a fight *tomorrow*? All we'll know is these super advanced strategies that there's no chance we'll be able to pull off. Why not teach us some techniques that'll be useful, say, *now?*"

Stillman is silent for a minute. "That is… a valid point, Miss Winters." He shakes his head. "Well, hopefully you won't find yourself in a battle any time soon."

"But what if we *do?*"

The bell rings and students start to leave the room. Professor Stillman seems relieved. "We'll have to discuss this more another time. Class dismissed."

The girl who sat next to me in Combat Skills walks beside me as I head to my next class. "Hopefully you made him rethink the things he's teaching us," she says with a sigh. "Man, that class is stupid."

"I wouldn't count on it," I say, walking a little faster to try and get away from her. My next class, Rainloft History, is on the other side of the school and it takes the whole three minutes they give us in between periods to get there. I don't have time for small talk.

To my dismay, she matches my pace. "So, what's your next class?"

"Rainloft History."

"That's, like, on the other side of the building from here, right?"

"Yup. I don't have a lot of time to get there, so I should probably…" I trail off, hoping she gets the message.

"Right." She pauses. "I'm Ava, by the way."

"Cool, I'm June—"

"Winters," she finishes. "I know."

I stop in my tracks. "Huh? How did you—?" I cut myself off and sigh. "Oh. Of course you do. Because of my brother."

I should have known. Ever since Atlas became the first student ever to escape the Rainloft two years ago, everyone knows my name.

"So how did he do it?" she asks, like a news reporter at a crime scene. "Did he tell you before he left?"

"No, actually," I reply, realizing with a grimace that Ava only wanted to talk to me because I'm Atlas's sister. I don't know why everyone assumes that he told me his plan before he escaped. I'm a Type Three and Atlas was a Type Two, meaning we weren't even allowed to interact with each other because rules are rules and who knows what could happen if different types so much as say hello to each other?

He left without any sort of warning. One day he was here, and the next, he was gone.

The bell rings, making me jump. Ava curses under her breath. "I'm late for class. See you tomorrow?"

"Bye," I murmur, already on my way to class. I walk as fast as possible without technically running, my heart beating faster with every step I take. *Shoot, shoot, shoot* is all that goes through my mind the whole way to Rainloft History. I've never been late to class before, and Professor Becker is my harshest teacher. I once watched her give a kid three months' worth of detention just for chewing gum during her lesson.

I'm out of breath by the time I reach her classroom. All eyes are on me the second I step inside, including Professor Becker's.

Professor Becker is a short, plump old lady with frizzy gray hair and cherry-red glasses with rhinestones along the edges. I don't think I've ever seen her smile, except for when she's handing out detention.

I stand there in the doorway, panting as she stands up from her desk and walks slowly over to me. Her mouth forms a thin line as she looks me up and down, her eyes narrowed. "Professor, I'm so so sorry, it won't happen again. I—"

"Miss Winters," she cuts me off. She watches me for an uncomfortably long time, and I struggle to keep my cool under the heat of her gaze. Finally, she sighs. "Your tie is loose."

I stare at her. "That's it?" I ask before I can stop myself.

"Yes." She waves me off. "Now go sit down."

I make my way towards my desk near the back of the room, smiling like I just won the lottery. Part of me expects her to turn around and sentence me to detention for life, but she doesn't. This is so unlike her that I'm almost concerned—I was two minutes late to class and she didn't even mention it?

Maybe she's letting it slide this time because I'm usually one of her best students? That has to be it. Putting that aside, I pull out my notebook and favorite pen to take notes on her lecture.

Becker clears her throat. "Miss Winters, your tie?"

"Right. Sorry."

I quickly adjust my golden-yellow uniform tie. Another one of the countless Rainloft Academy rules: all students must wear a uniform. That includes a blazer, a white button-down shirt, a tie, a skirt or pants or shorts and some (very uncomfortable) black shoes.

Each type wears a different color: Type Ones wear purple blazers the color of irises. Type Twos wear rainforest-green, Type Threes are stuck with mustard-yellow and Type Fours have dark teal. Type Fives wear uniforms the color of swimming pools in the summertime.

Professor Becker clears her throat. "Today you'll be starting a project on the founding of the Rainloft Academy," she announces. "Now, since we all know that Headmistress Avalon is our founder, remind me: for how many years has the Rainloft existed?"

A Type Two's hand shoots up. "Twenty-eight years."

"That is correct," Becker nods. "And how long did it take the headmistress to perfect the serum that gives you your powers?"

"Nineteen years!" a Type Four in the front row hollers.

Becker purses her lips. "That'll be a month of detention for speaking out of turn, Miss Adams, but yes—that's correct. It took her nearly two decades to finish the serum that would later become the baseline of the Rainloft Academy.

"For this project, we'll be diving deeper into the *why* of the founding. Now that you're in your fourth year, it's time you discover Headmistress Avalon's reasoning for starting the Rainloft." She gestures to a stack of textbooks on her desk. "You'll read from one of these Rainloft History textbooks. After thoroughly studying the book, you'll take what you learn from the reading and write a twelve-page essay on the reasoning for the founding."

I resist the urge to groan out loud. This is the fifth essay that she's had us write this month, and she expects them all to be unreasonably long.

It's almost like she's read my mind when she sighs. "I know that you've had to do a lot of writing assignments, so this time—just this once—I'll allow you to work with a partner of your choosing." At that, just about everyone in the room perks up. "Remember: I expect this essay to be your best work yet. You must cover every key detail of the founding and no less. And, as a reminder, if you choose to work with a partner, they must be the same type as you. You may begin."

Everyone starts shuffling around, chairs scraping the ground as people get up and break off into groups of two. "You have two days to complete the assignment," says Professor Becker as students swarm her desk to get their textbooks.

I know from the second she announces that we're allowed to work in pairs that I'm working alone. It's a no-brainer: all the other Type Threes in this class are about as easy to work with as a pen without ink. I'd rather do all the work myself than try and get along with one of those uptight snobs.

I scribble down a few notes on the founding as I wait for the textbook pickup area to clear out. *Avalon spent nearly twenty years of her life searching for a way to give ordinary kids superpowers,* I think. *If she spent that long trying, then she must have had a really good reason for it. What could that—*

My thoughts are interrupted when a textbook drops onto my desk, scattering my papers and making me jump three feet out of my chair. I look up to see a girl with dark skin and long, curly hair standing in front of me. Her violet uniform tells me that she's a Type One, which… wait…

"I need your help," she says firmly.

I gape at her, not sure whether to respond. Does she know that different types aren't allowed to speak to each other? She has to—teachers have been reminding us constantly since day one. Plus, Professor Becker just told us. Maybe she just hasn't been paying any attention whatsoever to the rules for the past four years?

I can't help but back away when she extends a hand to me. "I'm Kathryn Sharp. Ryn for short. Want to work together?"

I stare at her hand like it's a grenade about to blow up. "But—er—"

"Miss Sharp!" Professor Becker hisses. "You know the rule: *no interaction between different types!*" She shakes her head in disappointment. "I'll have to discuss further punishment with the headmistress, but know you're going to have detention for a *very* long time, starting tonight. Come to this classroom at midnight." She sighs and lowers her voice. "This is *outrageous*."

Kathryn (or whatever her name is) grimaces. "We'll talk after class," she mutters before going back to her desk.

I get absolutely zero work done for the rest of the period. It's not great, seeing as this is one of the only work days I have to complete the assignment, but I can't take my mind off of what just happened. Are the other Type Ones just so awful that she couldn't be partners with any of them? Why couldn't she have worked alone? And... *why me?*

Before I can blink, the bell rings. I gather up my supplies as slowly as possible, waiting to see whether that

Ryn girl waits for me. She *did* say that we'd talk after class, but she leaves the room without me. I can't help but sigh in relief.

But when I walk out the door, she grabs my wrist and drags me to the side of the hallway.

"It's June, right?" she asks, and I nod. "Great. So, do you want to partner up on the project or not?"

I hesitate. "Aren't we… um… isn't it, you know, against the rules?"

"Forget about the rules," Ryn waves a hand dismissively, brushing away my question like it's nothing. "Listen, if you do, there's this portrait of your brother in the Type One dorm wing. You'll know it when you see it. Meet me there tonight at midnight."

I finally find my voice. "Don't you have detention?"

She looks at me, her chocolate-colored eyes dead serious. "I'm not going."

And she walks away, leaving me to wonder what in the world I just got myself into.

Chapter Two

Before hardly any time has passed, I find myself walking down the dark Type One hallway, flashlight in hand.

I'm not sure what convinced me to sneak out at the dead of night—whether it was the fact that Ryn is expecting me or nothing but sheer boredom, I'm here now and I can't say I'm not regretting this decision.

My footsteps echo across the silent corridor, my heart pounding in my ears. I scan the mauve-colored walls with my flashlight, searching for the portrait that Ryn said to meet her by.

I can't get caught. My normally detention-free nights are on the line, and I have way too much homework in the evenings to give those up. By meeting Ryn this late, I'm violating more than one of the biggest Rainloft rules: leaving my dorm after eight o'clock *and* talking to a Type One. Breaking either one of those alone could earn me a full year's worth of detention. Who knows what could happen if a teacher finds me?

My light lands on an oil painting of my brother, maybe eleven or twelve years old at the time. In the portrait, his coffee-colored hair is swept to the side and his storm-gray eyes stare straight into my soul. He wears a jade-green uniform and a stone-cold expression.

Atlas and I are twins—same hair color, same eye color, same thick eyebrows that make us look serious all the time. He was the last Rainloft student I would've expected to escape—I always thought it would be Thomas or someone a little more, I don't know, strong-willed. Sometimes I still wonder where my brother is now.

"Gosh, you guys look scary alike," Ryn remarks out of nowhere, making me spring backward. She stands next to me with the RH textbook tucked under her arm, wrinkling her nose at the portrait.

"When did you get here?" I whisper, waiting for my heart rate to slow.

"Not important," she says, opening the textbook and flipping the pages. "Well, should we get started?"

"Hold on, slow down," I say and Ryn pauses, looking up from the book. "First of all, let me ask: why are you doing this?"

"You mean, why am I doing this project?"

"No, I mean why are you risking everything by doing this project with another type?" I question, keeping my voice low. "It's one of the most heavily-enforced rules there is here, so why are you so determined to break it?"

Ryn closes the textbook. "Have you ever wondered why that rule even exists?"

"So that we don't hurt each other with our powers?" I shrug.

"That doesn't make any sense," she says, shaking her head. "Point is, it's a stupid rule. So are so many of the other ones. Like, why aren't we allowed to pick who we sit with at lunch? It's like they're just trying to make our lives even more miserable than they already are." Ryn sighs, opening the textbook again. "So many things need to change, and this project is the first step.”

I stare at her. *“The first step?”* I repeat.

She looks up at me, exasperated. “You really have no idea what we’re doing here, do you?”

“Not a clue.”

She sighs again, closing the book and setting it down by her feet. “Okay, here’s the gist,” she begins. “This project is a chance to give the teachers a piece of our minds. By working with a different type on the essay, we can show them that nothing bad will come of it.”

“So, sort of like a rebellion?” I suggest.

“In a way, sure,” she nods. “It’s an opportunity to show them that their rules are pointless. And maybe—just *maybe*—they’ll change how things work around here.”

I think for a second. “Not to rain on your parade or anything, but I doubt that two people breaking one of the rules is going to convince them to rethink their entire system.”

Ryn smirks. “That’s why it’s *not* going to be just two people, and it’s *not* going to be just one rule.”

“What are you saying?”

“I’m saying that we can convince some of the other types to do the same.” She crosses her arms, smiling like this is the most brilliant idea ever. "And we're going to break more than one of the rules. So, are you in?"

My initial reaction is *Absolutely not,* but I stop myself and think. I still have four more years here, and I'm already sick of the place. If this is a chance to change the way things work around here… "I suppose it's worth a shot," I decide. "But don't make me do anything too crazy. I don't want to get into more trouble than I have to if this whole thing goes wrong."

"Perfect," Ryn grins. "And that leads me to my question: do you happen to know anyone here? Preferably a different type?"

I open my mouth to tell her *no,* but I stop myself, realizing that I do. "Well, there's this Type Four that I went to camp with one time," I say, and a memory comes to mind.

I was eight, and my dad had sent me to this cooking camp because apparently I couldn't whip up a decent dinner if my life depended on it. I was thrown into a giant kitchen with a bunch of other bright-eyed, bushy-tailed third graders, all ready to learn something new.

I have to admit—that camp *destroyed* me. All I had to do that day was make a pot of mac and cheese and I couldn't, for the life of me, figure out how to turn on the stove. I was on the verge of tears, twisting knobs and pressing buttons and almost setting the camp on fire.

And that's when I met Grayson. He was the teacher's son, so he was automatically the best chef in the class. He left his own mac and cheese unattended and came over to help me figure out the stove.

Maybe that wasn't the greatest idea—Grayson's noodles burst into flames and the fire department had to come put them out—but I was grateful nonetheless. However, that friendship didn't last very long. He moved halfway across the country and we quickly fell out of touch.

I was shocked when he turned up at the Rainloft a couple years later. Though, on our first day, we found out the hard way that different types weren't allowed to interact.

"Do you think you could convince him to do the project with a different type?" Ryn's voice calls me back to the present. "We're going to need as many people as possible to pull this off."

"I don't know." I can't imagine roping Grayson into this. He hardly ever broke the rules when we were kids, unless you count that one time when he accidentally drank one of the camp instructors' coffee. He apologized at least a hundred times.

"At least talk to him about it? We really—" Ryn starts, but she freezes, her eyes wide. "Do you hear that?"

"Hear wh—?"

She grabs me by the arm and pulls me down the hallway, keeping her head down. "Hey, what is—?" and then I hear it.

"Who's there?" Professor Becker's voice echoes down the corridor from behind us. "You'd better hope I don't find you!"

"Come on," Ryn mutters, picking up the pace. Suddenly, she stops, pointing to a potted pear tree at the side of the hallway. "Hide behind that."

I dive behind the plant without wasting a second, expecting her to follow, but she doesn't. Ryn stands there, in the middle of the hallway, unflinching as Professor Becker marches up and shines a flashlight in her face.

"Well, if it isn't Kathryn Sharp," Becker sneers, looking awfully pleased with herself. I watch from behind the plant, biting my lip. "May I ask, why are you out here, wandering the hallways when you're supposed to be in my classroom for detention?"

Ryn turns her head, shielding her eyes from the bright white light in her face. "I was sleepwalking," she says, somehow keeping calm as Becker's eyes bore into hers. I can't help but be glad it's Ryn and not me. If I were caught by any teacher—Becker or not—I'd be nothing short of a nervous wreck.

The teacher gives Ryn a once-over. "And if you were sleeping, then why are you still fully dressed?"

Ryn glances down at her uniform with a forced laugh. "I must have forgotten to change into pajamas before I went to bed. My bad!"

Becker gives a small *hmph* and lowers her flashlight. "Very well. Shall we head to my classroom, then?"

She puts a hand on Ryn's back and guides her down the corridor in the direction we came from. Before they disappear into the darkness, Ryn glances over her shoulder and mouths *Remember the plan.*

I hide in the safety of the pear tree's shadow for a few minutes, making sure the coast is clear and that no more bloodthirsty teachers are going to come strolling down the hall on the hunt for misbehaving students.

Still crouching behind the plant, I dig around in my blazer pocket and pull out a pen and a crumpled-up napkin from breakfast today. Resting the napkin on my knee, I scribble down a (barely legible) message:

Meet me by the big trash can in the dining hall at breakfast tomorrow

- J

Before going back to my dorm, I make a quick pit-stop by the Type Four wing and slide the note under Grayson's door. Chances are, he won't want anything to do with Ryn's plan, but why not ask? She was right: if we want to make even a little bit of a change, we're going to need as many people on board as we can get. It's worth a try, if you ask me.

When I get back to my room, I don't waste a minute before flopping into bed. I never thought breaking the rules could be so exhausting—I'm asleep the second my head hits the pillow.

The next morning, I stand by the garbage can, trying not to gag from the smell as I wait for Grayson.

Thomas walks up to dump his tray in the trash and looks at me like something his dog just tracked in from the backyard. "Why are you just standing there like that?" he demands.

"That's none of your business, is it?" I smirk.

He shakes his head as he walks back to our table. "Weirdo."

Before long, I spot Grayson wandering around like a lost puppy, my napkin note in his hand. I wave him over. "Hey, Grayson. Long time no see!"

He stares at me for a second, then his sea-green eyes light up with recognition and he walks hesitantly towards me. "Uh, hi," he mutters, eyes darting back and forth. "What are you doing? You know that different types aren't allowed to be talking to each other, right?"

I can feel the lunch lady's eyes burning holes into the back of my head, so I lower my voice. "Yeah, I'm breaking the rules. Now, there's something I need to talk to you about. Follow me."

I start towards the dining hall exit. In the doorway, I turn around to make sure Grayson is coming, but he's still standing by the garbage can. *Come on,* I mouth, beckoning him over. Reluctantly, he follows me out the dining hall and halfway across the school until I find my favorite spot in the whole building: a dead-end hallway that nobody else ever goes down. A giant window takes up most of the far wall and a little lavender plant sits on a table in front of it, bathing in the early morning sunlight.

I turn to face Grayson. Since I last saw him, he's gotten taller. Other than that, he looks exactly the same as he did six years ago—stocky build, sandy blond hair, freckles across the bridge of his nose and green eyes like sea glass. "You remember me, right?" I venture.

"Of course," he says. "Third grade cooking camp. You almost burned the place down. Now, do you want to tell me what's going on here?"

"Oh—right," I begin, slightly relieved that he hasn't forgotten who I am. "You know that ridiculously long essay Professor Becker is having us write? Well, yesterday, this random Type One walked up to me and asked if I wanted to work with her on it."

"A Type One? But that's—"

"Not allowed, I know. Anyways, I met up with her at midnight to discuss the project, and she told me that we were breaking the rules as a sort of…rebellion," I explain. "She thinks if we can get enough people to do the project with a different type, then the teachers will get rid of the rule that different types can't interact."

Grayson raises an eyebrow. "Okay… but how will breaking the rules get the teachers to change them?"

"I know, the whole idea is a little… out there," I admit, "but Ryn's convinced it'll work. She says we need as many people to do the project in order to make even a little bit of an impact. And this project is all we'll have to do. So, what do you think?"

"I…don't know," he says. "Professor Becker is the strictest teacher here. We could end up in detention for the rest of our *lives* by breaking that rule, and I've got to say— this whole plan seems a little far-fetched."

"I know," I say, "but we're going to be stuck here for the next four years of our life. Are you happy with the way things work around this place? All of the pointless rules?"

"Well, no, but—"

"This is a way to change things—or so Ryn thinks," I add. "If we're trapped here, then wouldn't you rather things be a little more… fair?"

"But what if we end up in detention?" he questions. "I don't have time for detention."

"We probably will, honestly, but a little detention never killed anyone. Right?"

I can see the gears grinding in his mind. "Please?" I press.

"Well, if this Ryn person thinks it'll help, then…" he sighs. "Why not?"

"Really? Wow, that was easier than I thought it would be." The bell rings, and students start to flood the hallways. "I'm sure Ryn will be happy. Let me know tomorrow how it goes, okay?"

"Got it," Grayson says as we leave the dead-end hallway. "It was good seeing you again, June."

"Good seeing you, too."

*　　*　　*

"May I have your attention, please?" Professor Becker's voice booms across the classroom, her lips pursed as she claps a ruler against her hand. "It has come to my attention that students have been partnering up with other types for this project." She lets out the loudest, most dramatic sigh I've ever heard. "This is *against the rules!* I explicitly told you yesterday that this is *not allowed.* So, if you are one of these students working with a type other than your own, I would *strongly* advise you to rethink your actions.

"Now." She clears her throat. "You may begin working. Turn your essay in to me once you're finished."

The class breaks into hushed chatter and Ryn drags a chair across the room, positioning it beside my desk. She sits and sets down a stack of papers.

"Hopefully you don't mind, but I wrote the essay last night," she says.

I gape at her. "You wrote the *entire thing*? All twelve pages of it?"

"Uh-huh." She slides the essay towards me. "Let me know your thoughts."

"Hold on," I say. "Didn't you hear what Becker just said? She knows what we're doing. We can't work together anymore."

She stares at me. "Are you kidding? This is a rebellion, June. We must persist."

"Whatever you say." At the top of the essay, the words **By Kathryn Sharp and June Winters** are written in impossibly neat cursive.

"Miss Sharp! Miss Winters!" Becker gasps. "Were you paying any attention to my announcement? *You can't work together*. Detention, both of you. Midnight tonight."

Ryn frowns. "We must persist," she mutters under her breath as she takes her papers back to her desk.

"I got Grayson to do the project," I report to Ryn in the hallway after class.

"Great," she says, rummaging through her bag and handing me all twelve pages of our (her) essay. "Will you read this after school today? Let me know your thoughts at dinner."

"At dinner? But we're not—"

"Yeah, *I know* we're not allowed to sit together for meals," she cuts in with an impatient sigh, "but you know how I said that we'll have to break more than one rule?"

I sigh. "Oh no. Please don't drag me into this."

"Come on," she whines. "Don't you want to be able to sit with who you want?"

The thought of sitting with Thomas and Fiona every day for the next four years makes me shudder. "Yeah, I do," I cave. "Fine. Where will we sit, though?"

"I'll find you," says Ryn, and she rushes off to her next class.

"Geez, the food here has *seriously* gone downhill," Fiona grumbles, wrinkling her nose at the bowl of salad in front of her.

"Yeah. June, you wanna grab us some—" Thomas begins, but he stops, staring at something past my shoulder.

"Hi, June," says Ryn. She stands behind me and Thomas gapes at her, his eyes wide. "Where should I sit?"

"Take one of *their* spots," I say, nodding towards Thomas and Fiona. Thomas scrambles out of his seat and leaves the dining hall so fast that he nearly knocks over his chair.

And then Grayson appears, carrying a bowl of what looks like nothing but lettuce. "I heard there was a rebellion going on?"

"Apparently so," I say, and nod towards Ryn. "Oh— Grayson, this is Ryn Sharp; Ryn, this is Grayson Campbell."

"What are *they* doing here? And why are you *talking* to them?" Fiona demands.

"Hey, how about you mind your own business?" Ryn glares at her. Fiona is up and out of the cafeteria in a matter of seconds.

Ryn and Grayson take their seats, earning lots of stares from the other Type Threes. "I didn't think you wanted to break the rules like this," I tell Grayson.

He shrugs. "I didn't either. But I thought about it and decided, what have I got to lose?"

"My thinking ex—" I begin, but someone clears their throat behind me and I freeze when I realize who it is. "A little birdie informed me that you three were breaking the rules," says Professor Stillman.

Thomas stands behind him with an overly prideful expression that makes me want to dump my salad on his head. "I'm the little birdie."

"Yeah, no duh," Ryn sneers.

"Typical Thomas," I sigh bitterly. "When's detention, Professor Stillman?"

"My classroom, after school tomorrow," he says. "I'm very disappointed in you, June. I expected better from my star student."

Ouch. Way to rub it in, Stillman. He walks away, leaving us with Thomas, who still has that stupid grin plastered across his face.

"Yikes. You guys are in *trouble,*" he smirks, stretching out the word *trouble* way too much. "I'll take my seat back now."

Ryn glares at him. "Oh yeah? Who said you could?"

"Uh, I did," Thomas scoffs. "You don't belong at this table, Type One, so go away. You too, Four. Or else."

"Listen, I don't want any trouble," says Grayson, starting to stand up. "So sorry for the inconvenience, I'll just—"

Ryn grabs him by the arm and yanks him back down. "Or else what?" she asks Thomas, a hint of amusement in her tone.

"Or else I'll… I'll… uh… I'll make you leave," Thomas says, grinning like this is the best comeback in the history of comebacks.

"Go ahead," says Ryn, smiling. "I'd like to see you try."

He just stands there, looking around. "That's what I thought," says Ryn, going back to her salad.

Thomas balls up his fists and grits his teeth, writhing with anger. He marches up to me, grabs the slice of baguette off my plate and chucks it at Ryn. With a sharp gasp, she ducks down at the last second, narrowly dodging it. The whole cafeteria goes quiet.

"My baguette," I murmur.

All eyes on her, Ryn slowly looks back up at Thomas, nostrils flared and eyes ablaze. "Oh, you're gonna pay for that," she snarls, rising to her feet.

Thomas's eyes widen and he backs away, nearly crashing into the Type Two table. "Don't hurt me! It was an accident!"

She gives a harsh laugh. "You mean, you launched that baguette at me… by accident?"

"Ryn, don't," I whisper.

I watch in horror as she eyes the giant bowl of ranch dressing on the table and it rises into the air. The dining hall is dead silent as Ryn uses her powers to send the bowl floating towards Thomas, breaking yet another of the biggest Rainloft rules: *no using your abilities outside of class.*

The bowl hovers above Thomas's head and he stares up at it, bottom lip trembling, eyes as wide as saucers. "*Now* can I have your seat?" Ryn asks, eyes locked on the dressing bowl.

Thomas gulps. "No way! I refuse to let you break the rules!"

"Alright, have it your way." With a flick of Ryn's wrist, the floating bowl of dressing is flipped over. My hand flies up to my mouth as Thomas is overcome by a landslide of ranch dressing, the creamy sauce splattering all over him and everyone within a five-mile radius.

There's a collective gasp. All eyes are on Thomas as he wipes the dressing out of his eyes, flinging it onto the floor. "I'm telling the teacher!" he yells, turning on his heel and wiping out on the giant puddle of sauce. I know it's against the rules and all, but I can't say I don't enjoy watching Ryn put Thomas in his place.

"No need," says Professor Stillman from the dining hall doors. He shakes his head in disbelief, his arms crossed. "I saw it all. Miss Sharp, come with me."

Grayson and I exchange a glance as Stillman escorts Ryn out of the dining hall, and I release the breath I've been holding. "Well, now I know why *that* rule exists."

Why midnight? I think as I make my way to Becker's classroom, the sound of my footsteps filling the empty hallway as I try not to collapse from exhaustion. *She couldn't have scheduled detention for, say, six o'clock? Seven? Eight?*

There are seven other students in the room when I walk in. That includes Ryn and Grayson, both of whom look just as tired and disgruntled as I feel.

Becker frowns. "You're late," she tells me.

It's 12:01.

I can't help but laugh. "Seriously?"

"Sit down, Miss Winters."

Why doesn't she call me by my first name? It's a lot shorter and would be easier for everyone. Fuming, I cross the room and sit down at my usual desk near the back. All eyes follow my every move and nobody says a word until I'm fully settled.

"You all know why you're here," says Becker. "All eight of you made the unwise decision to violate one of the most important Rainloft rules, and now you must pay the price." She picks up a stack of notebook paper and begins passing it out. "You will write the words '*different types must not interact*' five hundred times before you may leave."

"Five hundred?!" I blurt out before I can stop myself.

"*Six* hundred for you, Miss Winters," Becker glowers, handing me a few sheets of paper. *Of course* I had to open my mouth. Now I'm going to be here until midnight *tomorrow.* "You may begin."

I pull out my favorite pen and start writing.

Different types must not interact.

Different types must not interact.

Different types must not interact.

I stop when a pencil snaps from across the room. "This is ridiculous," says Ryn, throwing her hands in the air. Her chair makes an ear-piercing screech against the tile as she stands up and storms out of the room.

Heads turn in alarm. Becker's lips part and she stares at the door, her face pale with shock. "Well, don't just sit there!" she barks. "Someone, go get her!"

I drop my pencil and I'm out the door before Becker is even finished talking. "Hey—Ryn," I call, jogging to catch up with her. "Where are you going?"

Not slowing down, she shakes her head. "I don't know. Anywhere but here."

The edge in her tone makes me stop in my tracks. "What's going on?"

"What do you mean, *'what's going on'?*"

"You seem mad."

"Oh, do I?"

I sigh and run down the hallway to catch back up to her. "Ryn, what's wrong?"

Abruptly, she whirls around to face me and I step back. "I'll tell you what's wrong," she rages, "everything about this school! Actually, I wouldn't call it a school—

it's a prison. This place is a prison and we're all prisoners. And none of us deserve to be locked up!"

I stare at her. "Huh?"

"What I mean is *this isn't working,*" she says. "This whole breaking-the-rules-in-order-to-change-them thing? *It's not working.*"

"Well, not *yet* it's not," I correct her. "We just started breaking the rules, what, yesterday? It'll take time for the teachers to change things."

"But here's the thing: the teachers aren't *going* to change," says Ryn. "I was sent to Headmistress Avalon's office after the whole dinner fiasco, and guess what? She gave me detention for a year." She scoffs. "I have to sit in detention doing extra work from four o'clock to midnight *every single day.* And what's worse is she said that if I violate the rules one more time, there will be even worse consequences."

"So what I'm hearing is… the rebellion is canceled?" I can't help but feel a twinge of relief.

She shakes her head. "Oh, it's far from canceled. We just need to do something bigger. Something so big that they'll have no choice but to change the way things work here."

"What are you saying?"

She takes a deep breath and her eyes meet mine. "We need to escape."

Chapter Three

I can't help but laugh. "*Escape? That's crazy.*"

"But it's not," says Ryn. She starts pacing around the empty hallway and I have to turn my head to keep eye contact. "Just think about it! With the right plan and the right people, we could make it happen!"

"But… *how?*" I question. "There are so many teachers and Alumni all over the place. We wouldn't even make it *outside* without getting caught."

"June, we have *powers,*" Ryn says. "There has to be *some* way around that."

"Uh, we're also floating miles above the ground, in case you forgot," I remind her. "Even if we do make it past all the guards, what do we do then? Jump?"

"Maybe," she replies, even though I meant it as a joke. "Just… give me a day to work out the details."

"Ryn, only one person has *ever* escaped this place."

She stops in her tracks and points at me. "Exactly! Your brother did it. We can do it too!"

I sigh, folding my arms. "Look, if you want to try and escape, I'm not stopping you. I just think it's a little too risky."

"Fine," says Ryn, visibly deflating a little. "I get it, I guess. But…let me know if you change your mind."

I'm about to respond when I hear Professor Becker's high heels clicking on the tile behind me. I whirl around to face her. "Now what are you two doing out here?" she demands, hands on her hips.

"I just had to go to the bathroom," Ryn lies easily.

Becker eyes her, pursing her lips. "*Hmph.* Well, bathroom break's over, Miss Sharp. Back to my classroom, both of you."

She herds Ryn and I back into detention and we continue working on our assignment. I scrawl down the words Different types must not interact over and over again, paying absolutely no attention to what I'm writing. All I can think about is Ryn's idea.

I've never really thought about escaping before. Sure, I hate the Rainloft with every ounce of my being, but it's just never crossed my mind. It just hasn't seemed possible before. Like something on top of a tall shelf, sitting so high up that you don't even try to reach it. But maybe it's not impossible. It would definitely be risky, but maybe Ryn's on to something…

I'm still thinking about it when I finish up my assignment and turn it in to Professor Becker. By now everyone else is long gone, getting some much-needed sleep while I write the same sentence a hundred extra times. I guess that's what I get for opening my mouth.

It's past three o'clock in the morning when I finally get back to my dorm room, my hand ready to fall off and my eyelids heavier than a ton of bricks. I shrug off my blazer, crawl into bed and despite everything on my mind, I'm out like a light.

*   *   *

"Ryn wants to escape," I report to Grayson as we walk down the hallway, me on my way to Rainloft History and him heading to Advancing Teleportation.

He looks at me like I have two heads. "Is she insane?"

"Yeah, maybe a little," I admit, "but also kind of brilliant."

"So… you're going with her?" Grayson asks.

"Oh, no," I reply immediately, shaking my head, though I still haven't fully convinced myself that I'm not going to do it. "Way too dangerous."

"Right." There's a long pause. "Well, I should get to class."

"Bye." He goes into the Advancing Teleportation classroom and I walk the rest of the way to Rainloft History, still thinking about the whole escaping-the-Rainloft thing. *What if I do escape? What if I get to go back home? What if I could go to high school like a normal teenager instead of spending my life cooped up in this place?*

I step into Becker's classroom, expecting it to be full of students, but it's almost completely empty. The bell rings, but the only people inside are Professor Becker and Headmistress Avalon.

Wait. *Headmistress Avalon?*

She has her back turned to me, talking to Becker in a hushed tone. I back out of the classroom and glance at my watch—it's 5:16. *I don't have Rainloft History at 5:16.*

My heart rate picks up when I realize I'm supposed to be in Advancing Time Travel right now. I pivot and I'm about to make a mad dash to class when I hear my name from Professor Becker's classroom.

"…June Winters…"

Curiosity gets the better of me and I creep up to the door, crouching down by the doorframe just out of Becker's line of sight.

Am I eavesdropping on my teachers? Technically, yes. Is this a bad idea? Definitely. But don't act like you wouldn't do the same thing if you overheard two people talking about you behind your back.

"This… *thing* is becoming a problem," says Professor Becker, spitting out the word *thing* like it's a curse. "We need to do something about it."

"I think you're right," Headmistress Avalon whispers, concern edging into her normally calm tone. "I mean, a One, a Three *and* a Four working together?" she shudders. "Who knows what they're capable of?"

What we're capable of? What does that even mean? I lean closer to the door in order to hear better.

"Especially if they start putting their powers together," Becker says gravely. "They'd become too powerful for the good of this school. We have to put a stop to this."

"I know," says Avalon. "And I don't think detention is going to suffice."

"Well, what do you suggest we do?"

Avalon sighs, folding her arms over her long black dress. "Expulsion is our only option."

My heart lurches. *Expulsion?* No, that can't be right. Only one student has ever been expelled, as far as I know—Stan Grapeman, three years ago. Stan caused a lot of trouble—he spoke out of turn, used his powers outside of class and broke every rule in the book. Then one day he sent his teacher flying across the classroom with his mind and that was the last straw. Rumor has it that Avalon stripped him of his powers and threw him off the landing deck—no parachute, no harness, nothing protecting him from hitting the ground.

Then again, I did hear that from Thomas. But still— nobody knows what expulsion from the Rainloft entails, and I'd rather not be the first to find out—especially if that rumor is the truth.

Becker's eyes are wide, but she nods, only causing me to panic more. "You're right. Those three need to be stopped, and if expulsion is the best way to put an end to their little shenanigans, then so be it."

"I'm glad we agree," says Avalon. "We'll make it quick and discreet. Four o'clock tomorrow morning seems like a good time to do it."

"Do *what*?" I don't realize I've said that out loud until both women spin around to face me with the same wide-eyed expression on both of their faces. I clap a hand over my mouth. *Shoot.*

"Ah. Well, if it isn't Miss Winters herself," Avalon drawls, flashing me an eerie grin from behind her feathery black mask.

I scramble to my feet. "Er—I was… um…" All sorts of excuses and alibis fill my head, each one crazier than the last. *I got lost on my way to class and accidentally stumbled upon Professor Becker's classroom. I was walking by the classroom and talking to myself for some reason and you just happened to hear me. I'm not real— a Type Two is mind-controlling you right now.*

To my surprise, Avalon just waves it off. "No matter," she says. It's kind of scaring me how calm Avalon is being, especially when Becker's so furious that her face is nothing short of a wrinkly tomato. "We have a punishment in place. Go back to class, June."

I don't even bother trying to hide my confusion. "But, um… what's the punishment?" I venture.

Avalon smiles again. "You'll find out soon enough. But rest assured—you're going to regret eavesdropping on your superiors."

"Uh, okay," I manage, nearly tripping over my own feet as I turn around and bolt back down the hallway, my mind spinning. *What if that rumor about Stan isn't actually a rumor? Is that what they're going to do to Ryn, Grayson and me? Punt us off the landing deck and let us free-fall to our doom?*

I've heard the Stan legend countless times before, but it's always seemed too insane to be true. Too evil. But the way Avalon was acting…

My mind flips back to Ryn's idea and suddenly, making a break for it doesn't sound so risky. Staying here would be more dangerous than trying to escape, at this point.

I'm hit by a rush of excitement. This is *happening*. We're really getting out of here. Still, the question remains: *how?*

Ryn must have a plan by now. She has to. Or else… I shake my head to clear the thought from my mind.

Fingers crossed, I head towards the dining hall.

"What's your deal?" Thomas sneers through a mouthful of beef roast.

I stare at the doors of the dining hall, fidgeting with my bracelet and biting my lip as I wait for Ryn or Grayson to walk in. I realize I haven't even touched my food yet.

"Nothing," I murmur, not taking my eyes off the door. It's 7:02. I might only have nine hours left before Avalon throws me over the landing deck, and the thought is freaking me out.

I spot Ryn near the entrance and practically leap out of my seat, intercepting her before she gets to the Type One table.

"Hey," I start, still fiddling with my bracelet. "So, uh, I kind of changed my mind about the whole escape thing? Um, we have to get out of here by four o'clock tomorrow or else we're all gonna die."

Ryn stares at me, her tray of food hanging limply in her hands. "Come with me," she mutters, grabbing my arm and dragging me out of the dining hall, throwing her food in the garbage on the way.

Once we're outside, she spins around to face me. "Okay, *what??*"

"Well, I overheard Headmistress Avalon talking with Professor Becker," I explain, talking fast, words spilling out of my mouth. "She said that you, me and Grayson are becoming a problem, and that expulsion is the only solution, whatever that means, and you know the Stan Grapeman rumor—"

"Whoa, hold up," Ryn interrupts. "Why does Avalon want to expel all three of us? I broke more rules than either of you two."

"I don't know, she said we were becoming 'too powerful' or something now that we're 'working together'?" I shrug.

She narrows her eyes at me. "That doesn't make any sense."

"I know, but either way, we need to escape ASAP," I say. "So? Have you thought of a plan yet?"

"Uh, sort of?" she hesitates.

I nod hopefully. "Great. Do you think you'll be ready to leave by, say, midnight?"

"Probably?" Ryn takes a deep breath, running a hand through her hair. "Wow, this is *happening*."

"Yeah," I murmur. I can hardly believe it myself—a couple hours ago I was ready to spend the rest of my life in this place. Now there's not a thought on my mind other than how I'm going to escape.

The bell rings, releasing us from dinner. "We'll meet at that portrait of your brother in the Type One wing. Nine-thirty tonight," Ryn decides. "Bring Grayson."

"Got it," I say. "See you then."

I don't get any of my homework done. That's what I would normally be spending my evenings on—trying to finish all the essays and worksheets my teachers have assigned before the sun rises—but why should I? One way or another, I'm not going to class tomorrow.

Time flies by and soon enough I find myself creeping down the pitch-dark corridor, armed with a flashlight and on my guard for any teachers or Alumni wandering the halls. My heart thumps against my ribcage and I bite my lip, trying to keep my footsteps light and quiet.

Dread fills me when Professor Becker's voice echoes off the hallway walls. "Who's there?" she demands. "You know you're supposed to be in bed!"

I freeze, looking desperately around the area for a place to hide. My gaze lands on a giant statue of Avalon and I dive into the safety of its shadow.

I can't help but feel a twinge of annoyance as Becker charges straight past me. *Why is she always walking around the school at this time of night?* I think. *Doesn't she have anything better to do than hunt for misbehaving students? Like, I don't know, sleep?*

Once the coast is clear, I walk the rest of the way to Grayson's dorm. It takes me way longer than expected due to the insane number of teachers patrolling the corridors. I feel like a video game character, ducking and dodging enemies every five seconds.

Finally I make it to Grayson's room. I glance over my shoulder to make sure I haven't accidentally brought any stalker teachers with me, and then knock softly on the door.

Surprisingly, he answers right away. He's still fully dressed in the sea-green Type Four uniform, his tie loose and his blond hair rumpled from sleep. He rubs his eyes and squints at me. "June?" he starts. "What are you—?"

"We're escaping," I tell him shortly, keeping my voice low. "Ryn is waiting, so we have to go. Like, *now*."

He stares at me. "Huh?"

I shake my head and grab Grayson by the wrist, dragging him down the hallway behind me. "Okay," I whisper as I march down the hallway, looking and sounding much more confident than I feel. "So, long story short, if we don't escape now, we'll all be dead by morning."

"*What?*" he blurts out, jogging to catch up with me. "What do you mean '*dead by morning*'?"

"I'll explain once we're out of here," I say. We round the corner to the Type One hallway and there's Ryn, standing next to the same portrait of Atlas that I met her by before. She waves us over.

"*There* you are," she sighs. "What took you guys so long?"

"Becker was on the hunt again," I shrug. "So what's the plan?"

"To put it simply, we'll go out onto the Landing Deck—we might have to dodge some Alumni on the way—and then we'll jump," says Ryn, like this plan makes total sense.

"I just woke up five minutes ago," Grayson murmurs.

"Wait, *jump?*" I repeat. "As in… thousands of feet?"

"Well, not…" Ryn trails off, narrowing her eyes. "Do you hear that?"

I pause, and sure enough, the sound of Becker's voice comes floating down the hallway. "I heard that!" she bellows. "You little rule-breakers better get to bed before I find you!"

"Again?" I groan.

"It's only a matter of time before Becker tells Avalon. Before long there'll be a whole search party out to find us," Ryn grumbles. "Well? You two ready?"

No, I think immediately, but what other choice do I have? I force a smile and nod.

Grayson looks back and forth between Ryn and I, his eyes wide. "Wait, so we're just going to waltz out onto the landing deck and hope nobody notices us?"

Ryn sighs impatiently. "I have a plan. Just trust me, okay?"

The *click* of Becker's high heels on the tile floor gets louder by the second. "Uh, quick question," I whisper, "does anyone know where the landing deck *is*?"

Ryn looks at me like I've sprouted wings. "You don't?" she shakes her head. "Well, follow me then."

We end up playing a game of Follow-the-Leader down the winding Rainloft hallways and all the way to the doorway of the central lobby. My palms are sweating and my mind is spinning with worries: *What if we don't make it past the guards? What will they do to us then? What happens when we hit the ground... if we hit the ground...*

Once we've reached the entrance of the lobby, Ryn spins around to face Grayson and I, like a coach hyping up the team before a big game. "The doors to the landing deck are at the back of the lobby," she says, jerking her thumb towards the giant metal doors straight across the lobby from us. The room looks like a typical hotel lobby—plain-looking couches with boring pillows and shiny white coffee tables are scattered around. Dim sconces line the walls—they're just bright enough that I can see two Alumni, dressed in their trademark black leather uniforms, guarding the exit.

"What do we do about *them?*" I question, pointing at the guards. I realize my hand is shaking and quickly tuck it behind my back.

"Just—" Ryn starts, but then she freezes, her eyes widening. *"Shoot."*

I follow her gaze back to the Alumni—and realize that it's too late. I step back and watch one of them—a twenty-something-year-old man with eyes like a pit bull's—point towards us and start marching in our direction. The other one—an Alumna who looks like she could crush diamond with her teeth—follows closely behind.

"You know, maybe we should turn around," says Grayson, eyes fixed on the pair of giants slowly stalking towards us. I can't help but nod in agreement.

"Just use your powers," Ryn hisses, but I can hardly hear her with my heart pounding in my ears. Without warning, she jerks her head towards the Alumnus and he's sent flying through the air like a rocket. He lands with a *thud* that echoes around the lobby.

And then Ryn takes off, sidestepping the Alumna and tearing across the lobby like an Olympic gold medalist. She's reached the doors before I can blink. "What are you waiting for?" she calls. "Run!"

I force myself into motion, sprinting as fast as I can toward the metal doors. The Alumna is faster—just as I'm running past her, she grunts and thrusts a giant hand in my direction. My heart skips a beat when my feet freeze without me telling them to. *She's a Type One.* Before I even realize what's happening, the Alumna has me frozen in midair, my toes dangling five feet above the ground. Her telekinetic hold on me is so tight that I can hardly move or breathe. "Let—me—go!" I gasp, fighting to bring air into my lungs. It's no use—she's too powerful.

"I've gotcha now, little punk," the Alumna snarls, her eyes locked on me. She's so focused that she doesn't notice when Grayson appears beside her, holding a blue pillow from one of the couches. I watch as he smashes the pillow into the Alumna's face—*hard*—breaking her concentration. I crumble to the floor, gasping like a fish out of water. The Alumna clutches her nose and staggers backward. "Owww!" she howls.

Grayson's expression flips to concern and for a second, he looks ready to bring the Alumna an ice pack. "Er—sorry, I didn't—"

"Grayson!" Ryn barks from the doors. Her eyes are locked on the Alumnus—who's still lying on his back like a turtle—pinning him to the ground. "Hurry up!"

Grayson nods and appears by my side with a flash of blue-green light. For some reason, the fact that he can teleport hasn't crossed my mind until now. "You alright?" he asks, helping me up.

I nod, still trying to catch my breath. "Yeah—thanks." Out the corner of my eye, I catch the Alumnus slowly rising to his feet, despite Ryn's best efforts to keep him down. With his nostrils flared and his fists clenched, he looks like a bull, ready to charge at her.

But he doesn't. Instead, he stays put, looking Ryn straight in the eye. "Come here," he growls, his voice low and gruff. To my surprise, she does exactly that, obediently stepping away from the landing deck doors and strolling over to the Alumnus without a single protest.

Grayson realizes what's going on before I do. "Mind control. He's a Type Two."

A few feet away from us, the Alumna is regaining her senses. "You hold her off," I say, "I'll go help Ryn."

I take off, dodging the Alumna and heading for Ryn. She stands by the Alumnus, holding out her hands and patiently waiting while he binds her wrists together with some kind of pale blue rope. Once he's finished, he whips out a walkie-talkie and holds it up to his mouth.

I get there before he can say anything into it. Without fully thinking it through, I swat the walkie-talkie out of his hand and it clatters to the ground, shattering on impact.

The Alumnus turns and looks at me like I just punched his grandmother. "How *dare* you?" he snarls, his beady eyes glinting with fury.

I swallow hard, stepping back. Yeah, that may not have been the greatest idea ever. I scan the area for a solution, my heart pounding. *Too bad time travel is completely useless in a fight,* I think bitterly.

Ryn seems to be caught in some sort of trance, staring straight ahead with a faraway look in her eyes. She doesn't seem to notice that her hands are tied together or that the Alumnus is controlling her mind right now.

"Uh, Ryn?" I say tentatively.

"Good luck waking her up," the Alumnus rasps. "You'll have to get past me if you want your little friend back. And we both know that's not happening!" He tosses back his head, cackling like a mad scientist.

I see the opportunity. Without thinking twice, I pull back my fist and ram it with full force into his jaw. "Argh!" he squawks, tilting backward and landing flat on his back.

At that moment, Ryn snaps out of her trance and stumbles forward. "Oh, that was awful," she shudders, shaking her head. She looks down at the rope still tied around her wrists. "What—?"

"Here," I say. I walk over to her and unknot the rope with ease. Hey, my powers are totally worthless in combat, but at least I'm good at untying knots!

Once the rope is off, Ryn and I make a break for the exit. We reach the landing deck doors and I spin back around to see Grayson fighting a losing battle against the furious Alumna.

Ryn merely eyes the Alumna and she's sent flying across the lobby, giving Grayson a chance to blink over to us. "Thanks," he says, fixing his uniform tie.

"No problem." Ryn glances over her shoulder at the Alumna, who's lying on the ground next to the Alumnus. He's getting to his feet, a new walkie-talkie in his hand. "We have to go, *now*. You guys ready?"

As ready as I'll ever be, I think. Ryn shoves open the doors and we follow her outside.

The wind hits me like a tidal wave, threatening to blow me right back inside. Cool white floor lights line the deck, illuminating the long, empty area from the doors all the way to the far edge. Surprisingly, it's completely deserted. The only thing that stands between us and a plummet to our doom is the seventy-foot-long landing deck, and the thought twists my stomach into a knot.

Ryn presses forward. "The Alumni will be coming after us any second now," she shouts over the wind. "We have to be quick!"

We make it to the end of the deck way too fast, and every bit of me wants to turn around and bolt back inside. Looking over the edge makes my head spin—dark, swirling clouds block the ground below from view. The fact that there are clouds *below* us just shows how insanely high up the Rainloft floats.

"What do we do now?" I yell.

Ryn takes a deep breath. "We jump."

Both Grayson and I whip around to face her. "We *what?"*

"Just trust me!" she hisses. "It's now or never!"

One glance over my shoulder tells me she's right: a whole pack of Alumni is pouring out the doors, all of them dead set on bringing us back. "This is *insane*," I murmur.

"On the count of three, we jump," Ryn says urgently. As much as I hate it, I know that if we're going to do this, we have to do it now. It's either jump or get carried back into the Rainloft. While the latter isn't nearly as terrifying, I know that I'll regret letting them lock me up again. "One… two… three!"

And so, my hands shaking and my heart thundering, I step over the edge.

I end up doing a full gymnastics routine during the fall: flipping and twisting and cartwheeling all the way down. The different features of the city below tumble in and out of my vision and the wind howls through my ears, getting louder and louder the farther I fall.

I can hardly breathe. I can hardly form a full thought. I would scream, but I can barely open my mouth. At first I can pretend I'm flying, but as I gather speed and momentum, it starts to feel like my clothes are on fire.

But then, gravity seems to reverse itself. I'm about a hundred feet away from splattering on the forest floor below when I begin to slow down. All of that momentum vanishes and I'm left drifting down to the ground like a feather.

Floating slowly down to the treetops underneath me, I can't help but wonder: *Am I...dead? Is this what it feels like to be dead?*

A minute later, I'm left with my toes dangling above a rain-soaked patch of dirt. All of the sudden, I drop straight into a puddle of mud, instantly soaking my shiny black uniform shoes.

"No way," I murmur, taking in my surroundings. I'm in the middle of a clearing, surrounded by freakishly tall trees that scrape the star-flecked night sky. The air is thick and humid, telling me that it's rained here recently. The dirt floor is flooded and the screech of cicadas is inescapable.

There's a sudden *splash* noise behind me. I whirl around just in time to see Grayson wipe out in a giant puddle of mud, his pale cheeks flushed with wind.

"Holy cow," he says as I help him to his feet. "What *was* that?"

"It was me." Ryn's voice causes us both to spin around. She hovers there in midair, not even disturbing the mud around her when she drops gracefully to the floor. "My powers."

"Huh? But… how?" I question.

"When we got close enough to the ground, I used my powers to stop all three of us mid-fall," Ryn explains casually, combing through her windswept hair. "I was able to lower us down safely from there. See? I told you it would work."

"That's… kind of amazing," Grayson remarks.

"Yeah, it is," I begin, "but I have to ask: what do we do now?"

Before, the only thing I could think about was the fact that we were going to escape and how we were going to do it. I never really considered what would come after.

"Well, I *did* have an idea," says Ryn, turning to face me. "We find your brother."

PART II

Chapter 4

I remember the day Atlas escaped like it was yesterday.

It was midway through my second year at the Rainloft and I was sitting in my Beginning Time Travel class, trying not to fall asleep while my teacher droned on about an assignment we were to complete.

"Remember: it's important to have all the correct calculations when jumping back in time," Miss Bauer repeated for the hundredth time. "Especially—"

She never got to finish the sentence, because at that moment, the Escapee Alarm started blaring. I shot five feet out of my chair and couldn't help but cover my ears over the alarm's obnoxious screeching.

All of us stayed glued to our seats, looking up at Miss Bauer with wide eyes. Nobody knew what to do. This had never happened before. At that point, the little indicator light on the wall was nothing but a decoration.

Now, it flashed ice-blue light across the classroom, signifying that a student had escaped. "Er—nobody panic," said Miss Bauer, her tone ironically full of panic. "It's probably just a drill."

But then Headmistress Avalon's voice came booming over the P.A. system. "Attention, students and staff: this is not a drill," she announced. "A second-year Type Two is attempting to escape."

At first, I didn't think much of the fact that it was a Type Two the same age as me. My brother was one of twenty of them. In that moment, the only two thoughts in my mind were *Is that student going to make it out?* followed by *What happens if they do?*

"Everyone, please remain inside the classrooms," Avalon continued. "Stay calm; our Alumni have this under control."

We all made a beeline toward the big window, some of my classmates shoving each other out of the way to get a good view of the landing deck. I ended up at the back of the pack and had to stand on my tiptoes in order to see over Thomas's head.

"Who is it?" someone whispered. "Did they make it?"

Thomas snorted. "Please. If anyone's going to escape this place, it's gonna be me."

Out on the landing deck, I could just barely make out a sleek black Rainloft helicopter and a group of Alumni charging at it like a pack of bulls. "Look!" one of the other Type Threes shouted, jabbing his finger at the window. "It's that student! Inside the chopper!"

Sure enough, through the tinted passenger side window, I caught a glimpse of that trademark green Type Two uniform. Then the blades started spinning and the chopper rose up off the deck.

All of us watched from the classroom with bated breath. Whoever was in control of the helicopter drove it straight off the landing deck, sending it sailing down to the ground. The swarm of Alumni stopped at the edge, watching helplessly as the chopper disappeared beneath the clouds.

Thomas broke the silence. "Who in the universe *was* that?"

As if on cue, Avalon's voice came booming over the P.A. system again. "I'm sure you're all wondering what, exactly, just happened," she said, and there was something different behind her voice, an emotion that I couldn't quite place. Sadness, maybe? Defeat? "Well, one of our Type Twos somehow managed to mind-control an Alumna. The student convinced her to pilot one of our helicopters and bring him down to the ground inside one."

The group of Alumni was still standing on the landing deck. None of them seemed sure of what to do next.

"We're going to bring him back." Now there was nothing but sheer determination in Avalon's tone. "Whatever it takes, no matter how we do it, we're going to bring Atlas Winters back to the Rainloft."

And then there was silence. I didn't need to look around to know that everyone was staring at me.

"No way! It was your *brother*?" Thomas asked, gaping at me. "*That* little shrimp?"

"Um… yeah," I said, even though I could hardly believe it myself. "Yeah, it was."

Atlas's great escape was all that anyone could talk about for way too long afterward. Droves of Alumni flew out of the Rainloft every day for a year, tirelessly searching every nook and cranny of the ground below just to find my brother.

From the rumors I've heard floating around, they did find him. A few times, actually. Yet he always managed to evade capture—whether it was the fact that he was really good with his powers or nothing but dumb luck, Avalon never did manage to bring Atlas back.

"So… quick question," I say as Ryn, Grayson and I trudge through the muddy forest. It's so humid that the air weighs on me like a ton of bricks, and my hair is plastered to my forehead with sweat. We've been out here walking for way too long, and I'm practically melting. "How are we supposed to find Atlas?"

"Well, for starters," says Ryn, "we need to make it out of this forest."

"Which could take multiple days because we have absolutely no clue where we are," I point out, wiping my sweaty brow with the back of my hand. Thank goodness the sun isn't up. Otherwise, I'd be toast.

Ryn sighs, kicking at a clump of mud. "It won't be *that* long. We're close to the end, I can feel it. Anyways, is there a certain place where your brother used to hang out a lot? Maybe a restaurant or a park or something?"

I think for a second. "Our house?"

"Well, maybe that's where we'll find him," Ryn suggests.

I look at her sideways. "Maybe, but personally, if I were to escape the Rainloft, I don't think I would hide in *my house*. That's the *first* place the Alumni would look."

"But Atlas has mind-control powers," Grayson chimes in, clearly catching on to Ryn's train of thought faster than I am.

Ryn stops in her tracks and points at him. "Bingo!" she exclaims. "I wouldn't put anything past this guy. June, say he *did* decide to hide at home. If the Alumni showed up at his doorstep, he could have sent them away with his powers! Think smarter, not harder, right?"

"I guess so?" I *could* get on board with Ryn's glass-half-full mindset, but in the back of my mind, I know that we've been really lucky so far. We somehow managed to escape the Rainloft *and* reach the ground completely unscathed, and I can't shake the feeling that that luck is going to run out eventually. Plus, what are the odds that we find my brother, who is basically the world's most wanted criminal, *in his house?* As much as I want to believe it, not everything is going to go our way.

"Hold on." Grayson stops suddenly, holding up his index finger. "Do you hear that?"

I pause to listen, and sure enough, my ears are greeted with the sweet sound of somebody's car alarm blaring in the distance. If there's a car nearby, then that must mean—

"Humanity," Ryn gasps. She turns to smirk at me. "I told you we were close."

Without any sort of warning, she takes off running in the direction of the alarm. As miserable as it sounds to run in this kind of heat, Grayson and I are left with no choice but to go after her.

The trees cut off abruptly behind a row of houses. I emerge from the forest to find myself in what seems to be somebody's backyard—a grassy lawn the size of a football field, directly behind a brown-brick home that looks identical to the ones around it.

Through a gap between the houses, I spot Ryn standing on a sidewalk up ahead. I cut through the gap, Grayson at my heels.

"Do either of you recognize this area?" Ryn asks immediately once we slow to a halt next to her.

I open my mouth to say *no,* but stop myself. Looking around—the quaint little houses lined up against a winding brick road, the perfectly-manicured front lawns—I'm overcome with the sense that I've seen this place before. I recognize this neighborhood almost like I've only ever seen it from pictures.

The realization hits me like a truck. "This is my neighborhood," I murmur.

Both Ryn and Grayson whip around to face me. "For real?" Ryn asks.

"Yeah," I breathe, even though I can hardly believe it myself. I peer down the sidewalk to my left. "And if I remember correctly…my house is just down that way."

"That's wild," Grayson marvels. "What are the odds that we land less than a mile away from where we need to be?"

"Yeah," I say vaguely, not entirely sure what to make of this situation. I have no idea how I've never realized before that the Rainloft hovers almost directly over my neighborhood. "What are the odds?"

Without wasting a second, Ryn starts strolling down the sidewalk in the direction of my house. "Well?" she says, looking over her shoulder at Grayson and me. "We need to get moving—the Alumni can't be far, and I'd rather not get hauled back up to the Rainloft again."

"Right." On the way, I trip over my own feet more times than I'd like to admit because I can't stop looking around. The neighborhood is exactly how I remember it—the tree sprouts that my family helped plant a small eternity ago have hardly grown an inch. My neighbor, Mrs. Laughlin, still has her holiday decorations up, even though it's the middle of April and the sun gets so bright during the day that you'd need to wear multiple pairs of sunglasses if you plan on staying outside for longer than a minute. I smile, remembering Mrs. Laughlin's response when the HOA got mad at her for leaving the lights up year-round—she sprayed them all with a garden hose.

And then we reach my house, and I'm hit with a whole tsunami of memories. There are so many good ones: Atlas and I posing for first-day-of-school pictures on the front porch, Atlas and I playing basketball in the driveway, Atlas crying to our parents after I accidentally-on-purpose launched the ball straight into his face.

But there are bad ones, too. One look around brings back a whole truckload of memories that I'd stuffed in a box and shoved somewhere in the back of my mind. Most of them are memories of *that night*—the sleek black

Rainloft helicopter parked in the street, the flooded lawn squishing under my feet, the look on my dad's face as he watched his only remaining family get taken away.

My dad. Suddenly, it occurs to me that my dad might actually be inside that house. *And maybe even my mom.* I can't stop the thought from crossing my mind, even when I know that's darn near impossible. When my brother and I left for the Rainloft, she had already been missing for a year. It was pretty clear that, wherever she was, she wasn't coming back.

And that brings about another batch of sad flashbacks. At first I thought it was bittersweet, being back here. But now, my mind is flooded with nothing but bad memories and all it feels is *bitter.* I can't think about any of the good times without being reminded of the fact that there's no going back to the way things were. As much as I want to hit rewind and stop all of it—my mom's disappearance, the Rainloft—from happening in the first place, I know that's not happening and the thought makes my heart hurt.

Grayson seems to notice. "You okay there, June?"

I shake my head to clear my mind. "Just peachy," I say, plastering on an award-winning smile and forcing myself to walk past the gray SUV in the driveway and up to the front door.

My house is entirely average—it's neither big nor small, made mostly of brown brick with a black roof and accents. But still, my heart rate gets faster with every step I take towards it, because I have no idea what I'm walking into. I could see my family for the first time in *four years*. It might not look like that long on paper, but once you've lived it, it feels like an eternity has passed. Don't believe me? You try it—go four years without any sort of family in your life, and then we'll talk.

I can't help but wonder: *what will they think of me now?* Especially now that I'm basically a fugitive for escaping the Rainloft? If my dad answers the door, will he let us in? Or will he call the police and have us sent right back up there?

I reach the front entrance way too quickly. For a second I just stare at the door's chipped brown paint, not really sure whether to knock or ring the doorbell or just walk in. It feels strange to knock at *my own* front door, but it would be even weirder to just waltz in like the last four years never happened.

"Um, earth to June?" Ryn's voice draws me back to reality. "Are you going to knock, or should I?"

"Oh, yeah." I raise a fist and knock on the door before I can think twice. With a deep breath, I step back to where Ryn and Grayson are standing and wait.

It must only be a few seconds, but it feels like multiple hours have passed before the door finally swings open. When I see who's behind it, I stop breathing. And I'm pretty sure he does, too.

There, standing in the doorway, is Atlas. *In his house,* just as Ryn had predicted. He looks exactly how I remember him—brown hair, silvery-gray eyes and thick eyebrows that make him look dead-serious all the time. Instead of the jade-green Type Two uniform that I'm used to seeing him in at the Rainloft, he wears a leather jacket over a plain white T-shirt and jeans. He and I just kind of stare at each other for the better part of a minute.

Ryn breaks the silence. "You two really do look alike," she remarks.

"Who are you?" Atlas demands, his pale eyes fixed on mine.

I glance between Ryn and Grayson, even though that question was clearly aimed at me. "Uh… I'm your sister?" I say, my voice ticking up at the end like I'm asking a question. "I'm June. Do you re—"

"No," Atlas cuts me off, his voice razor-sharp. "Who are you, really?"

That one throws me for a loop. "Well, I'm—"

"We're former Rainloft students, like you." Ryn steps up next to me, extending her hand to Atlas, who looks at her like she just dropped from the sky. "I'm Ryn Sharp, this is Grayson Campbell—" she gestures to Grayson, who gives a small wave. Ryn nods toward me and continues "—and this is your sister. The three of us escaped this morning and we were wondering if you could help us out a little."

My brother's hand is still gripping the doorknob, his knuckles paper-white. "You have thirty seconds."

"Thirty seconds?" I repeat, searching his face for an answer. When we were younger, I could read him like a book. Now, it's impossible to tell whether he's happy, mad, surprised or something entirely different. "Thirty seconds to *what*?"

"You know what I mean," Atlas says forcefully. "Turn around, get back in your little helicopter, fly away, and *leave me alone* if you know what's good for you."

"You don't believe we're actual Rainloft students," Ryn realizes, narrowing her eyes at Atlas. "Well... who do you *think* we are?"

"I've seen every trick in the book," says Atlas, leaning against the doorframe. "Whether this is some kind of mind-control stunt or if you're trying to lure me out there so that a pack of Alumni can kidnap me and drag me back up to that place, I would advise you walk away before one of you gets hurt."

"Atlas." I look him square in the eye. "I'm your sister. I wouldn't trick you like that—you can trust me."

He still doesn't look convinced. "How do I know that I'm not being mind-controlled into seeing you right now?"

"You're not," says Ryn, impatience creeping into her tone.

"And why should I believe *you*?" asks Atlas, arching an eyebrow.

"Just… we're real." Ryn thinks for a second. "Here. I'll prove it to you."

She glances over her shoulder at the car parked in the driveway, and then closes her eyes. The rest of us watch her expectantly, but nothing happens.

"Er—Ryn?" I say tentatively. "I don't think—"

"Quiet," she snaps, and I shut my mouth.

Suddenly, the car's alarm starts howling, its headlights flashing wildly, making me jump and waking up everyone within a ten-mile radius.

It doesn't take long for the neighbors to stir. Across the street from us, a lady steps out of her house, clad in a fluffy pink bathrobe and matching slippers. She looks ready to breathe fire. "Will one of you four turn off that dang car alarm?" she shouts over the car's obnoxious shrieking.

Ryn folds her arms and looks to Atlas, clearly pleased with herself. "Well?" she says. "Other people can see us too. You're not being mind-controlled—*we're real.*"

At that moment, something visibly clicks in my brother's brain. His eyes go wide and he closes the front door softly behind him, walking straight past us. "Come with me," he mutters.

Ryn, Grayson and I follow him across the front lawn and over to the side of the house. Once we're in the shade and out of the neighbors' sight, he spins around to face us, eyes ablaze.

"What were you thinking?" he hisses. "You can't just jump off the Rainloft, then walk around looking like *that* and expect nobody to notice you."

For some reason, it hasn't occurred to me before now that the three of us are still decked out in our full Rainloft uniforms, Grayson and I covered in dried mud. Odds are, news of our great escape has already gotten around. If anyone sees us, the uniforms are a dead giveaway that we're not supposed to be down here.

"Well, we haven't exactly had a chance to change," Ryn protests.

"People will probably just think they're costumes," I say. "The important thing is, what do we do now?"

Atlas shakes his head and starts pacing. "I don't believe it," he says, a hint of amusement in his tone. "You escape the Rainloft and come *here*, expecting me to *help* you." He stops in his tracks, looking back at us. "Well, for starters, you can't just *walk around in public.* You're fugitives now. If anyone recognizes you, you'll be back up there by nightfall." He sighs. "If you're dumb enough to think otherwise, then *I can't help you.*"

"We're not *dumb*," Ryn snaps back. "Nobody has recognized us yet."

"Yet," Atlas repeats. He narrows his eyes at her. "I get the sense that you're the leader of this little band. So, tell me—*why*?"

"Guys," I cut in, exasperated. "Arguing isn't going to help anything!"

Ryn and Atlas both still look outraged, so Grayson steps in. "Okay, so we all clearly have some explaining to do, and multiple different opinions on this whole…situation. What if we discuss it all—in a slightly less hostile way—over a late-night snack?"

The very mention of food makes my stomach growl. I haven't realized how hungry I am before now. But before I can say anything, Atlas frowns. "A late-night snack? Where are you going to get *that*?"

Suddenly, a memory pops into my mind: me, Atlas and our mother, sitting around a table, a mountain of fresh pastries in front of us. That's where we would go every Wednesday night after dinner, when our dad—a surgeon—had to work late: a little bakery where the entire staff knew us by name. It wasn't all that surprising that they knew us so well, as the bakery was hidden somewhere behind a massive grocery store and we were one of approximately three families that knew it existed, but it was still nice.

I grin. "What about Granny Marie's?"

Atlas just sighs. "Marie's is a *public place*. You three can't *go* to public places."

"Come on, Atlas—nobody ever goes there," I reason. "And nobody's going to recognize us; It's only been a few hours since we escaped. I kind of doubt that news will have gotten around that quickly." I pause. "Also, a Granny Marie's cookie sounds incredible right now."

He still doesn't look convinced, so Ryn suggests, "What if we take a vote? All in favor of going to the bakery, say *'aye'*." After she, Grayson and I say it in unison, she shrugs. "Oh, well. Looks like you're outnumbered."

"In case you forgot, I'm not part of this group," says Atlas. "I have no reason to risk *everything* just to help you when you're more than likely to get yourselves captured either way."

"But you can't just *let* us get taken back up there," I say. "You know a lot more about this whole 'escapee' thing than we do, and if I know you at all, you wouldn't just leave us to fend for ourselves."

Atlas considers that. "How good are you with your powers?"

"Well, mine got us down here," says Ryn. "June was crowned *Most Promising Type Three* and, oh, Grayson hit an Alumna with a pillow."

After a second, Atlas sighs, finally caving. "Fine."

One painfully awkward fifteen-minute walk later, I find myself walking through the door to Granny Marie's, overcome by another landslide of bittersweet memories. The little bell that jingles as we walk in, the sweet aroma of frosted pastries and fresh-baked bread, the cozy acoustic music playing from speakers above my head— it's all exactly as I remember it. Call me an idiot for waltzing into a public bakery with my gang of fugitives, but sometimes you have to do impulsive things like that. Plus, you've never smelled Granny Marie's bread. The scent is like laughing gas at the dentist's office—it makes everything else disappear.

A quick scan of the dining area tells me that we're the only ones here, save for one guy sitting at the counter, scrolling on his phone and sipping on coffee. "See?" I mutter to Atlas. "It's practically empty."

Granny Marie's was always my favorite place as a kid. Before her disappearance, I would beg our mother to take us there for a cookie after dinner every single night and even in the morning before school sometimes. Some may say the bakery looks a little old or run-down, what with the retro decor, flickery light-up menu boards behind the counter as well as tables and chairs that I'm pretty sure came from some ancient 80s diner, but I've always loved it here. The owner, Marie, would insist that we call her 'Granny' and treat Atlas and I like her own grandkids—she'd constantly ask us how school was going and tell us stories about her cats. She even memorized both of our food preferences (I was obsessed with sugar cookies; Atlas loathed them).

"I'll be with you in a jif!" Granny Marie's melodious voice drifts out from the open kitchen door, as sugary-sweet as the pastries in the glass display case behind the counter.

I grin when my eyes land on a table off to the right side of the room. There was never anything special about it—it was just a random table, neither at the edge of the dining area nor in the center—but every time we came here with our mother, without fail, that was the table we ate at. The number of memories the sight of that table brings back is overwhelming.

"It's weird, isn't it?" I mutter to Atlas. "Being back here?"

I expect an answer, but he completely ignores my question and strolls over to a table on the left side of the bakery. "This one will work," he says, pulling out a chair and sitting down.

I follow his lead for lack of anything better to do. Ryn, Grayson and I take our seats around the circular metal table and I cringe when my chair makes an ear-piercing *screech* sound as I pull it out.

Almost as if on cue, Granny Marie walks out the kitchen door, rescuing us from any potential awkward conversation. Her eyes are glued to the notepad in her hands as she bustles over to our table. When she finally looks up, she freezes and almost drops the notepad she'd been holding. "Oh my word," Granny Marie murmurs with her thick Southern accent, her wide blue eyes bouncing between Atlas and I in turn. Her silvery hair is pulled back in a tight bun, just the way it was styled every time we came here as kids. I'm pretty sure her entire uniform is exactly the same, too—she wears a visor that matches her dirty-pink dress and an off-white apron with faded coffee stains all over it. "This can't be."

I'm not entirely sure what to do here but I'm fighting the urge to stand up and give her a hug, whereas Atlas hardly even looks up from the menu. "You don't know us," he says shortly. "And you think their uniforms are costumes."

That earns him a weird look from everyone at the table. However, Granny Marie's utterly-bewildered expression flips to a peachy-sweet smile within about half a second. "Hello, welcome to Granny Marie's," she says, suddenly oblivious to our true identities. "Aren't you dears a tad young to be here without parents?"

I'm too busy trying to comprehend what just happened to realize that she asked a question. "Well," Ryn starts to say. "We—"

"We got separated from our parents," Atlas cuts in, still looking down at the menu. "We were all walking around the city, and somehow, we lost track of them. They told us to meet them here if we got split up."

I realize that Atlas is just as good a liar as Ryn, if not even better. When we were kids, that was never the case—in fact, I can't remember him telling a single lie. Not to me, not to our parents, not to anyone. Then again, maybe he was just such a good liar that nobody ever caught him in the act.

"Oh, you poor dears," Granny Marie gushes. "Well, can I get you somethin' to eat while you wait for your parents?"

"But… we don't have any money," Grayson points out, earning himself a look from Atlas.

Granny Marie just smiles and waves that off. "Oh, don't worry about it, dear. Whatever you want, it's on the house."

"Thank you, ma'am," says Ryn.

"I'll have a glass of chocolate milk," Atlas orders. "Hot."

Marie maintains the same cheery grin as she scribbles that down and takes the rest of our orders (a croissant for Ryn, an eclair for Grayson and a classic sugar cookie for me). Before going to put our orders in, she faces Ryn, Grayson and I and says, "I like the costumes. They're very realistic."

My eyes follow her as she walks off and disappears into the kitchen. I wait until the door stops swinging behind her before I turn to Atlas. "What was *that*?"

"What was what?"

"That," I repeat, gesturing at the empty space where Granny Marie stood just a second ago. "You brainwashed her without even looking in her direction. I thought you had to look people in the eye to mind-control them. Also… you don't like chocolate milk."

"Maybe I do," says Atlas. He finally tears his gaze from the menu but starts staring out the window rather than meeting my eyes.

I open my mouth to ask what could possibly be so interesting about a deserted parking lot, but Grayson stops me. "How about we focus on what we came here for?" he suggests. "Which is… explaining! So! Who wants to go first?"

"My vote's on Atlas," I say, eyeing my brother. "You have a whole lot more to explain than we do."

"I second that," says Ryn.

We all look at him expectantly, but he just sighs. He picks up one of the paper napkins on the table and starts tearing off shreds of it. He would do that all the time when we went to restaurants as kids. Nervous habit, I guess. "I escaped two years ago," he says, his voice low. "Alumni chased me for a while, but eventually they gave up and left me alone."

"But where did you hide that whole time?" I interrogate. "How did you stay hidden?"

"Powers," he says shortly.

Before I can ask any further questions, Granny Marie appears by the side of our table, concern etched across her features. "Are you sure your parents are comin'?" she asks. "Do you want me to call 'em and let 'em know you're here? If you have one of their numbers, then I can—"

"No, that's okay," Ryn interjects. "They'll be here soon enough, we can wait."

"Are you sure?" Marie presses. "I'd hate for—"

"We're sure," Atlas says forcefully. "They'll be here."

Granny Marie lingers uncertainly around our table for a second, then turns and retreats to the kitchen. "That was harsh," Ryn says to Atlas once Marie is out of earshot.

Atlas sits back in his chair, his steely gaze still on the window even though there's nothing out there worth staring at. "It's your turn to explain," he says.

After a beat of silence, I speak up. "There's not a whole lot to explain on our end of things," I shrug. "Basically, back at the Rainloft, Ryn thought it was time for a change, and we decided to do a group project together in order to, you know, defy the teachers and prove that nothing bad will come of interaction between different types. All we got from that was a whole lot of detention, but Ryn decided that we just needed to do something bigger in order to make a difference. From there, things spiraled, we escaped, and now we're here," I finish, turning to my brother. "See, that was a good explanation. Yours… not so much."

"Why?" asks Atlas.

I raise an eyebrow at him. "Well, you left a lot of details out, and I still have so many—"

"I mean, why did you do it?" he says, his cold gray eyes finally meeting mine. There's something different behind his tone, but I can't quite figure out what it is. It's almost condescending, in a way. "Why did you escape?"

"Because we wanted to make a change," Ryn says confidently. "And give Avalon a piece of our minds. I figured that if she had more students escape, then maybe she would start to realize how much we hate it there. How twisted and horrible the Rainloft really is."

Atlas just sighs, shaking his head. "What?" Ryn asks defensively.

He gives a harsh laugh. "You really thought escaping would change Avalon's mind," he murmurs, his tone full of amusement. "You really thought that three students could make a difference."

"We can," Ryn snaps. "Three students—"

"No," Atlas interrupts, his gray eyes stone-cold. "Nothing that *you* could do will change the ways of the Rainloft."

I'd been so engaged in this conversation that I hadn't even noticed Granny Marie standing by the side of our table, four different dishes balanced precariously in her arms. "I've got snacks!" she chirps, gently placing our food in front of us. Atlas's eyes are still locked on Ryn's and they both look ready to start a deadly food fight, but Granny Marie doesn't seem to notice. "You enjoy, okay?" she says. "Let me know if you need anything at all, dears."

The second Marie steps back into the kitchen, Ryn speaks up. "Then we'll do something bigger."

We all turn to face her. "What?"

"If escaping wasn't big enough, then we'll do something bigger," she elaborates, and I can see the gears grinding in her brain. Suddenly, she looks up. "What if we bring it down?"

"What do you mean, 'bring it down'?" I repeat uneasily, because I'm pretty sure I know what she means but the thought is too farcical to wrap my head around at the moment.

"I mean, *bring it down*," she says confidently. "As in, bring down the Rainloft. For good."

I wait for Atlas to burst her bubble and shoot that idea to the ground, but he doesn't. His steely gaze is fixed on the window again, and his knuckles are paper-white as he grips the handle of his mug with one hand. I follow his gaze, but still, I don't see anything but an empty parking lot.

Before I can ask what he's looking at, Granny Marie comes drifting over to us. "So, what were y'all doin' in the city today?" she asks, pulling a fifth chair up to our table and sitting down. Atlas is still staring out the window for no apparent reason, but if she finds that strange, she doesn't let on.

"We were, uh, shopping," I tell her when nobody else bothers to respond. I'd rather focus on finding a solution to our current predicament than come up with an entire fake alibi for how we ended up here, but then again, Granny Marie gave us all this delicious food *free of charge*. The least I can do is try and make small talk. "School starts soon, so we were shopping for supplies."

Granny Marie cocks her head at me. "But… it's the middle of April. I thought school didn't start 'till August."

"Right," I say hastily, cursing myself for saying that without checking the date first. School at the Rainloft is year-round, so after a while you just kind of lose track of what month and season it is. Plus, Rainloft students are prohibited from going outside for risk of plummeting to our doom, so 100-degree heat and negative-twenty-degree cold feel exactly the same to us.

"We were just, er, doing all of our school shopping early. Before all the good stuff gets picked over. You know, early bird gets all the best pens, right?" I laugh nervously, then stuff my mouth with cookie to keep from blabbing anymore.

"Um, June?" Ryn says tentatively, notes of apprehension in her voice. "We should probably get going. Like, soon."

I narrow my eyes at her, completely in the dark. My brother's hand is still wrapped in a death-grip around the handle of his mug, and Ryn and Grayson both look alarmed. "Why?" I ask, talking around a bite of cookie. "We don't need to…"

I trail off when Ryn gives a subtle nod towards the window. I look out there, and still don't see anything out-of-the-norm at first. But I nearly choke on my cookie when a shiny glint catches my eye.

It's almost invisible against the obsidian sky, but it's there. A sleek black helicopter parked in the center of the otherwise-empty parking lot, its monstrous blades jutting out into the darkness. I'm instantly taken back to that night—an Alumnus dragging Atlas and I down our flooded lawn, being ordered to climb into the helicopter, looking back and seeing our dad standing in the doorway.

The jingle of the tiny bell on the door calls me back to the present. My heart stops when I look over my shoulder to see two figures—a tall, blonde-haired woman and a not-so-tall bald man—clad in slick black uniforms and tool belts equipped with everything an Alumni could possibly need to do their job, which includes a weapon that resembles a handgun but isn't one. In Rainloft History class one day, we briefly went over the weapon that Alumni use, but I can't recall what it's called or how it's different from a regular gun. I wasn't exactly paying attention that day, because frankly, I thought, would there ever be an instance when I needed to know the difference between one potentially-deadly firearm and another that's equally as dangerous?

Now I'm wishing I had listened a little more closely that day, because these Alumni both have one hand on their weapon, they're looking straight at us and I have no idea what could happen to me if I make one of them mad.

"Oh, I wonder what they're here for," Granny Marie says to us, still completely unaware. "I'll just be one second."

She rises from her seat and crosses to the door, greeting the Alumni without an ounce less of pep than she welcomed us with. "Welcome to Granny Marie's," she says. "To what do I owe the pleasure?"

The Alumnus starts talking to her in a hushed tone, so I can barely make out what he's saying. I watch Marie's smile fade more and more by the second. "But… they said they were separated from their parents," she says, her eyes bouncing between the Alumni and our table.

"How did they find us?" Grayson murmurs.

"I don't know, but we've got to get out of here," urges Ryn. "Marie's distracting them, so now's our best—"

"Keep your head down," Atlas cuts in, his tone razor-sharp. His eyes are on the table and he's still gripping his mug.

"What?" I ask frantically. "Why—?"

"Just do it," he grits out. I still don't get the point, but there really isn't any other way out of this, so I follow his lead and bring my gaze down to my half-eaten cookie on the table in front of me.

For half an eternity, the only sound beside my heart pounding in my ears is soft conversation between Granny Marie and the Alumni. Finally, their discussion comes to a stop and I can hear slow, heavy footsteps approaching from behind me.

Each step sends my heart rate soaring higher and higher. I stare down my cookie as I wait for the pair of Alumni to reach our table, but they might as well be walking in slow motion. Their footsteps sound careful, I realize—cautious, even. Almost like they're afraid of us, though it couldn't be more backwards.

When they come to a stop, it's the Alumna's voice that sounds from behind Atlas. "Hands in the air."

I obey immediately for fear of what could happen if I don't. I can't see them, but I assume that Ryn and Grayson do the same.

"That means you, too, Winters," the Alumnus says gruffly. I sneak a glance up at the Alumni to find that both of them are standing behind my brother. The man is holding a roll of pale-blue rope, and the woman is pointing her gun at Atlas.

My heart skips a beat. There's no way this is legal. Nobody—not even a Rainloft Alumnus—would shoot a kid. That just doesn't happen. Right? "Um, Atlas?" I hesitate. "You might want to—"

"Hey, Barry. Linda. Long time, no see," Atlas says to the Alumni. His eyes are still glued to the table, his left hand still gripping the handle of his mug, and he doesn't seem fazed in the slightest by the fact that someone is aiming a loaded gun at his head.

"Now's not the time for salutations," The Alumna (Linda?) barks, her hold on the gun steady. "You need to put your hands in the air. I'm armed."

"And I'm not," Atlas counters, speaking faster than my brain can process what's happening. "I don't have a weapon, ergo, I can't hurt you. So why don't you lower the gun?"

"Because we've been here before," says the Alumna, her tone full of impatience. "I've already played every single one of your little games, Winters. So put your hands in the air. *Now*."

"You know, Linda," Atlas says slowly, "I heard that you shot Barry in the heart."

For a fraction of a second, the Alumna looks just as confused as I am. But then, without a moment's hesitation, she points the gun at the Alumnus's chest and pulls the trigger. There's a deafening *bang* and a blinding flash of light. Someone yells "Get down!" and before I can think twice I'm on my hands and knees under the table. The whole bakery erupts into chaos and about a thousand different things happen within the same millisecond—Barry goes limp and hits the floor with an earth-quaking *thud*. Ryn springs backward out of her chair and Grayson drops to the ground next to me. Atlas leaps to his feet and sprints for the counter, ducking past the Alumna, who's now targeting him and repeatedly firing her gun in his direction but missing every time. Bullets ricochet off the brick walls, blast holes through the metal tables and shatter the light-up menu boards behind the counter.

My ears are ringing and the only thought in my mind is *somebody just got shot.* I turn to face the Alumnus, expecting a bloodbath, but to my utter disbelief, he's already getting to his feet. There's no blood, no open wound, no evidence to suggest that he just got shot. In fact, he seems fully aware, and his fiery eyes are set directly on me and Grayson.

"What do we do?" I whisper desperately. The Alumnus is gripping his gun with one hand, and I get the feeling that trying to escape won't end well for us. But at the same time, staying under this table like sitting ducks is just as dangerous.

"No idea," says Grayson, evidently coming to the same conclusion. "Maybe just do what he says and, uh, avoid making him mad at all costs?"

"Yeah, good plan."

"I won't shoot unless you give me reason to," says the Alumnus, raising one hand but keeping the other braced around the grip of his gun. "I need you both to put your hands up and slowly step out from under the table. N—"

"Hey, idiot," Atlas calls from the opposite side of the bakery. The Alumna whips around and fires her gun at him, but he dodges the bullet by at least a foot. Keeping his eyes on the Alumnus, he nods toward our table. "Can you break that mug against your head?"

I watch as Barry's expression goes blank and he strolls over to the side of our table, where Atlas had been sitting just a minute ago. I try not to wince as he picks up the full mug, raises it up and smashes it with full force into his head. The mug cracks but doesn't break, and piping-hot chocolate milk is sent cascading down the brainwashed Alumnus's shiny bald head. He yelps in pain, but the mug isn't broken yet so he strikes it against his forehead again—hard enough that he loses his balance and falls to the ground.

"Go, now!" Atlas shouts, pointing at the counter.

I will myself to get up and leave the safety of our table while the Alumnus is down, then run as fast as my feet will carry me, swerving past the Alumni and all but diving behind the counter. Grayson follows closely behind me.

Cautiously, I stand up and peer over the granite countertop just in time to see the Alumna finally snap.

"Alright, that's it," she snarls, dropping her gun. Practically writhing with anger, she eyes one of the tables near ours and jerks her head toward Atlas. The whole table is sent hurtling at lightspeed across the dining room, whizzing past me and landing with a thunderous *boom* just inches away from Atlas.

"Type One," Grayson murmurs.

With a grunt, the Alumna glances at the table-less chairs and sends them soaring straight at my brother, who narrowly dodges them. Then she goes for a different table, then the chairs around it, sending them all airborne. She's so busy ravaging the dining room that she doesn't notice when Atlas slips out of the way and crosses to the other side of the bakery.

"Today—today is the day, Winters," the Alumna huffs, sending another set of chairs flying at the massive pile on the opposite side of the room, "that you quit haunting the thoughts of every single Alumnus that's ever failed to capture you. Today, I'm finally going to get the job done."

Somehow, she still doesn't realize that Atlas is standing a few feet away from her. In one fluid motion, he grabs a knife off our table, strides up behind the Alumna and sticks the blade in her back.

Everything goes dead-silent. I can't stop my hand from flying up to my mouth.

Atlas just pats the Alumna on the shoulder. "Hate to break it to you," he says, "but I'm afraid that day will have to wait."

Another moment of shell-shocked silence allows me to pick up a sound that I hadn't before—sirens. Distant at first, but getting louder and louder every second that we stand here with the pair of incapacitated Alumni.

"Cops," Ryn murmurs, the blood draining from her face.

Atlas curses under his breath. "Marie must have called them," he says, glancing at the kitchen door. "There's an exit in the back. We need to go."

"But what about them?" I gesture uneasily toward the Alumni, both of whom are now lying unconscious in pools of their own blood. "We can't just leave them like that, can we?"

"What do you suggest we do, call them an ambulance?" Atlas bends down to wrench the knife from the Alumna's back, then turns and heads for the kitchen door. "The cops will deal with them," he says. "We just need to get out of here."

Through the window, I can see a cop car pulling up to the bakery, flashing its wild blue-and-red lights across the parking lot. Before I know it I'm following Atlas through the kitchen, Ryn and Grayson right behind me.

On our way to the back door we pass Granny Marie, on the ground, pressed up against one of the ovens. She looks positively thunderstruck, and every ounce of me wants to give her a hug. Instead I just whisper an awkward "sorry" and keep walking.

I hadn't realized how good it would feel to get out of that building until the cool, fresh night air hits my face. Atlas doesn't stop long to savor it, though—he just keeps on marching forward, across the deserted back parking lot and towards the lights of the city.

"Okay, what *were* those things?" asks Ryn, jogging to catch up with Atlas and glancing over her shoulder at the wrecked bakery. The lights are still flickering inside and I can see police rushing into the scene of the crime. "The guns, I mean?" Ryn clarifies.

"Those were Sim guns," Atlas says absently, not slowing down. "They're designed to look and sound like pistols, but the bullets can't do any real damage if you get hit with one. They just simulate the pain of a real gunshot wound."

"But if they hurt just as much as a real gunshot, how come that Alumnus was able to get right back up after getting hit?" I question.

"Because he's an Alumnus," Atlas replies shortly. "They're trained to withstand the pain."

"Huh." We walk in quiet for a while, putting more and more distance between us and the law every second. I keep looking back, expecting hordes of police to be chasing after us, but nobody ever comes.

After a minute, I stop in my tracks. "Wait," I say, narrowing my eyes at my brother. "Where are we going?"

"Into the city," he answers. "To the Springfield Train Station."

"A train station?" Grayson asks. "Why?"

With a sigh, Atlas slows to a halt in the middle of the parking lot. He looks directly at Ryn. "Because you were right," he says.

"I was right?" Ryn repeats slowly. "I mean, obviously, but… what was I right about, exactly?"

"It's our only option, at this point," Atlas mumbles, turning away from the rest of us. "We can't keep running. *I* can't keep running."

"So what are we going to do?" I ask, trying not to sound too impatient.

Atlas turns to face us again, eyes on the asphalt driveway. When he looks up, there's an unmistakable look of determination in his eyes. "We need to bring down the Rainloft," he says finally. "For good."

Chapter Five

"Dozens of trains leave Springfield every day," says Atlas, bowing his head against the chilly city breeze. "Nine times out of ten, there'll be at least one heading up to Lebanon."

"Great. And… what's in Lebanon, exactly?" I ask, cramming my hands deeper into the pockets of my Rainloft blazer as we hike up the sidewalk. We're in downtown Springfield by now, and the one thing I remember about April in this city is that the weather flips like a light switch—one minute the temperature will be perfect, and the next, it will have dropped twenty degrees and you'll be a walking iceberg. The buildings lined up against either side of the street don't do much to block out the sharp wind, and my breath forms misty clouds in the crisp, cold air in front of me.

"The Rainloft Management Facility," Atlas answers, glancing back over his shoulder—making sure we haven't brought any unwanted cop cars along with us, presumably. "The Facility is a place where Alumni manage the Rainloft from the ground," he explains. "It's also where they keep the helicopters when they're not being used to take people to and from the ship. If I can get someone at the Facility to bring us up—"

"Then you can get one of the Rainloft pilots to bring it down," I finish.

"Bingo." Atlas cranes his neck to get a better view of the buildings in front of us. Not too far ahead is the enormous Starview Shopping Mall—one of the very few places in Springfield that our parents deliberately refused to take us. When I asked them why, they would always reply with some line about how harmful the mall was for the smaller shops in downtown Springfield. Apparently, a large handful of the shops were shut down because the Starview was robbing them of all their business.

Size-wise, if every other building is a pebble, then the Starview is Mount Everest. It has to have at least fifty different stores inside, plus an enormous parking garage. The giant neon sign above the front entrance casts a blue glow on the road, providing the only light besides that from the bright white street lights lined up along the sidewalk.

As we walk, I run through Atlas's plan in my head multiple times because there's no way it could possibly be that straightforward. "That sounds… easy enough," I say slowly, still searching for holes in the plan. But the sheer scale of Atlas's powers makes it difficult to find any at all.

For another few ticks the city is quiet, except for the sound of our footsteps against the cement. After a minute, it occurs to me that I still have questions. "So, um, why are we bringing down the Rainloft?" I ask.

"Because it's either that or spend the rest of time running from Alumni," Atlas replies plainly. "It took some time, but I've come to the realization that none of us will be able to lead normal lives as long as the Rainloft is afloat."

"But… why not?" I question. "Didn't you say that when you escaped, Alumni chased you for a while, but then left you alone? Why couldn't we just hide until they get bored of trying to find us, and then, well, get back to normal life?"

"That's not how this works," says Atlas, shaking his head. "You do realize that, in this day and age, escaping the Rainloft is the single most egregious crime you could have committed? Give it an hour, and you'll be all over the news. There's nowhere you can hide without somebody calling the cops on you."

"I don't understand," Ryn sighs, her breath forming a frosty cloud in front of her. "What's so horrible about what we did? We were taken up there against our will, we were unhappy, so we left. Simple! Avalon is the only real criminal here. I mean, she *kidnaps* kids and forces them to do her bidding for the rest of their lives!"

"Well, when you put it that way, it's bad, but she had good intentions," Grayson shrugs. "Avalon started the Rainloft in a time when crime rates everywhere were through the roof. She agreed to use her groundbreaking serum to create crime-fighting heroes and provide protection for the world below, in exchange for a hundred kids each year. There's hardly been a single criminal since then."

"*We're* the criminals now," I realize, the truth finally sinking in. Just a few hours ago, I was studying to become a crime-fighting superhuman. Now I've committed the most unspeakable crime there is.

"Our only option now is to bring it down," Atlas says resolutely. "It's the only… hold on."

He slows to a halt in the middle of the sidewalk, holding up his index finger as a signal for the rest of us to pause as well. I stop in my tracks and open my mouth to ask what he could possibly be stopping for right now, but after a second, I hear it, too. *Sirens*.

"Oh no," I mutter, my heart rate picking up. "What do we…?"

I trail off when Atlas starts walking again, this time at a slower pace. "Keep going," he orders, keeping his eyes to the ground. "Don't be suspicious."

Reluctantly, I start walking, even though part of me thinks things would turn out better for us if we just let the police catch up and turn ourselves in. I used to watch this police crime drama with my mother (our dad insisted that I was too young and didn't want me watching it, so naturally, we waited until after he had gone to bed to turn it on), and after sixteen seasons of that show, I can safely say that running never goes over well for the criminals.

The shrill sound of police sirens only gets louder as the cop car approaches from behind us, and before long, it's close enough that its wild blue-and-red lights are right in my face and I have to look away to keep from going blind. My heart hammering, I refrain from looking up at the car as it drives up to us and try to act like I'm taking a totally normal, late-night walk around the city rather than running from the law because I just watched my brother stab someone.

I'm braced and ready for the police to stop, but to my utter disbelief, the car whizzes straight past us. I release the breath I didn't realize I'd been holding. "That was almost bad," I manage, forcing a nervous laugh.

"Not 'almost'," Atlas corrects me with a sigh, looking up at the police car. "It *is* bad."

A little ways down the street, the car skids to an abrupt halt. A wave of dread washes over me. "They saw us," Ryn murmurs.

Hastily, I scan the area in search of a solution. My eyes immediately land on a narrow alleyway a few feet ahead, between a little red-brick shop and the enormous Starview mall. "There," I say, pointing it out.

I hear the door of the police car slam shut as I lead the group down the alley, trying to keep as quiet as possible as we head for the back of it.

Just as I had hoped, there's a door to the mall at the very end of the alley. "Jackpot," I grin, reaching out for the doorknob. My smile instantly fades when I try to turn it and realize that—of course—the door is locked.

I can hear the cops yelling and their footsteps pounding against the sidewalk, louder as they get closer to us. I bite my lip and frantically jiggle the doorknob, hoping for some kind of miracle, but it's no use. "*Shoot.*"

"Hang on," says Grayson, and in a sudden flash of light, he disappears. A second later there's a *click*, then the heavy metal door swings inward. Grayson steps aside to let us in. I'm well aware that this isn't the time or place to be wishing that I had different powers, but seriously: time travel is *useless* compared to all the other ones.

After we all pile into the building and Grayson pulls the door shut behind us, darkness closes around me like a fist. For a second we stand there in quiet, listening to the cops' muffled conversation outside the door: one says "I swear I saw 'em run down here", the other replies with "Well, guess you were wrong" and that's the end of that discussion. Their heavy footsteps fade as they leave the alley.

I turn around from the door and blink a few times. As soon as my eyes adjust to the darkness, my jaw hits the floor. "No way," I murmur.

We're standing in a food court the size of about twelve football fields combined. There are dozens of different fast food restaurants around the perimeter of the dining area, from *Taco Tuesdays* to *Casey's Cakery* and *The Burger Buffet*. The restaurants and stores are labeled with bright neon signs that provide the only light as far as I can see. Modern-looking booths with glossy white tables and giant plants in quartz vases are scattered around the dining area. On the opposite side of the food court, mostly concealed by shadows, is a monstrous escalator that leads to the second floor.

Aside from the Rainloft, this has to be the single most amazing building I've ever been in. I can finally see why it was so popular back when I lived in this city.

A *click* and a bright white light from behind me calls me back to the present. I turn to see Atlas holding a flashlight, illuminating the area around us and nearly blinding me. He nods toward a shelf unit next to the door, stocked with flashlights, walkie-talkies and other gear that

I assume belongs to the mall security guards. "Take what you need," he says, striding past the rest of us toward the center of the food court.

"For what?" I ask.

"Well, we're here." Atlas's voice echoes around the deserted food court as he scans the area with his flashlight. "Now's as good a time as any to stock up on supplies."

"Stock up on supplies?" I repeat skeptically. "You mean… we're going to shoplift?"

Atlas pauses for a second. "Yeah," he says simply. "That's exactly what we're going to do."

I'm still not a big fan of that idea, but Ryn is already raiding the security guards' stash. "Come on, June," she says, handing me a flashlight. "We're already in a hole. There's no getting out of it, so why not have some fun?"

"'Have some fun'?" I repeat.

"We can't wear these uniforms forever," Ryn grins mischievously, motioning down at her violet Type One uniform. "They're a dead giveaway of who we really are. Here, I know a few stores."

Without any further explanation, she grabs my wrist and drags me across the food court in the direction of the escalator. "Try not to get yourselves killed," Atlas calls after us.

I follow Ryn up the escalator, even though I still have no idea where we're going or what we're doing there. Before long we're on the second floor, surrounded by department stores galore. Just like the restaurants in the food court, each shop has a colorful neon sign above the entrance, lighting up the area and making the tile ground look like a dance floor.

"Oh, you have a Halle Ross here?" Ryn gasps, pointing out a store to my left with a bright red sign.

"Apparently so?" I shrug. "Also, who's Halle Ross?"

"Ha-ha, good one," says Ryn. When I just keep staring at her blankly, her eyebrows shoot up. "You seriously don't know who Halle Ross is?"

"No clue."

She looks at me like I just sprouted wings. "Haven't you ever been in a mall before?"

"Never," I say. "So who's Halle Ross?"

"Only the greatest designer of our time," Ryn scoffs like that's more obvious than the fact that grass is green. "Her shop was my favorite place in the world when I was younger."

She starts walking toward the entrance of the store. "Well, it sounds like a cool place," I start, "but we're supposed to be gathering supplies, not shopping for clothes, right?"

Ryn just waves that off. "Grayson and Atlas will take care of that," she says. "Plus, shopping for clothes is just as important. If anyone sees us in these uniforms, we're toast. We need to blend in with the public."

I open my mouth to protest, but she's right. We're much more likely to be caught dressed like this.

"Fine," I sigh, but Ryn is already walking into the store. I jog to catch up with her.

I feel like a real criminal now, crossing the threshold into the dark, deserted Halle Ross shop. The room is pitch-black apart from the dim display lights beneath the mannequins that make the well-dressed plastic models look like they're telling scary stories. For some reason, I get the unnerving feeling that mall security is going to jump out from behind one of the clothing racks and arrest us.

Ryn, apparently, doesn't notice. "June, look," she exclaims, elbowing me in the arm.

"At what?"

"Clothes," she says in awe. "Clothes that *aren't* itchy old uniforms. I don't know how long it's been since I've worn something other than this."

"Well, yeah," I start, "but you can't just—"

"Watch me."

Before I can say anything else, Ryn rips an entire row of clothing off its rack and disappears into a changing room. Before I can blink, she comes out wearing a lilac Halle Ross crewneck with matching shorts and high-top sneakers bedecked in rhinestones. They remind me vaguely of disco balls and I kind of love it.

"Oh, what the heck." Five minutes later we strut out of that store looking like Halle Ross models, abandoning our old uniforms completely.

"Okay, maybe you were right," I admit, looking down at my brand-new fleece sweatshirt. It's a nice cream color and I can imagine this is what being hugged by a cloud feels like. "It *is* nice to wear something that's not a stuffy school uniform for once."

"See? What'd I tell you?" Ryn gloats, pushing her new sunglasses further up her head. "You better not doubt me again after this."

"I won't. Probably."

Suddenly she gasps and stops in her tracks, pointing out an expensive-looking shop with a purple neon sign that reads *The Perfumery.* "We're going in," she decides, marching up to the store's entrance.

"Okay, new clothes was one thing," I stop her, "but do we really need *perfume*?"

"What did I *just* say?" She turns to face me, walking backwards towards The Perfumery. "Don't doubt me."

Giving up, I roll my eyes and follow her into the shop. Inside are several glass cabinets and tables with immaculate displays of ornate perfume bottles. The cheapest scent I can find has a price well into the triple digits, and the chandelier above me looks more expensive than my house.

"So… what are we doing in here?" I ask, shining my flashlight around the store. The translucent perfume bottles catch the light, casting colorful shadows wherever I aim it.

On the opposite side of the shop, Ryn is already on her knees, looking through one of the fancy display cases. "Found it," she says, standing up and cradling a purple bottle of perfume in her hands.

I cross the room and look over her shoulder at the perfume. "Vanilla Lavender," Ryn reads off the side of the bottle. Then her voice goes soft. "This was my mother's favorite scent."

It's hardly noticeable, but there's something different behind her tone—I can't quite put my finger on it, but I think it's almost melancholy. Though I could just be imagining that, because it's gone as quickly as it came.

"Here, smell it," she says, holding the bottle up to my nose and then spraying it straight in my face.

The perfume smells amazing, but its fumes sting my eyes and burn my nostrils. "Hey!" I laugh, then seize the nearest bottle, hold it up to Ryn's face and spray her with a giant flower bomb.

She staggers backward, blinking the perfume out of her eyes. "Oh, you'll regret that," she warns, raising her sweet-scented weapon.

I turn on my heel and start to run away, but I hardly make it two feet before I trip over my clunky new fur boots and fall on my face. I take Ryn down with me and we both burst out laughing on the fancy tile floor.

Ryn and I have raided just about every single shop on the second floor before we head back to the food court. We end up behind the front counter of The Ice Box, which is—according to the faded banner that takes up ninety percent of the back wall—Springfield's number-one ice cream parlor.

"What flavor do you want?" asks Ryn as she scoops her own strawberry ice cream into a waffle cone from the kitchen. "I've got chocolate, mint chip, strawberry, and… that's it."

"Mint chip, please," I say.

"Really?" she asks, giving me a weird look. I nod and she shakes her head, leaning over the cooler to scoop my ice cream. "Well, enjoy your toothpaste."

I smile and take the cone from her. "I will, thanks."

Ryn perches on the edge of the counter and I lean back against it. We enjoy our ice cream in silence for a few minutes, until I offer "Trade?" and we swap cones.

"I wonder where Grayson and your brother ended up," says Ryn with a laugh. "Think they've been abducted by Alumni yet."

"Is that even possible, at this point?" I question, licking my ice cream and staring at the wall. "Like, at the Rainloft, they make the Alumni out to be these mega-powerful, godlike beings, but Atlas took out two of them at once and made it look easy."

"True." There's a beat or two of silence before Ryn speaks again. "Was he always like that?"

I turn to face her. "Huh?"

"Your brother, I mean," she elaborates. "Was he like that, as a kid? That… intense?"

"Not at all," I tell her, thinking back to when we were younger. The Atlas I knew growing up would always refuse to step on ants because 'small lives matter too'. An hour ago, I watched him take out two human beings without a second thought. "People change, I guess."

"Uh-huh."

Both of us are quiet for a while as we finish off our ice cream. I pop the end of the cone into my mouth, dust off my hands and just as I'm about to help myself to another scoop, there's a *bang* from across the food court.

I look up just in time to see the back door swing open and a group of people hustles into the mall—three angry-looking mall cops armed with flashlights and walkie-talkies.

Before I have the chance to fully register what's going on, Ryn grabs my wrist and pulls me down behind the counter. The guards' footsteps echo across the food court and my heart jumps into my throat. *Security cameras,* I realize, my eyes landing on a tiny camera in the upper corner of the ice cream parlor. *That's how they knew we were here. Why didn't we think of that* before *we stole half the mall's inventory?*

"What do we do?" I whisper hastily, my back pressed up against the counter. I can hear footsteps quickly approaching our hiding spot, and my mind has gone completely blank. "Any ideas? Because I've got nothing."

"Follow my lead," mutters Ryn. She turns around, peering over the countertop at something on the other side of the food court. Before I'm able to pinpoint exactly what she's staring at, there's a deafening *clang* as the taco shop's heavy metal cash register hits the tile floor.

The mall cops immediately flock to that area, the blinding spotlight created by their combined lamps turning the taco shop into the star of the food court. "And now we run," says Ryn. "Front doors, *now*."

"*Run?!*" I ask frantically. I can barely even see the front doors from where we are now, and the odds that I make it there without A) running out of breath and passing out or B) falling on my face without any specific cause are next to nil.

"We have to go," says Ryn, her gaze set on the entrance doors. "Now."

And then she takes off before I have the chance to share my thoughts on that plan. Every part of me wants to stay hidden in the safety of the ice cream parlor, but that would probably end just as badly as running would, so I force myself to my feet and make a mad dash for the front doors.

Don't think, just run, I tell myself, gaining more and more momentum each time my feet strike the ground. My heart racing, I cut across the dining area, swerving past tables and chairs that are positioned, in my opinion, *way* too close to one another.

Ryn and I are mere yards away from safe harbor, and just as I start to think, *hey, I might actually make it,* my foot catches on the leg of a chair and all hope goes out the window.

I let out a sharp gasp as I fall flat on the ground, throwing out my hands and barely saving myself from a nosedive into the tile. Within an instant, all the guards' lights are on me.

"Hey, stop right there!"

Ryn gets to me just before the mall cops do and yanks me back onto my feet. "Stay calm," she mutters as the trio of security guards gallops up to us.

"Hands in the air," one of them demands, pointing his flashlight at us like it's a gun. Next to me Ryn obeys and raises her hands up in front of her, so I decide to follow her lead.

"Now," says the guard—*Hank,* according to his nametag. His tone is patient and articulate, but should we mess this up, he looks ready to send us to jail for the rest of our lives. "Can either of you ladies tell me what you're doing here at this hour?"

"Well, my friend June here—" Ryn motions to me so I smile and give a little wave "—you see, today is her birthday. There are these Halle Ross boots that she's been wanting for months—no, *years* now. And I, being the wonderful and generous friend that I am, wanted to come here early and get them for her before they sold out."

The security guard narrows his eyes. "So you decided to break into private property at two o'clock in the morning and *steal* the shoes?"

I nod and put one hand over my heart to look convincing. "I really wanted them."

"We're really sorry, sir," says Ryn. "It won't happen again. We'll just get out of your way and you guys won't have to worry about us anymore."

She starts strolling towards the exit doors and I follow her. I'm in complete disbelief that that actually worked, but I give her a discreet little victory high-five as we head for safety.

Of course, Hank bursts my bubble. "Hold it."

Ryn sighs as we turn back to face the guards. "What is it, sir?"

"You know, I haven't seen you two around before," says Hank, a puzzled look on his face. "Could you tell me where you're from?"

"Are you asking us where we live?" Ryn asks. "Because, I'm sorry, but my parents always told me not to share that information with strangers."

"Is that so?" says Hank, stretching those words out way too long. I get the feeling that something's wrong even before he continues, "Or are you just avoiding the question? That seems like a logical thing for an escaped Rainloft student to do."

My heart drops. Hank's hand moves to something on his toolbelt that I'd failed to notice before—a Sim gun. Immediately, my hands fly up into the air, but Ryn hardly even flinches. "What?! How did you know? Who *are* you?" she interrogates.

"If I were you, I'd stop asking questions and put my hands in the air," says Hank, swiftly pulling out his gun and pointing it directly at Ryn. "Or else I will shoot."

Looking straight down the barrel of his gun, Ryn's confident expression falters a bit. "Am I supposed to be afraid?" she demands, but it comes out sounding like a genuine question. "That's not even a real gun."

"It hurts just the same," the security guard says impatiently, his lips forming a thin line. "Now you'd better put your hands in the air if you know what's good for you, because I'll shoot."

"I have no doubt you will." Out of nowhere, my brother strolls onto the scene, hands in his pockets, Grayson trailing uncertainly behind him. "But what are the odds that you actually land the blow?"

"Winters," Hank says gruffly, shifting his aim to target Atlas.

"Jackson." Atlas gives the 'security guard' a once-over. "Nice costume."

Ryn's voice draws me out of the conversation. "Any idea what's going on right now?" she whispers in my ear.

I catch something from Atlas about an incident at some taco restaurant, and then Hank/Jackson/whoever he is gets defensive and replies with "That kid's family was sufficiently compensated, and you know that."

"No clue," I mutter.

After another minute of cryptic conversation, Ryn sighs. "This is pointless," she says. "We need to get away from them."

"What are you going to do?" I ask uneasily, because I get the feeling that I won't like her answer.

"Oh, don't worry about it," she says under her breath, eyes locked on the 'mall cops'. "Just run for the door, okay?"

"Ryn—"

Before I can stop her she jerks her head to the side, sending Hank flying straight into one of the other guards, knocking them both over like a pair of human dominoes. The second guard loses his grip on the flashlight and it skids across the floor, landing inches away from Ryn's feet. "No!" Hank yells from the ground. "No, you stupid girl!"

Without missing a beat, Ryn swipes the flashlight off the ground and pivots, her new Halle Ross sneakers squeaking on the tile floor. She's reached the front doors before I can blink. "Guys, come on!" she shouts across the food court.

Atlas just stares at her for a second, at a loss for words. He almost doesn't notice the third security guard creeping towards him like a monster out of the shadows, but at the very last second he looks over his shoulder at the guard and "Halt, Stuart" is all he has to say to make the disguised Alumnus stop in his tracks. Atlas starts heading for the exit and Grayson teleports over there, so I do the same. I break into a jog towards the doors, swerving between all the tables and chairs scattered around the food court.

"Stop right there!" Hank commands. Against my better judgment I slow down and look back to see him on his feet now. For a fleeting second our eyes meet and he shouts "I order you to stop!"

I'm about to ignore him and bolt for the exit when suddenly I get the overwhelming urge to *stop running*. My feet quit moving without me telling them to and now Hank's voice is all I can hear. It fills my ears and echoes through my mind, commanding me to *stay put*.

Just as I'm starting to panic, Atlas turns back and jogs up to me, looking me straight in the eye. "It's mind control," he says, his voice cutting through the deafening echoes of Hank's. "Don't listen."

And just like that, I snap out of it. Hank's voice disappears and I stumble forward a little, my feet no longer locked in place. I can't help but shudder. I've seen other people get mind-controlled before, and it's scary enough to witness, but it's an entirely different thing when you're the one being brainwashed.

Atlas is already at the front exit with Ryn and Grayson, so I force myself to run the remaining distance over there. I'm about to shove open the doors and get the heck out of there when Ryn murmurs "No way."

My hand still on the cold metal door handle, I turn to face her. Her eyes are wide and the security guard's flashlight is hanging limply from her hand, pointed at something across the food court from us. I follow its beam up to a giant wooden clock that I'd failed to notice before, hanging high above the dining area. "Ryn?" I say tentatively, trying to stay patient. "What is it?"

"That… clock," she says. Her voice sounds small and oddly far away. "I don't believe it."

"Now is not the time for this," Atlas growls. "We have to go."

All three Alumni are now making their way towards us, each step they take causing my heart rate to skyrocket. But Ryn's feet stay planted firmly on the ground, her flashlight aimed straight at that inconspicuous clock. "No, it isn't," she murmurs, shaking her head. It's almost like she's disconnected from reality—she doesn't hear Atlas or I and she doesn't notice the trio of Alumni that's ready to knock us senseless if we don't move soon. "It can't be."

My eyes bounce back and forth between Ryn's petrified expression and the massive clock. There's nothing noticeably special about it—it's just a plain wooden clock with a barely-visible '3S' engraved into one of the hands. "Ryn, come on," I whisper hastily, eyeing the Alumni. "We really, *really* need to—"

"Kathryn Sharp."

My heart plummets. *We're too late.* The main Alumnus (Hank?)'s voice booms across the mall, his eyes locked on Ryn's. All I can do is watch as her gaze drops from the clock and her eyes meet the Alumnus's. Hank looks all too satisfied with himself as he tells her, "Capture your friends for me."

He pulls something blue and metallic off his tool belt and tosses it to Ryn, who promptly catches it. With a vacant expression, she spins to face the rest of us, and only then do I realize what she's holding—handcuffs.

By the time I'm able to register what's happening, it's too late. She makes to grab my wrists and cuff them together, but I manage to jerk away. "Atlas, turn her back!" I shout. Ryn's eyes are boring into mine like lasers. She seems dead set on locking me up, and all I can think to do is back away from her.

"Ryn," Atlas says hastily, turning her attention from me to himself. "You're being mind-controlled, don't—"

"Don't listen to Winters," Hank commands firmly from a distance away. Visibly torn between who to listen to, Ryn looks back and forth between him and Atlas for a second, not paying any attention to Grayson or I. My eyes land on the set of handcuffs dangling from her hand and without fully thinking it through, I seize the opportunity and smack them to the ground.

That small little action lights a fuse and Ryn practically blows up. She eyes the heavy metal cash register that she knocked off the taco shop's counter just moments ago, and with a flick of her wrist, it's sent hurtling at lightspeed straight at my face.

I dive out of the way and the cash register makes a deafening *clang* as it strikes the tile floor just inches to my left. By the time I'm able to get to my feet Ryn's holding out her palm, a scary-looking kitchen knife levitating above it.

"Ryn," Atlas says cautiously, and her head whips in his direction. "Don't throw that."

Ryn's expression flickers for a second before the Alumnus tells her "Throw it. At whatever cost, you need to *capture them*!"

Ryn's eyes immediately lock on mine and she rotates the knife so that its tip is pointed directly at me. My heart stops. Mercilessly, she sends the blade whizzing straight at my face. I'm almost able to dodge it, but it makes a clean cut across my cheek.

I turn my head to see the knife clatter to the ground a few feet behind me, then I spin back around just in time to see Ryn eye the light-up sign above the ice cream parlor. With a flash of neon light it's ripped off the wall, and Ryn flings it in our direction.

We all manage to dodge it but before it even hits the ground, Ryn's torn the bright green sign off the taco restaurant wall and hurls it at us.

Completely out of control, she throws sign after sign at us and each one smashes into the ground with a deafening *crash* and a shower of sparks. All I can think to do is dodge them. "Atlas, *what do we do*?" I shout over the chaos, scrambling out of the way of a flying neon burger sign.

The sign hits the ground with a burst of sparks, lighting up Atlas's face. For the first time since we found him, he looks genuinely unsure of what to do. "Talk to her," he shouts, ducking out of the way of a light-up cookie.

"*Me* talk to her?" I repeat.

"Yes, *you* talk to her."

"But *you're* the one with mind-control powers, why don't *you* talk to her?" I yell.

"Did it look like that was working to you?" he shouts irritably. *"Talk to your friend."*

Uneasily, I realize that the persistent *crash* of neon signs has come to an abrupt stop. Slowly, I turn to face Ryn. Her eyes are set on an entirely new target that I hadn't even noticed was there before—a sleek black car, on display in the center of the food court.

Ryn points the palm of her hand straight towards it and the car starts to shudder. It quakes for a second and then slowly starts rising into the air, bright neon lights reflecting off its shiny exterior.

Cautiously, I take a step towards her. "Ryn," I start. Her head whips back in my direction, but her hand stays pointed straight at the floating car. "Listen to me."

The room is dead-silent apart from the echo of my voice. "This isn't you," I tell her. "That Alumnus—he's in your head. You have to kick him out."

Her expression is somewhat strained, like using her powers to lift something as heavy as that car is draining her energy. "You wouldn't do this to us," I say, suddenly painfully aware of what could happen to me if she does decide to throw that car. "We're your friends. *I'm* your friend. Your best friend. I think."

I shake my head. "At least I'd hope so. You're *my* best friend, anyways."

And just like that, she's out of it. The life returns to her eyes and she loses her hold on the car, sending it plummeting toward the ground. I stagger back and prepare to go deaf as soon as the car crashes to the ground.

Only, it doesn't. Gravity stops and the car freezes in midair, just inches above the tile floor. Her outstretched hand shaking, Ryn holds it there and eyes the Alumnus.

"Don't you dare," he breathes, all of the cockiness gone from his expression. Both of the other mall cops have ditched him by now and he cowers in the shadows, holding his hands up innocently. "You'll regret this. Believe me, *you will regret this.*"

"Really?" Ryn growls, her voice strained. There's an unmistakable glint of vengeance in her eyes. "Because I don't think I will."

Her hand snaps over in his direction and the car is sent hurtling through the air like a football. It takes the Alumnus out completely, crushing him underneath it.

As soon as she hears the *crash,* Ryn staggers backward and takes in a sharp breath. She stares at the scene with a look of pure shock across her face. The car is completely destroyed—all the windows are all shattered and thick black smoke pours from the engine. If we weren't already in trouble with mall security, then we definitely are now.

Ryn turns back around. She surveys the area—all the smashed, smoking light-up signs and various other things she attempted to murder us with—and immediately winces. "Did… *I* do all that?" she asks uneasily.

"Yeah. Yeah, you did," says Atlas, not a trace of sympathy in his voice. He steps over what used to be the *Casey's Cakery* sign and starts heading for the doors without another word.

I glance between Ryn and Grayson. "I guess we should probably, uh, get going," I say. "That train will be getting here soon."

They both nod, and the three of us follow Atlas out the mall doors. Stepping into the icy night air, we set out for the train station.

*   *   *

By the time we get to the train station, the moon is high in the sky, looming large above the now-quiet city.

152

Springfield has hardly seen a shoplifter since the Rainloft was implemented. We're probably all over the news by now, what with our high-dive act off the Rainloft, blowing up a bakery, raiding a mall and nearly obliterating multiple security guards. When people wake up in the morning and turn on their TVs, they'll be shocked to their cores. Despite the weight of it all, I can't help but laugh a little. I've broken more laws in the past two hours than most people do in their entire lives.

The antique clock on the wall tells me that it's just past three. If the tiny, wrinkled schedule taped up next to the clock is correct, then the next train to Lebanon won't be here until three thirty.

The station is completely deserted—guess there aren't many people like us with an urgent need to hop on a train to Lebanon in the dead of night. The dim yellow lights along the edge of the ceiling cast a warm glow on the empty platform, and our footsteps against the tile floor are the only sound for seemingly miles.

Atlas is leading the group along the edge of the platform. His hands are in his pockets and he looks deep in thought. Now that I think about it, neither he nor Ryn has said a word since we left the mall. None of us have really spoken much—we're all a little tired, given that it's three in the morning and we've hardly slept in two days—but this prolonged silence is uncharacteristic for Ryn.

"So… Lebanon," I venture, trying to break the tension. "Is there anything cool there? Besides the RMF?"

"There sure are a lot of Alumni there, I can tell you that much," Atlas says dryly, eyes on the floor. "Many of them being Type Twos. We should all know how to handle those properly."

Ryn stops in her tracks. "What's that supposed to mean?"

With a sigh, Atlas stops and turns to face the rest of us. "I had things under control back there. Tell me, what made you think it was a good idea to fling a highly lethal Alumni across the room like some sort of frisbee?"

"Oh, please. You didn't have things under control," Ryn scoffs. "You were having a full-on *conversation* with that guy, like you two were best friends or something."

"It was all a part of the process," Atlas says, his tone full to the brim with irritation. "Some Alumni, specifically Twos, are better trained to resist mind-control, so it takes time to get to them. And making casual conversation is the most efficient way to do that."

Ryn folds her arms in front of her. "I don't get it."

"Of course you don't," Atlas mutters with a bitter laugh. "How naive of me to think you were smart enough to understand."

"Did you just call me *dumb*?"

"Hey, not to butt into this super meaningful… highly productive argument or anything," Grayson says tentatively, "but whatever happened in that mall, can't we just move on from it? Let the past be past and focus on *now*?"

"What he's trying to say is that this is stupid," I elaborate bluntly. I'm too tired to deal with their pointless bickering. "Why don't you two just go and sit in opposite corners of this station and don't talk to or look at each other until the train comes? How's that sound?"

"Fine by me," says Atlas. He turns on his heel and strides off.

"Ugh, you are such a *child*," Ryn fumes, storming off in the opposite direction.

Grayson and I are left standing in the middle of the platform. After a beat of awkward silence, Grayson says, "I feel like we should go talk to them."

"Do we *have* to?" I ask, only half joking. "They're scary when they're mad. Both of them."

"Agreed," says Grayson. "But if *this* argument never gets resolved, the problem is only going to get worse and they're just going to keep on fighting."

"It's really annoying how smart you are." I let out an exaggerated sigh, watching Ryn stomp off with her arms crossed over Grayson's shoulder. A smirk crosses my lips. "I call dibs on Ryn!"

"Hey, no fair!" he protests. "Atlas is your *brother*."

"Yeah, and he's terrifying."

Grayson grimaces. "You're so good at talking to people," I add. "You've got this!"

He raises an eyebrow at me, but starts walking— almost as quickly as a tortoise caught in quicksand. "Good luck!" I call after him.

Once he's a good distance away, I turn back in Ryn's direction and decide to make my way over there.

Ryn is perched at the very edge of the platform, her brand-new disco ball sneakers dangling over the railroad. The train will be here before long and part of me wants to ask her to move because there are tons of other seating options in this station that are a thousand times less dangerous, but I refrain. She hardly even looks up when I sit down next to her.

"Your brother's awful, you know," she says, her voice low. "I can't believe you two are related."

I laugh a little. "Yeah, I can't either, sometimes."

The dim lights cast a golden glow on her face, making her look almost ethereal. We're both silent for a long moment, and in my head I weigh whether it's worth it to ask risky questions. But I decide now's as good a time as any and start, "So… that clock."

Just like that, all the anger drains from her eyes and her expression goes blank. I wish I could swallow my words. "Never mind. Forget I said anything."

"No," she says with a sigh of resignation. Her eyes wander to the now scabbed-over cut across my cheek. "I tried to hurt you guys. All three of you. The least I owe you is an explanation."

She takes a long breath in, and I listen intently. "My parents built that clock," she says, like it's some sort of earth-shattering truth that's going to flip my world upside-down. "I saw their brand logo on one of the hands."

"Oh," I say. "That's really cool."

"No, it's not." Her eyes go back to the deserted railroad tracks beneath us, and a hint of anger returns to her voice. "I hate how that happened. I hate how I let that awful Alumnus make me hurt you guys in front of my parents' clock. I hate it.

"Their business was the most important thing in the world to them—second to me, of course," she continues, a faint smile crossing her lips. "*Three Sharp*, that's what they called it. Because our last name is Sharp and there were three of us. Anyways, they made all kinds of clocks—some tiny ones, like the kind that people would have in a bedroom or a classroom, and some giant ones. Like the huge brass one at the mall."

"Uh-huh," I nod along, still not sure where this is going.

Ryn continues, and her voice sounds far away, like she's lost in a sea of memories. "I was really little then, but my parents let me help with the construction process all the time," she says wistfully. "My job was always burning the little *3S* logo into the clock hands. Don't ask why they trusted a nine-year-old with fire, that's beside the point.

"I loved being a part of Three Sharp. Every day, I'd go to my little elementary school and brag to all my classmates that I had my own job and made really epic clocks for a living. They were obviously super impressed." She sighs. "My parents were amazing."

"That's awesome, Ryn," I smile, but it fades when I realize that she's been speaking in the past tense this whole time. "They… *were* amazing?"

She bites her lip and nods, still looking down at the tracks below us. Then she finally meets my eyes. "My parents are dead, June."

I can't stop my jaw from dropping. "They're—they're dead?" I repeat a little too loudly, cursing myself for not having anything better to say. "That's terrible. How? What happened? I mean—I'm really sorry. I had no idea they were… you know…"

I trail off. Ryn's just been watching me struggle, wearing this smile that's weary but amused at the same time. "Are you done?"

"Yeah," I say, looking down. "Sorry. I'll be quiet now."

"I was ten when it happened," she continues. "It was within a week of my birthday and a couple months before I was picked to go to the Rainloft."

"That… must have made for a really rough year," I comment.

"No kidding," she says bitterly. "Anyways, that morning, my parents woke me up early. They told me that I'd be spending the day at my grandparents' house, because they had some work business to attend to. I didn't believe that for a second and spent the entire car ride to my grandma's asking questions. They refused to tell me the truth, but… I found out myself later that night."

"So where were they really going?" I ask hesitantly.

"They were going to protest against the Rainloft," she says simply. "I heard everything on the news at my grandma's house. Hundreds of people from all over the country made signs and met up in Lebanon to protest against the Rainloft—peacefully."

"Peacefully?" I repeat.

"Uh-huh. All they did was gather outside the Rainloft Management Facility and hold up handmade signs with messages about why the Rainloft should come down. That was it." She takes a deep breath. "And Avalon killed them all for it."

"The Lebanon Massacre." A memory jumps into my mind—my dad, Atlas and me, gathered around the TV, watching a horrified news reporter walk around the scene of the crime. Atlas and I both knew that we shouldn't have been watching it, but our dad was too shocked to chase us out of the room. Now that I'm older, I see the incident from a whole different lens. "But… how did she get away with it?" I ask. "It's illegal to kill nonviolent protesters. Freedom of speech, remember?"

"Yeah, no duh, June," Ryn sighs. "But you know how it is. Avalon's too powerful. The control she has over this entire country is absolutely ridiculous. She knew it was illegal—*everyone* knew it was illegal—but people were just too afraid to stand up to her.

"Avalon killed them," Ryn repeats, contempt laced through her voice. "All they were doing was speaking out against what they believed was truly *wrong,* and she dropped a nuclear bomb on them." She shakes her head. "And I will never, for the life of me, understand why *anyone* thought that was okay. People just let it happen and forgot about it after a few weeks. How is that even *possible*?"

"It shouldn't be," I tell her, stating the obvious because I can't think of anything better to say. "Avalon shouldn't be in charge of everything, not if *that's* the way she wants to run the world."

"Obviously," says Ryn. "And that's why *we're* going to be the ones to stop her. Bring down the Rainloft and end her reign of terror. For good."

"Yeah," I hear myself saying. "Your parents—all those people—they won't have died for nothing."

She looks at me, a hint of surprise in her expression. Then she smiles. "Thanks, June."

"No problem."

And for just a second, I forget just how impossible of an idea bringing down the Rainloft really is. I forget that there's a ninety–nine percent chance that we'll all be back up there by morning and for a second, I start to believe that maybe—just maybe—we'll pull it off. We'll never know what we're capable of unless we try, after all.

We sit there in quiet until the rumble of an approaching train scatters my thoughts. I get to my feet and help Ryn up just in time for the train to pull into the station. "You ready?" I ask.

She flashes me a confident grin. "I was born ready."

We look at each other and then, despite the situation, despite the weight of everything, Ryn starts laughing. I give her a funny look but I can't help but join in, and by the time Grayson and Atlas find us we're laughing our heads off.

And for the first time since we jumped off the Rainloft, I start to think that maybe there's hope for us after all.

Chapter Six

The Baytrack Train turned out to be nothing like I expected.

First of all, I was pleasantly surprised to find out that it was a Bed and Breakfast train—meaning they would have a huge breakfast buffet set up in the morning (free of charge for those who paid for their tickets as well as anyone that brought with them a certain wanted criminal who's really good at getting what he wants). That's what I was looking forward to, since all I'd had to eat for a very long time had been half a cookie and an ice cream cone.

Overall, the train is nice. There's a large dining car and somehow we ended up in one of the largest cabins available. Then again, this was a train, so our 'luxurious stateroom' turned out to be a cramped seven-by-seven-foot box with two sets of bunk beds that folded out from the walls. The thin mattresses felt sort of like cardboard and I did notice a faint musty smell when I walked in, but I wasn't bothered. I didn't need a five-star hotel, I just needed a place to sleep.

This was one thing that Ryn and I didn't agree on. "What *is* this?" she complained when she sat down on one of the mattresses.

"It's a bed," Atlas replied. "Made for sleeping."

I hadn't slept in multiple days and I couldn't wait to crawl into bed, but it still took me a while to fall asleep. The rock-hard mattress or the fact that my face was less than a foot away from the ceiling and my claustrophobia was really starting to kick in definitely could have contributed to the problem. But millions of thoughts were running laps around my head—the whole Granny Marie's fiasco, everything that happened at the mall, the conversation I'd had with Ryn not too long before, our crazy plan to bring down the Rainloft and the even crazier idea that we could actually do it. Those thoughts spiraled through my mind and kept me staring at the ceiling for what felt like multiple hours. By the time I actually began to doze off, the sun was starting to creep above the horizon.

Now the sun is high in the sky, peeking through the blinds of our tiny window. It has to be at least noon and I'm still in bed, contemplating whether it's worth it to get up or just sleep until tomorrow morning now that I'm finally comfortable.

But then I catch a faint whiff of the breakfast buffet and my eyes pop open. I sit up and look around the room just to discover that I'm alone. Great. They all ditched me for pancakes.

I climb down from the top bunk, struggling not to let the unpredictable rattle of the train buck me off. I tug my hair into a messy ponytail and slip into the furry boots that I picked up from the Halle Ross store last night, then leave our room. The ground rumbling beneath my feet, I follow the scent of fresh breakfast down to the dining car.

The dining room isn't much, but it's nicer than I expected it to be. There are dozens of booths along the walls, most of which are occupied. Atlas is sitting at one of the tables, but Ryn and Grayson are still at the breakfast buffet near the back of the room. They wave me over and

I cross the room, the scent of buttery pancakes making my mouth water.

"You're awake," Ryn exclaims, handing me a plate. "You must have been really tired. It was twelve thirty when we left the room and you were *still* asleep."

"I *told* them we should wait for you, but Ryn kept saying she would die of starvation if we waited any longer, so that was that," says Grayson with a shrug. Ryn whirls around to hit him with a pair of tongs.

"Oh, don't worry. I'll get over it… someday," I tease, making my voice sound as heartbroken as possible and wiping away invisible tears. Both of them laugh. It's interesting to me how, even after everything that happened yesterday, we're able to go right back to normal. It's almost like nothing ever happened—the incident at Granny Marie's and everything with Ryn at the mall could've been merely a dream.

Once we're done piling our plates with pancakes, eggs and various other ordinary breakfast foods that we haven't had the luxury of since before being selected for the Rainloft, the three of us head to the booth where my brother is already sitting.

"So, how long 'til we get there?" I ask as we sit down, realizing too late that I sound like a little kid on a long car ride.

"It'll be a while," says Atlas. "I don't expect we'll stop until at least this time tomorrow."

"Then we've got some time to kill."

I look out the small window above our table, watching the barren countryside whiz by. Nobody speaks again for a while. Maybe it's because we're all too busy enjoying our food. Or it could definitely be due to that pesky elephant that's been repeatedly popping up every time Ryn and Atlas are in the same room. I assume it's the latter, because as it turns out, the breakfast smelled a heck of a lot better than it tastes.

"So what's the plan once we get to Lebanon?" I ask, trying to spark up a conversation. "Where do we start once we get off the train?"

"To put it simply, we'll walk to the Rainloft Management Facility," Atlas explains. "Then we'll walk up to one of the employees and I'll have them take us to the helicopters. We'll walk up to the helicopters and I'll tell one of the pilots to fly us up to the Rainloft." He pauses. "Basically, all you have to do is walk. I'll do all the talking."

Immediately, Ryn shoots him a look. "So you're telling me that you're going to bring down the Rainloft all by yourself, with the *power of words*?" She scoffs, shaking her head. "We're not completely useless, you know. We know what we're doing."

The corners of Atlas's mouth tick up in amusement. I can see where this is headed, so I try to steer things in a different direction. "Hey, why don't we try an icebreaker?" I blurt out. "Everyone say your favorite thing about, I don't know, the person sitting across from you."

The two of them look at each other across the table. Atlas frowns and Ryn opens her mouth to protest, but I cut her off. "I'll go first. Grayson," I say, shifting my gaze in his direction. "You're an amazing chef. The spaghetti you made at that second-grade cooking camp was the best I've ever tasted."

"Why thank you, June," Grayson grins. "You're not so bad yourself. Once you figured out how to turn on the stove, your mac and cheese turned out incredible."

I laugh a little, then turn back to the others. Atlas looks mildly disinterested, but Ryn looks like she's trying to set him on fire with her eyes. "So which one of you two wants to go first?" I ask enthusiastically.

Atlas's cold gray eyes flit over to Ryn. "I will," he says bitterly. "It's amazing to me how you act like you're in charge of us all. Because the only decisions you've made so far have been so reckless and impetuous that you've landed us mere inches away from capture more times than I can count in the last twenty-four hours. Now, if you'll excuse me, I'm going to do something that's actually worth my time."

Abandoning his breakfast plate, he stands up and leaves the dining car. "Well *some*one's cranky," says Ryn, cutting into a pancake.

I glance between her and Grayson. "I'll be right back," I mutter, sliding out of the booth and going after Atlas.

I catch up to him in the hallway of one of the sleeper cars. He hardly acknowledges me as I fall into step with him, fighting a little to keep my balance with the rocking of the train. He sighs after a second. "Why are you following me?"

"You know, that was uncalled for," I say.

"It was the truth," he says flatly. "There's no denying that."

We're both silent for a couple of seconds. "Can you just try to be even remotely civil to her?" I plead. "She hasn't had it easy."

"How so?"

I open my mouth, ready to spill everything that Ryn told me last night, but stop myself. It took so long for her to open up to *me* about everything that happened to her and her parents. Even though I don't see anything potentially embarrassing or degrading about that story, she told me in confidentiality. There's no way she'd be happy if I revealed everything to Atlas of all people.

But then again, maybe with more context, he'd be able to understand her better. Maybe he'll see her side of things and they'll be able to finally coexist without breathing fire at each other every three seconds.

Putting aside my loyalty to Ryn, I take a breath. "Her parents died when she was little," I confess. "They were killed by Avalon, in the Lebanon Massacre. I think that's why she's so set on bringing down the Rainloft. She wants to do the thing her parents died trying to accomplish, and it makes perfect sense."

To my utter disappointment, Atlas's expression doesn't change. "Everyone has a sob story," he says decisively. "That doesn't make it okay that she tried to murder us all with light-up taco signs."

I stop in the middle of the hallway for a second, frustrated. "Can't you at least *try* to see her side?" I press.

"We'll never be able to bring down the Rainloft if we can't work as a team."

"I'll try," he says, rather unconvincingly. "Now, if you don't mind, I'm going to do something that's actually productive."

I consider asking him what that *something* could possibly be, but change my mind. "Fine," I grumble, then turn around and head back to the dining car.

Ryn and Grayson are still eating when I get back to the booth. They both look up at me expectantly as I sit down. "He'll get over himself," I tell them, hoping it's true. "Eventually."

A few hours later I'm in our room, laying on my stomach on the claustrophobic top bunk and trying to read a boring Baytrack Railroads pamphlet. After everything that happened yesterday, I thought it would be nice to have a little break from all the craziness and just lounge around on the train for a day. But trying to get comfortable on a train turns out to be a hundred times harder than I expected—my bed just might be worse than sleeping on the ground, so sleeping isn't really an option unless you're completely exhausted. I try to fill the time by flipping through railroad brochures, but every time I finish reading a line, a sudden jerk of the train jars my thoughts into chaos and I have to start all over again.

Sick of reading the same monotonous paragraph about *Why You Should Choose Baytrack for All Your Travel Needs*, I close the pamphlet and sigh dramatically. "I'm bored," I announce.

"Really?" asks Grayson. He's the only other person in the room, sitting on the bottom bunk of the opposite bed and filling out a random crossword puzzle he found in a drawer. I can tell it's a hard one, based on the way he's staring it down. "Would you rather be fighting Alumni right now?"

"No," I mumble, shifting to lay on my back. "It's just weird having so much free time. I feel like I should be doing homework or writing some sort of essay right now."

"Do you *want* to be doing schoolwork right now?"

"No!" I say quickly. "But think about it. When was the last time you really had a break? You know, a real, official break when you didn't have a whole mountain of homework that needed to be done the next morning?"

He puts down the crossword and thinks for a second. "Before I got taken up to the Rainloft?"

"Exactly," I say. "It's not that I don't *like* having free time. I just have no clue what to *do* with it."

"I get that."

I stare at the ceiling for a minute. It's quiet without Ryn or Atlas here. As soon as we got back to the room after breakfast, Ryn left to go 'explore' and Atlas is still off doing who knows what in some other part of the train.

"Do you think we'll do it?" I ask.

"Do what?"

"Bring down the Rainloft." I sit up again and face Grayson. "Do you think we will?"

He considers that for a second, putting his pen to his lips. "I don't know," he decides. "The whole idea sounds insane on paper. But with all four of our powers combined…"

"Yeah. And maybe I'm crazy, maybe I'm just tired and losing my mind or something," I ramble, thinking out loud, "but honestly, I think we can do it. And I think it'll be easy."

For some reason, that realization doesn't bring me as much satisfaction as I expected it to. I don't know why—I hate the Rainloft. Even before I was chosen, I've never been okay with it. And that's been the plan this entire time: we'll bring it down, and Avalon's reign of terror will come to an end.

I should be thrilled. So why is there still a part of me that's not?

Before I can think about it too much, I shove the thought out of my head. I'm probably just tired. Exhaustion can make you irrational, right? "I can't wait," I say, more to myself than Grayson. Then I turn back to him. "So what do you think things will be like after we bring it down?"

"Weird," he says after a second. "Definitely different."

Suddenly, thousands of different *What If?*s hit me at once. "What if they just build a new Rainloft?" I question. "What'll even happen after we bring it down? Will we go to high school just like all the other teenagers or will we go to, I don't know, *jail*?"

"I hope not," Grayson cuts me off before I can worry any more. "But how about we cross that bridge when we get to it? Let's just focus on getting it done before we worry about what happens after."

I shoot him a look, then sigh. "I guess."

That doesn't stop me from coming up with tons more unanswerable questions. I lie back on my rock-hard mattress, thousands of worries spiraling around my mind. What would things even be like without the Rainloft looming above it? I've never known a Rainloft-free world, and the vision is both terrifying and endlessly exciting at the same time.

It scares me because the Rainloft was created for a reason. From what I've gathered from news reports and history books, Lavon had exploded into chaos and crime rates were up to the point where Avalon's miracle serum was the only solution. Without Alumni to keep things in order, would the world go right back to the way it was? Or has society learned its lesson by now?

As frightening as it is, the possibilities are amazing. I could go to high school. *Normal* high school, where you get to learn algebra and play instruments and join clubs. I won't have to worry about learning to harness my useless powers and I'll be able to touch grass any time I want. I'll have teachers that I don't like but none that I absolutely despise, like the overwhelming majority of Rainloft professors. I could be a normal teenager for once.

I sigh happily, my head swirling with visions of math tests and underwhelming school lunches. Things are finally going to change—for better or for worse.

*   *   *

"I love tortelloni," says Ryn enthusiastically, bouncing on the balls of her feet as we wait in line for the pasta bar. "I don't even know why. It's just so good." She turns to me. "What about you, June? What's your favorite type of pasta?"

"Um—I'd have to go with penne," I decide, trying to match her energy.

"Ooh, penne *is* good," she beams. "I'll have to get some of that too."

For whatever reason, she seems to be in a better mood than she's been in all day—and that's more than I can say for the rest of us. "Okay, I get that you two've got a passion for spaghetti, but you're holding up the line," Atlas complains from behind me. Ryn rolls her eyes and moves forward to the dinner buffet.

Once we've all gotten our pasta, we head back to the same booth we sat at for breakfast. Nobody says anything for a while. I don't even think it's because of the lingering awkwardness between us four—though that definitely still exists. It's just that there really isn't anything good to say. The only thing that matters is our goal of bringing down the Rainloft, and we've already been over the plan multiple times. Nothing that any of us could say would be even remotely as important as that, so we just eat in silence.

There's a large television at the center of the wall, and on it a news reporter drones on about the economy or whatever it is news reporters talk about these days. Clueless passengers around us talk in monotone and stuff their mouths with food. The train clatters along on the tracks and the star-flecked night sky whizzes by out the window.

For the first time all day, I feel sort of comfortable. But that peace is gone just as quickly as it came when the words *Breaking News* flash across the TV.

Immediately, all eyes are on the screen. A horrified news reporter stands in front of Granny Marie's bakery, blinking red-and-blue lights lighting up her face. The bakery windows are shattered and inside the building, all the furniture is overturned. "This is Channel 13 News coming to you live from Granny Marie's and we have some breaking news for you," says the reporter, her tone full of urgency. "Yesterday, three students—Grayson Campbell, Kathryn Sharp and June Winters—escaped from the Rainloft Academy."

There's a collective gasp. "It's unclear exactly what led to this," the reporter continues. "But they've already managed to wreak havoc on two of Springfield's local businesses. I'm here now with Marie Johnson, who happened to be inside her bakery at the time of the incident."

The camera pans over to a distressed-looking Granny Marie. "So, Marie," the reporter begins. "Would you mind explaining *what in the world* went down last night?"

She hands the mic over to Marie. "Well, let's see," she says, a tremor in her voice. "There were these four kids that walked into the shop last night. Told me they'd been separated from their parents or somethin'. They were real nice, real polite about everything, so I made up some food for 'em, free of charge. Talked to 'em for a while, then these… these *people* walked into the bakery. With—with *guns!* An' they told me somethin' about the kids, can't remember what it was, but then… they tried to shoot at the children! Oh, it was awful, absolutely awful…"

The news reporter nods, her expression full of sympathy. "I'm so sorry this happened. Can you tell us what these kids looked like? And did you happen to recognize any of them—either the kids or the people with guns?"

Marie thinks for a second. "I didn't recognize any of 'em, no… the adults had on some shiny leather uniforms, now that I think of it, they may've been members of the military or army or somethin'... As for the kids, they were wearin' these colorful school uniforms. Well, three of them were, at least. The fourth was dressed somewhat like a member of a biker gang."

"And you're sure there were *four* of them?"

"Uh-huh," Marie nods with a forced chuckle. "I may be old, but I reckon I can still count."

The news reporter turns back to the camera. "Well, there you have it," she says. "There was a second incident reported at the Starview Mall, over in downtown Springfield. An Alumnus was found in the food court, crushed beneath a display car. Fortunately, a security camera managed to catch a photo of them walking out of the   mall."

At that, a grainy photo flashes across the screen. It's really blurry, so it's hard to make out our faces, but it's definitely us. Ryn and I are decked out in Halle Ross clothes, and there's blood streaked across my cheek. Each one of our expressions is some mix of shock, exhaustion and—more so in my brother's case—irritation.

That photo stays plastered across the screen for way too long, and then the camera finally goes back to the news reporter. "The fourth fugitive's identity has yet to be confirmed, but there's speculation that it could be Atlas Winters—whose sister, June Winters, was one of yesterday's escapees."

The whole dining car breaks into hushed chatter. On the TV, the news reporter turns back to Granny Marie, looking at her strangely. "As you can see, there seems to be something off about Marie's memory, as Lavon hasn't had a military since before the Rainloft. Could this be the start of another mind-control epidemic, reminiscent of the one caused by Winters when he first escaped two years ago?"

Marie looks completely lost. "What?" she asks. "Dear, what on earth are you talking about?"

"We don't know much more than that," the reporter says, looking squarely at the camera. "All we know is that these four individuals are highly dangerous, and we need all hands on deck to return them to the Rainloft, where they belong. Lavon, we *can't* have a repeat of Winters' big stunt a couple of years ago. If you see them, be extremely careful and contact the Rainloft Management Facility as soon as possible. If you play any part in returning these criminals to the Rainloft, you will be generously rewarded."

The channel abruptly flips to some sort of serene nature documentary—a stark contrast to that bombshell of a news report. For a split second I can't help but think, *hey, I'm on the news*. But the chatter rising up around me calls me back to my senses. All eyes are on us now, and the passengers at the booth across from us are pointing and slowly inching toward the far side of their seats.

"Uh, guys," Ryn whispers uneasily, eyes darting around the room.

"It's not the first time," Atlas mutters, and then to everyone's surprise, he stands up. This small little action draws all the breath from the room and now everyone's attention is on him.

"That's Atlas Winters!" someone squeaks out.

Atlas turns in that direction, hands in his pockets. "Actually, no," he says. His tone is unbelievably calm— if I were in his position, I think all those stares would melt me. "You don't know who I am. In fact, you don't know who any of us four are. We're only harmless travelers, on a much-needed vacation from everyday life—just like you."

Just like that, everyone visibly relaxes, believing that lie without a single doubt. They all return to their dinners, shoveling pasta into their mouths like Atlas just extinguished every worry in their minds.

Atlas lowers himself back to the booth and continues eating his lasagna like nothing happened, even though the rest of us are still staring at him.

"So that's it?" I ask. "They're just going to believe that, forever?"

"You saw Marie on that news report," he says simply. "Ordinary people are easy to brainwash. They're gullible. They'd believe the world was ending if I wanted them to."

"And whatever you tell them, they'll just believe that for their entire *lives*?" Ryn asks, narrowing her eyes. "So you could make someone think that, I don't know, dogs can fly…and for the rest of time, whenever they see a dog they'll expect it to launch into the sky like a rocket?"

Atlas looks up at her with an expression of genuine concern. "Yes. If for some insane reason I wanted to make someone think chihuahuas were a species of bird, I could do that."

Ryn shakes her head and twirls her fork around in her spaghetti. "That is *messed up*."

"It's a means of survival," says Atlas dryly. "Sometimes there's no other option."

And he leaves it at that. That one sentence brings an infinite number of questions to my mind, but I decide not to voice any of them.

It's strange—Atlas is my own twin brother, but it feels like I don't know him at all anymore. Sure, it's been two years since I've seen him and four since we've actually talked, but four years shouldn't be enough to turn someone's entire personality on its head. Time shouldn't have that much power.

But then again, maybe it wasn't the doing of time alone. The last two years of Atlas's life are a total blank to me. I have no clue what he's gone through or where he's been for all this time. In the last two years, he could have died and come back to life again. Maybe battling Alumni is a part of his daily routine. Yesterday I watched him kill two of them—and something tells me they aren't the only casualties of his 'mind-control epidemic', whatever that means.

But maybe he's been living a completely normal life this whole time. He could be going to high school. Taking math tests, going to football games, maybe even dating. He could be married for all I know. With mind-control, the possibilities are literally endless.

It's just weird—we were really close as kids. I remember our mom telling us once that we were caught in an endless game of follow-the-leader—wherever Atlas went, I would follow, and vice versa. But he's an entirely different person now. It doesn't make sense.

I can only hope that it won't last forever.

*　　　*　　　*

After lying in bed and staring at the ceiling for another small eternity, I sit up and rub the bleariness from my eyes. Through the window, the barren countryside has finally faded into picturesque fields of lush grass, dotted with colorful flowers that make the whole scene look like something out of a movie. Based on the stories I've heard about Lavon's capital city, I can tell we're nearing our destination.

Atlas is nowhere to be seen, but Ryn and Grayson are both still asleep and I can't help but feel a twinge of envy. Trying to make as little noise as humanly possible, I climb down the rickety metal ladder and cringe when it groans loudly beneath my feet.

I slip out of the room and close the door softly behind me. Just like I did yesterday, I follow the scent of fresh breakfast down to the dining car, dragging my feet along the carpeted hallway. I pass by a bubbly couple, chattering away with infinitely too much enthusiasm for eight o'clock in the morning and practically skipping down the halls. *How great it must be to get a full night's sleep on this dumb train,* I think to myself, stuffing my hands in my pockets.

I keep trudging down the hallway, avoiding social interaction at all costs and complaining to myself about how long this darn hallway is. I'm just a few steps away from the dining car when someone's hand around my arm jars me from my thoughts.

The hand yanks me off to the side of the hallway and I stumble over my shoes, my shoulder hitting one of the stateroom doors.

"Sorry, kid, didn't mean to startle you," says a voice, and only then do I look up to see who the hand belongs to. It's an older man—maybe late sixties or early seventies—with snow-white hair and thick tortoiseshell glasses.

"Atlas," I call down into the dining car, assuming this guy saw the news report but wasn't in the room for my brother to brainwash him.

"Oh, don't worry, I'm not going to turn you in," he says, swatting that thought away with one hand. His other one is still clamped around my arm. "I just wanted to say thank you."

"'Thank you?'" I repeat, narrowing my eyes at him and trying to get my heart rate to slow.

"Figures. You probably don't get that a lot," he says. "Well, thank you. For all that you do for this world."

None of this makes any sense to me, but maybe it's just my extreme sleep deprivation translating all his words into gibberish. "Um, you're welcome," I say.

"Calm down, I'm not going to call the cops on you," he says, reading my mind. "I'm just beyond happy that I finally have the opportunity to say this to one of you. This world wouldn't be the way it is without you Rainloft kids, and I know what you have to go through is awful, but I'm so grateful that you do it. Really, we all are."

I nod along, tilting my head. "Yeah?"

"I don't approve of what you four did," he states, his smile falling a bit, "but I'm glad for this opportunity. So, thanks again. Tell that to the other two."

"Okay," I say, still nodding for lack of anything better to do. "You're welcome."

He squints at me. "You really do look like him, you know. I see so much potential in you, June—it's a shame you're related."

At that, he drops my arm, turns around and walks away, leaving me wondering what in the world just happened. Not thirty seconds later, a different voice calls me to my senses.

"What are you staring at?" asks Atlas from beside me. "You look like you just rolled off a building."

"That—that guy," I stammer, pointing in the old man's direction. "He just *thanked* me. He said he was *grateful* for what Rainloft students do. And…he promised not to turn us in."

Atlas frowns. "He was lying to your face."

"You think everyone is lying," I accuse, folding my arms.

"Not true," he says shortly. "I only think that when people really *are* lying. Which is most of the time. People are constantly lying."

I shake my head, turning back to the dining car. "Forget it. I'm going to get breakfast."

"I'm not stopping you."

And then we part ways, Atlas heading back down the sleeper cars and me following the delicious smell of pancakes to the dining room. The fresh, buttery aroma is the one thing bringing up my mood when literally everything else is trying to drag it down.

I'm halfway across the dining car, just a few paces away from breakfast paradise when the familiar rumbling beneath my feet comes to an abrupt halt. I stagger forward a little but manage to grab on to the corner of a booth.

All at once, everyone looks up from their food and starts complaining loudly. "Aw, c'mon, what are we stoppin' for?" the guy in the booth next to me complains. "Ain't no way we're in the city yet."

Then the door to the conductor's car screeches open and my heart freezes. A woman walks into the dining car, her presence bringing a cold chill into the room. Her sleek black heels dig into the mold-green shag carpet and she wears a dark trench coat over her billowing dress. Coffee-brown hair cascades down her shoulders, a feathery black mask concealing most of her face.

Immediately, I turn on my heel and sprint back down the hallway, praying that she didn't see me. I almost run straight into Atlas, who turns around with a sigh.

"Avalon," I say, my thoughts spinning faster than my mouth can put them into words. "Avalon is here. She just walked onto the train."

He cranes his neck to get a better view of the dining car, then curses softly. "Come on," he mutters, turning around and heading back through the sleeper hallways.

"Wh—can't you just mind-control her?" I whisper, jogging to catch up with him. "Tell her to get off the train and leave us alone?"

"You don't understand," he hisses. "Avalon is the most powerful human being in Lavon and quite possibly the entire universe. She can't be mind-controlled, she'll just resist."

"How do you know that? Have you ever *tried*?"

"Yes, actually," he says impatiently. "And it didn't go well. Our best shot now is to pretend we're not here."

"'Pretend we're not here'?" I repeat.

Then we reach the very back of the train, a dead-end with a big metal door that has the words 'No Entry' spray-painted in white across its surface. Without hesitation, Atlas grabs the metal handle and pulls it open, letting in a gust of wind that nearly bowls me over.

"What are you doing?" I shout over the wind.

"I'm getting us out of here," he says, walking out onto the train's balcony and beckoning for me to follow. There isn't one part of me that thinks this is a good idea, but it's either this or go back and let Avalon capture me, so I reluctantly step outside.

The wind whips my hair in my face and I immediately stumble over to the flimsy railing, grabbing on for dear life. We're on a bridge probably a hundred feet above the ground and this balcony is way too narrow for my liking.

Atlas reaches back inside the train and flips a latch on the door, locking it before he pulls it shut.

"You just locked us out!" I yell frantically.

"Would you just trust me for one second?" he snaps, pointing around the corner of the train car. What I failed to notice before is that the balcony wraps around most of the train, stretching down the line of sleeper cars. "We need to get the conductor's car, and there's a door inside from the balcony."

For a second I wonder why he knows that, but he's already heading down the balcony so I follow him. I grasp the tiny metal railing with one hand and keep the other one on the train's wall to steady myself.

The soft scent of flowers rises up from the fields below us and mingles with the overpowering smell of engine smoke, filling the air with a sickly-sweet aroma. I can't not worry about what would happen if I were to fly off the train altogether.

"If we can reach the conductor, I can get him to kick Avalon off the train," explains Atlas, rescuing me from my thoughts. "I'll get him to find her and tell her that we're not even here."

"Great," I say, "and what should I do?"

He thinks for a second. "Just stand off to the side and try not to be a distraction."

"Okay," I grumble. "Glad I can help."

It takes way too long to get to the conductor's car, but after a lot of walking, we finally reach the fabled outside door. Atlas leans back against it, pauses to mouth *don't be a distraction*, then pushes it open and strolls inside like he owns the place.

The conductor's car is small. There's a large panoramic window along the front wall, and in front of it is a control panel. The conductor is reclined back in his chair by the control panel, picking at his fingernails with his fancy hat halfway over his eyes. I don't think he even sees us come in.

"Morning, sir," Atlas says casually. "Sorry if I'm interrupting anything, but I've got a small favor to ask of you."

The conductor spins around in his seat, his eyes wider than the train's wheels. "Hey, kid, you're not supposed to be in here," he barks.

"I know," says Atlas, hands in his pockets. "We just had a small complaint about one of the other passengers."

The conductor's brow furrows. "And what's that?"

"See, there's this lady on board—her name's Avalon. She's causing a massive disruption," Atlas explains, his voice full of concern. "I think she was carrying some sort of gun. Sir, I'm scared for the safety of your passengers. This lady looked *dangerous*."

"She's not gonna shoot anyone," the conductor says, leaning forward in his chair. "She's just lookin' for those kids that escaped. She'll be gone before you know it."

"Sure," says Atlas, nodding slowly. "But you need to kick her off."

Suddenly, the conductor's eyes light up with realization. "You're right," he gasps. "I can't believe I didn't see it before. She's a threat to this train's security!"

He turns to look squarely at Atlas. "Thanks for lettin' me know, son. I'll go tell her to leave right now."

He starts to rise from his chair, but then the door to the dining car slides open and my heart skips a beat. "There's no need," says Avalon in her euphonious tone, floating into the room and bringing with her a gust of frigid air that didn't come from outside. "You may have a seat, Robert, I won't be long."

The conductor falls back into his chair, obediently turning back to the control panel and going about his business like the single most powerful woman in the world didn't just stroll into his office. It's almost like she's brainwashing him the way I've seen Atlas control numerous people before.

And then it hits me: *Avalon is a Type Five.* I knew that—I've known it for longer than I can remember—but it's never really clicked with me what that means. She can mimic the power of any Rainloft student with nothing but a glance in their direction. She basically has all four of the other abilities, and that amount of power is terrifying in the hands of someone like her.

Avalon turns to face my brother and me, and I can't help but take a step back. "Hello Atlas," she says, her voice eerily calm. "June."

"Avalon," says Atlas. I can tell he's trying to keep cool, but there's a tension hidden behind the cocky smile he gives her. "To what do we owe the pleasure?"

Avalon tilts her head, her barely-visible eyes bouncing between the two of us. "You two have grown so much," she says, her tone almost wistful. "It feels like just yesterday that you were little first years, wandering the halls of the Rainloft, trying to find your classes on time." She pauses. "Look at you now."

"Okay, cut the crap," Atlas snaps. "If you're here to stuff us in a helicopter and drag us back up to your glorified Alcatraz, just get it over with. No one's stopping you."

Avalon looks at him with an expression that seems very out-of-place in this context—it's almost like the way a mother would look at her child on their graduation day. "As much as I'd love to do that, we both know you'd never let me."

"So why are you here?"

She smiles behind her mask, then her beady eyes slide over to meet mine. A chill runs down my spine. "June," Avalon drawls, and then she extends her hand to me. "I'd like for you to take my hand."

My eyes bounce between her hand and the expectant look on her face. "What?" I ask apprehensively. "Why?"

"It's impossible to explain," she says, her outstretched hand unwavering. "There's something imperative I need to show you. All I require is your trust."

"My trust?" I say, my voice sounding unintentionally small. "Why would I trust you?"

"Because I'm afraid there's no other option at this point," she says, faint notes of urgency creeping into her tone. "I'm not trying to pull one over on you, June. That wouldn't benefit either one of us. All I'm asking is for you to trust me."

You could cut the tension in the room with a knife. My mind is still trying to make sense of this tangled mess of words being thrown at me and everyone else is dead-silent. I sneak a glance at Atlas, who's watching this whole thing play out with a wary look and one hand braced around the door handle. Our eyes meet for a second and he arches an eyebrow.

"No," I say, turning back to Avalon. There's an unwanted hint of uncertainty in my voice, so I clear my throat and say it again, this time with more confidence. "No. I'm sorry, but I just don't see any way I could trust you."

Avalon pulls back her hand. "Very well," she says calmly. "I suppose I'll have to try again another day."

Her eyes briefly lock with mine. It's nearly impossible to see behind her mask, but I can almost swear she winks at me before she disappears, leaving behind nothing but a few stray feathers.

"What was that?" I ask after a few beats of silence.

"That was Avalon," Atlas says shortly, crossing the small room and stooping down to pick up one of Avalon's feathers. "The old lady is a walking riddle. She'll say the simplest things in the most roundabout way imaginable and she'll never get to the point if you don't get there for her."

Before I have the chance to respond to that, the door to the dining car swings open. I immediately jump backward, expecting Avalon to come waltzing back into the room, but instead it's Grayson who pokes his head inside.

"There you are," he says, his tone full of relief. "Ryn and I have been looking all over for you two. We thought for sure Avalon got you."

"Yeah, I sort of thought so, too," I say weakly.

He scans the room, his eyes landing on the conductor, Atlas and me in turn. His eyes narrow more and more by the second. "What's going on?"

"Nothing of note," Atlas replies briefly, pocketing the feather and strolling over to the conductor. "You can start the train now," he tells him, then turns around and heads into the dining car.

Grayson and I exchange a glance, then follow him through the doorway. Not a second after we cross the threshold, the engine roars to life beneath my feet and the train starts slowly inching along its tracks.

I snag a mini waffle from the breakfast buffet and smile to myself. As confusing as that was, we just managed to evade capture yet again—and that was *Avalon*. She could've caught us with ease but didn't bother trying. The reason *why* is beyond me, but I can't help but think: if the mother of the Rainloft herself let us go, maybe—just *maybe*—that means Alumni are done chasing us. After two whole tries, they've given up and decided that nothing they can do will put an end to our reign of terror. If that's the case, it's a straight shot from here to our goal of ending the Rainloft once and for all. There's nothing stopping us now.

At least that's what I keep telling myself.

Chapter Seven

I fell asleep as soon as we got back to our room. Cardboard mattress, blinding sunlight, noisy roommates and all—I climbed up to my bed and passed out the second my head hit the pillow. I couldn't help it. And don't ask how I ended up asleep in these conditions and laid awake for eight hours in a dark, quiet room just a little while before. Sleep has a bad habit of coming in the most inconvenient times imaginable. I could've hibernated for multiple days if the train hadn't arrived in Lebanon a mere two hours later.

"This is so exciting," Ryn gushes next to me as we move slowly down the sleeper car hallways, caught in the traffic jam of people flowing through the front doors. Her Halle Ross sunglasses are pulled down over her eyes and her curly hair hangs loosely around her shoulders. She looks like a regular tourist, headed to the city to visit family or go swimming or whatever it is people go to Lebanon to do. "Today is the day. The Rainloft comes down *today*."

"That's wild," I marvel. "This all feels like a dream, really. I keep thinking I'm going to blink and wake up back in my stuffy old dorm room."

"And you'll have a whole pile of homework on your nightstand that's due in ten minutes," Ryn adds spitefully. "*Believe* me, you're not the only one who feels that way."

"Thanks for riding," one of the employees repeats over and over again in monotone as she scans tickets and ushers passengers off the train. Once the four of us reach the doors, she wrinkles her nose and hits us with a stare hard enough to pierce diamond. "You need tickets"

"Sure," Atlas says dryly. "But you're going to let us off anyways."

The employee heaves the most dramatic sigh I've ever heard and swipes her hand carelessly in the direction of the door. "Thanks for riding."

Atlas grins at her. "Thanks for your hospitality."

Ryn, Grayson and I follow him down the train's metal steps. The second I step outside, the sun hits me like a bus and my hand flies up to shield my eyes. "The sun is so *bright* here," I tell Ryn, squinting in an attempt to see through the blinding light. "Maybe it's a sign. The sun is shining, so that means today's going to be…"

The second my eyes start to adjust, I trail off and my mouth falls open. "Whoa."

Lebanon City is something straight off of a postcard. We're standing in a small glass train station at the edge of the cobblestone town square, surrounded by pastel-brick buildings and monstrous skyscrapers. There's a massive fountain at the center of it all, and the water bubbling out from the top is crystal-clear and glitters in the sunlight. I'm not sure why it is—maybe I'm just used to the stuffy train by now—but the air here is so crisp and so fresh that part of me just wants to stand here, close my eyes and drink it up for a day.

But directly across the plaza from us, looming over the city and eclipsing every other building in sight is the

Rainloft Management Facility. It casts an ominous shadow over the sunny city and reminds me vaguely of something out of a horror movie. It's that one gloomy-looking, fog-shrouded house in an otherwise picture-perfect neighborhood—the one that kids make up scary stories about and avoid at all costs.

Though in the movies, nine times out of ten, the house's owner turns out to be a sugary-sweet old lady, misjudged and misunderstood by all her neighbors. All I can do is hope this is one of those cases—and not one of the rare scenarios where the house is inhabited by monsters.

"This place is *insane*," Grayson murmurs, taking in the city as we follow the flow of tourists out of the train station and into the town square. Most of them pile into one of the countless rental cars lined up along the road, so we weave around them to reach the city's core.

Once we get to the fountain, Atlas spins around to face the rest of us. "Okay," he starts, clapping his hands together like a coach explaining the team's next play. "This should be relatively simple, as long as we do everything right. And by that, I mean don't say or do anything until after the Rainloft is ancient history. Any questions?"

"One," I say, raising my index finger. "Are we allowed to breathe?"

Atlas shoots me a classic *you're-wasting-my-time* look. "Yes. You're allowed to breathe."

"What if you need help?" asks Ryn, one hand on her hip. "What if your whole plan crashes and burns and you end up in handcuffs? Do you want us to just stand there and watch it happen?"

"If I need backup, I'll say something," says Atlas. "But that's even less likely than June keeping her mouth shut this whole time."

"Hey," I protest. "That's not fair."

"Is it really all that simple, though?" asks Grayson. "I was just thinking—if the Rainloft is so easy to bring down, why hasn't someone gone out and done it already?

"*This* is the simple part," Atlas says, then his tone drops so that it's more like he's talking to himself than any of us. "Each phase before this has been even closer to impossible than the last. Harder than your microscopic brains   could   begin   to   comprehend."

"What?" I ask, narrowing my eyes. "You mean that train ride? What was so hard about—"

"That's beside the point," he cuts me off. "Any more   useless   questions   or   are   we   all   clear?"

I glance between Ryn and Grayson, then shrug. "I guess we're good?"

It comes out sounding like more of a question than I intend it to, but Atlas doesn't seem to care. "Good," he says, then turns on his heel and starts heading for the Rainloft Management Facility. The rest of us trail behind him.

After a second, Ryn catches my attention. There's something about the way she strays a little ways behind the rest of us and how she repeatedly scans the plaza with a wary look in her eyes that tells me something's off even before she says it.

"June, this is where it happened," she tells me, her voice low.

I open my mouth to ask what *it* is, but then it hits me. "Oh. This is where it happened."

"Uh-huh." Her gaze bounces between the colorful stucco buildings surrounding the bustling plaza. "They must've rebuilt it. This place was a disaster after the bomb hit."

"Are you sure this is the exact place?" I ask.

"Positive." She frowns and jerks a thumb over her shoulder. "I saw that fountain on the news report that night. It was mostly destroyed, but it was definitely that fountain. It had the same little dolphin statue at the top."

I look back, taking in the massive fountain. "And they rebuilt it?" I ask. "The exact same fountain?"

"The *exact* same one," she says with a bitter laugh. "I can't believe they did that. They just rebuilt this whole place. Like, I'm sorry, Avalon, but you can't just blow up an entire city and then pretend nothing ever happened. *That's not how that works*."

I sigh, shaking my head. "There's something wrong with Avalon," I decide. "There's something wrong with the world."

"You think?"

"Guys," Atlas interjects from a few paces ahead of us. "Think you could walk any faster?"

"Sorry," Ryn grumbles, then she turns to look at me with a mischievous glint in her eyes. "Guess we need to pick up the pace."

Without any sort of warning, she turns on her heel and starts skipping toward the entrance of the RMF. "Hey, wait for me!" I shout, taking off after her. Grayson laughs and Atlas calls after us, but we pretend we can't hear him.

We reach the entrance of the building way too fast. What I'd failed to notice before, though, is that there's a guard stationed by the facility's doors. Ryn and I skid to an abrupt halt in front of him, and I stagger back a little as soon as we do.

"Oh, hi," I say, plastering an innocent smile across my face. The guard—*Roberts* is the name I read off his nametag—is at least twice my height, so I have to look up to meet his eyes. "Sorry. Didn't see you there."

He squints at us both for a second, then takes in a sharp breath when the realization hits him. "It's you," he murmurs, his hand immediately moving to his tool belt. I can't tell whether he's reaching for the walkie-talkie or the barely-visible Sim gun right next to it. "You're the escaped students."

"Hold on, hold on," Ryn says hastily, eyes on the Sim gun. "Yeah, we're those students, but there's a reason why we escaped. The Rainloft is awful. Avalon is vile and cruel and I think you know that, don't you?"

The guard stares at her, his hand braced around the gun's handle. "I work for Avalon. *Willingly.*"

"Yeah, you do," says Atlas, striding up to the scene. Instantaneously, the guard's eyes go wide and he swipes the gun off his belt, pointing it straight at him with a white-knuckled grip. "But I think you're about to have a change of heart."

"Your tricks won't work on me, Winters," the guard snarls. "Don't even bother trying."

"Put the gun down, Roberts."

And he does. Like an obedient golden retriever, the guard kneels down and places the gun gently on the cobblestone floor.

"We're going inside now, alright?" Atlas says. "And you're not going to stop us."

The guard shakes his head. "No, I'm not."

"Great."

Just like that, we're in. That poor guard opens the door and holds it, waiting until we're all inside to close it softly behind us. "Thank you," I tell him weakly as I pass by.

It's painfully obvious that the RMF was built by the same people as the Rainloft. And take it from me: these people are *not* interior decorators. This place is hardly a step up from a cardboard box. The walls are painted the most boring shade of beige I've ever seen and the flooring is the same tile that covers every room in the Rainloft. There are fold-up chairs lined sloppily along the wall and metal end tables piled with stacks of Rainloft magazines, sort of like a waiting room in a doctor's office. A vending machine displaying a pathetic assortment of snacks is shoved in a corner, its dull hum filling up the loud silence.

The only trace of effort put into the decorating comes from a random kid's painting hanging at the far end of the room. I can't tell exactly what the drawing *is*—it's either a roller skate or a horse on wheels, take your pick.

A lady sits at the front counter, and from what I can tell, her mood matches this room perfectly. The corners of her mouth are turned downward and the bright blue light from her computer reflects off her wire-framed glasses as she sits rigidly at her desk. "Welcome in," she intones as we step inside, not bothering to look up from her work.

Atlas looks to the three of us and nods toward the line of fold-up chairs. "This won't take long," he mutters.

"We're still not useless, you know," Ryn protests. "We could help. You're not the only one here with powers that—"

"Your cooperation is much appreciated," Atlas says through gritted teeth, then motions in the direction of the chairs again. "Now go sit down."

Ryn opens her mouth to argue, but instead she rolls her eyes and reluctantly slumps down in one of the chairs. Grayson and I take the two seats to her left while Atlas heads for the front desk.

I lean forward in my chair and watch it all unfold: the receptionist lets out a tiny shriek when she looks up to see

Atlas. She sits there with her mouth hanging open until he says something barely audible from where I'm sitting, then her shoulders visibly relax. They proceed to chat casually for a few minutes, like a grocery store cashier would with a completely average customer. Then the lady nods, stands abruptly, then disappears through a door behind the counter.

I narrow my eyes, trying to figure out what could possibly be happening right now. Atlas stands there for a short eternity, drumming his fingers on the counter while he waits for the receptionist to return.

"Think that vending machine works?" Grayson asks next to me, pointing toward the sad vending machine stuffed in the corner.

"Probably," I guess. "We don't have any money though, do we?"

He grins, then pulls a five-dollar bill out of absolutely nowhere. "Found it on the ground outside," he explains, then his smile drops. "It probably belongs to someone, though, we should—"

"It's fine," I interrupt, plucking the money from his hand. He follows me over to the vending machine and I scan its contents, grinning when my eyes land on a fat bag of gummy worms right in the middle. "Jackpot."

I take Grayson's order, then punch both numbers into the keypad. We stand back and watch as my bag of gummies drops from its shelf, and then to both of our dismay, Grayson's candy bar gets stuck. "Come on," he groans.

"Here," I say, then gesture for him to step back. Without really thinking it through, I pull my leg back and kick the machine—*hard.*

All I get from that is a probably-broken foot. The chocolate bar doesn't budge, and I'm just about to give up hope when Ryn struts over. "Stand back, you amateurs," she mocks, and with a flick of her wrist, the vending machine starts quaking and nearly every single item is dislodged at once.

Food starts spilling out from the machine like an avalanche of sad off-brand candy. For a second the three of us just stare at each other, and then we all burst out laughing.

"Guys!" Atlas's voice cuts through the fun like a dagger. "*What are you doing?*"

"Sorry, master," Ryn says, her voice dripping with sarcasm. "We'll clean it up."

I stoop down to grab my gummy worms, then rip open the bag and eat them as I walk over to the counter where Atlas is still waiting.

"Want one?" I ask, offering him a worm. He raises an eyebrow at me and I shrug, popping it into my mouth instead. "Your loss."

At that moment, the door behind the desk swings open and the receptionist bustles into the room, an oddly giddy grin on her face. "Good news!" she sings, her mood completely flipped since I last saw her five minutes ago. "We have a shipment of school supplies we're sending up to the Rainloft via helicopter tomorrow morning. I'm certain they wouldn't mind if the four of you hitch a ride!"

"That's amazing," I exclaim, my heart lifting. But then it sinks a little when I register exactly what she just said, and I turn to Atlas. "Wait, tomorrow morning? What are we supposed to do until then?"

"Oh, don't worry, hon," the receptionist gushes. "You can stay the night here."

I stare at her. "Here?"

"Of course. It's no big deal," she says enthusiastically, swatting away my question like it's nothing. "We have several floors of suites here for all of our employees who work longer shifts. I'm sure we've got a room or two available."

"Wow," I say, not entirely sure how to react. "That's… incredibly convenient. Thank you."

She smiles sweetly at us, then bends down to rummage through one of her desk drawers. "Aha!" she exclaims, pulling out a small card and holding it up like it's something precious. "Suite 718. Perfect size for four kids like yourselves."

She slides the room key across the counter to us and Atlas takes it with a nod. "Don't tell anyone about us, alright?" he orders. "Especially not your coworkers. Can you do that?"

"Absolutely," she says, nodding eagerly. "Have a wonderful day, you two."

Not thirty seconds later, the four of us are piled inside of an elevator, on our way up to one of the very top floors of this monstrous building. "I can't believe it," Ryn squeals. "Our plan is *finally* in motion *and* we get to stay the night in a luxury suite. This *literally* couldn't get any better."

"Don't get your hopes up," says Atlas, watching the little meter above the doors as the floor number steadily ticks up. "If that receptionist lets it slip to one single person that we're here, then we're screwed."

"But odds are, that's not going to happen," I say, trying to keep the mood up. "Let's just enjoy the evening, shall we? It *is* the last night before the Rainloft comes down, after all."

The elevator *dings* and its doors slide apart, unveiling a dark, empty hallway with several doors lining its walls. Our room ends up being at the very end of it. Atlas pulls out the room card and swipes it along the electronic doorknob, then the lock clicks and the door swings open.

After seeing that beige disaster of a lobby, I'm fully expecting to walk into a ten-by-ten foot cardboard box with furniture. And I would've been totally fine with that—anything is better than that train. But when the light flashes on, my jaw drops.

This room is like a full-blown mansion stuffed inside of a skyscraper. I can barely see the end of it from where we stand now—there's a full kitchen and living space and doors in each corner that I presume lead to four different bedrooms. They must've hired the world's best interior designers to decorate this place, because the attention to detail is insane. There's a giant vase at the center of the dining table holding beaming sunflowers and lilacs that match perfectly with all the different throw pillows and blankets strewn across the sofas. The room is homey and relaxed, but at the same time I'm fully convinced that someone came in and measured the precise distance between one dining chair and the other and the exact angle that the pillows rest on the couches.

"Holy cow," Grayson murmurs, voicing my reaction for me. "*This* is our room?"

"It's not a room, it's a castle," I say, and for a second I think I might still be asleep on the train because this looks like something out of a dream. Then again, sleep wasn't exactly a thing that happened on that train, so this has to be real.

But of course, Atlas is hardly impressed. "Whatever you do, don't leave this room," he instructs shortly. "And don't get too comfortable. We'll be out of here before the sun rises tomorrow."

He turns around and leaves the room before any of us have a chance to ask where he's going. "Wow. Isn't he just a ray of sunshine?" Ryn scoffs.

"Forget about him," I say with a brush of my hand. "He can do what he wants, but we have this whole room to ourselves now. Why don't we have some fun? Explore a little?"

Grayson shrugs. "Sounds like a plan to me."

And so we do. Each of us claims a bedroom—mine is still bigger than an average hotel suite and I'm pretty sure the bed alone is bigger than our entire stateroom on the train. According to that receptionist, these suites are intended for the Alumni here that work too long of shifts to go all the way back home afterward. I know I probably wouldn't want to spend my entire life in this place without leaving, but I can't help but think: this wouldn't be a bad job to have. Sure, you'd have to get over the fact that you're working for Avalon, the woman who singlehandedly destroys the lives of a hundred ten-year-olds and their entire families every year, but this room might just make up for that.

I fill the time easily. I start by taking the longest shower of my life. I crank the water heat all the way up—Rainloft students don't have the luxury of hot water, so every shower I've taken in the past four years has been short and frigid. Here, it's like having my own personal sauna, and there's an endless assortment of bakery-scented soaps that smell way too good to resist. Once I'm squeaky-clean and smelling like a sugar cookie, I find a book in one of my nightstand drawers that just so happened to be my mother's favorite. At least, it *was* her favorite five years ago, before her disappearance. As a kid, I would constantly beg her to let me read it, but she'd always decline because I was 'too young'. Now, the further I get into the book, I start to realize *yeah, I'm still too young for this*, but it's so good that I just don't care.

I get roped into the story and before I know it, two hours have passed. The only reason I put the book down is because the faint scent of something spicy drifts to my nose and draws me out of my room. Grayson is at the stove, stirring a giant pot of thick red liquid that I assume is chili, and Ryn is perched at the edge of the dining table holding a spoon full of it.

"Whatcha makin'?" I ask, fighting to keep my mouth from watering.

"Oh, there you are." Grayson spins around to face me with a gargantuan spoon in hand. "It's chili. I found the ingredients here and thought I'd make some for dinner, as long as you all like it."

"Try it," says Ryn. "I don't care if you like chili or not, it's incredible."

Grayson prepares a spoonful and with a flick of her wrist, Ryn sends it levitating in my direction. I catch it with a laugh. "Showoff."

"Hey. We're not at the Rainloft anymore," she says defensively. "I'm allowed to show off all I want."

I hold the spoon to my lips and as soon as the chili hits my tongue, my bones fill with warmth and I'm reminded suddenly of everything that's good in the world. "It's amazing," I say to Grayson, nodding my head in thought. "But do you want my honest opinion?"

"Shoot."

"It needs more spice."

He and Ryn both look at me strangely. "Seriously?" asks Ryn.

"Yeah," I say, striding into the kitchen and scanning through all the different ingredients splayed across the counter. My eyes land on a small bottle with the word 'spice' written on it and I immediately grab it and bring it to the big pot.

"Wait, wait, wait," Grayson says hastily, swiping the bottle from my hand before I can pour it into the dinner. "This is a family recipe—Campbell Spicy Chili. I *already* added more black pepper than the recipe calls for."

I hit him with my best puppy-dog eyes and pinch my fingers together to symbolize a tiny amount. "Just a little more spice?"

He caves even faster than I would've expected. "Fine," he sighs. "Just a little."

"Thank you!" Grayson reluctantly hands over the bottle and I pop off the cap, holding it over the pot and sprinkling in as much pepper as possible before he can cut me off. But I'm forced to stop when it slides up out of my hand and starts floating high above the stovetop.

I shoot Ryn a look over my shoulder. "Really? Do you have to use your powers for *everything*?"

"Yes," she says shortly, guiding the spice bottle through the air and back down to the counter. Then she faces me. "Why don't you? I've never seen you use your powers. It seems like time travel would be super useful sometimes."

"It would seem that way," I frown. "It's absolutely useless in combat, though. Whenever Alumni show up, it always feels like I'm bringing an inflatable balloon sword to a gunfight. You guys can send the guns flying out of their hands with your mind or teleport out of the way of the bullet, but what can I do? Travel to a different time when the fight isn't happening?"

Grayson thinks for a second. "Yeah, maybe our powers would be more useful in *that* context," he says slowly, "but yours are probably really helpful at other times. What if you're, say, trying to solve a murder? You could travel back to the time of the incident and catch the killer in the act."

"That's dark," Ryn comments, but then her eyes light up. "Ooh, could you go back and have a conversation with your past self? That would be so great. There are *so* many things I would tell myself to and not to do."

"I guess you could," I say. "We were never allowed to do things like that at the Rainloft, though."

We're all quiet for a couple of minutes. Grayson stirs the chili, then takes out a spoonful and hands it to me. "Taste   this."

I do, and then nod. "It's perfect," I tell him, even though it could still use some more pepper.

"Great. Thanks."

Then he turns his back to put something in the dishwasher, and I seize the opportunity. In one swift motion, I snatch the bottle of spices, pull off the top and dump the entire thing into the pot.

When he turns back around, I hide the bottle with one hand and flash him a thumbs-up with the other. "It's perfect," I say again. "That's a perfect amount of spice."

Half an hour later, we're all gathered around the dining table with piping-hot bowls of chili in front of us—including Atlas, who just returned from a mysterious outing to who knows where a few minutes ago. I can smell the spice rising up from my dish in thick waves of steam.

"Hopefully it tastes okay," says Grayson. "I had to make do with the ingredients I found lying around here."

"I'm sure it'll be great," I assure him, then I fill my spoon and hold it to my mouth. It's just as good as it was earlier, only this time with an ample amount of spice. "It's amazing," I say honestly. "Best chili I've ever had."

"Is it really?" Grayson asks. "Well, now I have to try it."

As soon as he does, he holds a hand to his mouth. "Holy cow," he breathes. "That's a lot of spice."

Immediately, Ryn reaches across the table to grab a bottle of hot sauce. She unscrews the top and starts pouring it into her chili.

"Be careful, it's really hot already," Grayson warns.

She looks at him like he just told her to jump off a building. "Oh, is it?" She makes eye contact with each one of us as she shakes basically the entire bottle of sauce out into her food, daring us to challenge that. We all watch as, without hesitation, she holds the bowl to her mouth and takes a long sip.

Her hand flies up to her mouth. "Oh, my gosh," she gasps, her chair scraping against the tile as she scrambles to her feet and sprints for the refrigerator. I can't hold back my laughter as she yanks open the door and fumbles around for a jug of milk, her eyes watering.

I'm so caught up in watching Ryn struggle that I hardly even notice Atlas. When I turn to face him his cheeks have gone just about as red as the chili itself.

"Wh—it's not even that spicy!" I protest.

He's clearly trying to fight it, but after a minute he loses to the chili and stands up, making a break for the kitchen. Ryn leans over the kitchen island, still recovering, and slides the jug of milk across the counter to Atlas. He pours himself a shaky glass, downs it in one gulp and then slams the cup down. "Why?" he groans, wiping his mouth with the sleeve of his jacket.

"Grayson!" Ryn shouts frantically, shooting lasers at him with her eyes. "The chili was good as it was! Why'd you have to go and add a whole *gallon* of pepper?"

"It wasn't Grayson," Atlas sighs, his gaze falling on me.

Immediately, all eyes are on me and I throw my hands in the air. "Hey, it's not my fault! I'm basically immune to spice."

"I know," he shoots back, arching an eyebrow at me from behind the kitchen island. "You can't tell the difference between a dash of pepper and literal fire." He turns to Ryn and Grayson. "She puts hot sauce on chocolate chip cookies."

"That was one time!" I yell. "And you're the one who doesn't even *like* cookies! What kind of psychopath doesn't like *cookies*?"

"Wow," Ryn remarks. "You two really are siblings."

Atlas and I look at each other for a second, and I can't help but snort at the sheer absurdity of this whole situation. It doesn't take long for the others to join in. Even Atlas laughs a little, and now that I think of it, I haven't seen him smile once, at least not genuinely, in almost half a decade.

I can't quite place what it is, but something about this moment feels momentous—it's like the payoff when a divided sports team is finally able to band together and score their first goal. They may not *win* the game, per se, but it's the fact that they were able to cooperate for once and score any points at all that matters.

Maybe it's all in my head, but something tells me that we'll get there. One of these days, we'll win the game, and the possibility alone is enough to put all my other worries to rest.

Half an hour later, I'm alone. Ryn insisted that this room feels like a furnace and dragged Grayson down to the front desk with her to ask about air conditioning. I opted to stay here and clean up the kitchen, and Atlas is out on the balcony (one of the three we have within our room).

By now, all the night's excitement has settled down to a cozy quiet. A cool breeze drifts in from the open windows and faint city noises sound from far below. Once I've run the dishwasher and polished the already-cleaner-than-my-dorm-room-ever-was kitchen for the second time, I'm left with nothing to do. My eyes wander to the balcony door, and I take a step in that direction, but then my feet stop moving without me really telling them to.

I shove the thought out of my mind and keep walking. *This is stupid,* I tell myself. *Atlas is your brother. There's no reason for you to be scared of him. That's stupid.*

Blocking out the voice in my head telling me that *this is a bad idea,* I pull open the balcony door and step outside. When I catch sight of what Atlas is doing, I almost stop in my tracks again. In his hands is a RMF-brand pen and a small leather-bound notebook—which I recognize immediately.

I put aside my shock for the time being and move to lean against the railing next to him. "Dear diary," I mock. "Today I learned that Campbell Spicy Chicken is, in fact, spicy."

That earns me a glare. "Really?"

"What?" I shrug innocently. "I'm your older sister. It's my job to make fun of you."

"Hate to break it to you," he says, "but a nineteen-second age gap doesn't make all that much of a difference."

"Sure it does. You're just not old enough to realize it yet."

A hint of a smile playing at his lips, he tucks the book away in the pocket of his jacket. "Is that the journal Mom gave you?" I ask before I can think better of it.

"Yeah." He doesn't offer any more than that.

It's almost surreal seeing that old thing again. The notebook was his version of my pearl bracelet—the last gift Mom gave him before she vanished. In that year after her disappearance, Atlas would write in it all the time. It didn't matter whether or not he had anything to write about. Journaling just suddenly became his new favorite hobby. I knew he'd taken it up to the Rainloft, but I never would've expected him to still have it. I was sure by now he would've lost it or got bored of it or filled out all the pages, but apparently I was wrong. "Huh."

Looking down makes my head spin. We're near the top of Lebanon's tallest building and the skyscrapers that I thought stretched into the clouds from the ground look short from here. Streetlights and cars' headlamps shine through a misty fog blanketing the dark city, and the people roaming the streets are nothing but specks.

My eyes stray from the breathtaking downtown and over to Atlas's hand rested on the railing—or, more accurately, the streak of red along the back of it. "Is that blood?" I blurt before I can stop myself. "Are you *bleeding?*"

Immediately, he draws back his hand and looks off into the distance. "It's chili."

"Yeah, pretty sure I can tell the difference between chili and blood, thanks." Before I can think twice, I'm on my way inside. "I'll be right back."

I end up in my bathroom, searching the cabinets. *Surely, if they have thirteen different cookie-scented shampoos here, they'll have some sort of first-aid equipment.* Laser-focused, I scan the contents of my drawers and pile my arms with all the medical supplies I can find. I don't even know how bad it is—I realize too late that maybe I should've found that out before raiding the room for supplies—but at this point, I decide it's better to be safe than sorry and head back out onto the balcony.

Atlas watches as I lower myself to sit cross-legged on the cold stone floor. "Sit," I order. When he raises a brow at me, I return the look and add "That wasn't a suggestion."

Reluctantly, he sits down across from me. Surrounded by an entire doctor's office worth of supplies, I meet his eyes and wait, purposefully making it so uncomfortable that he has no choice but to roll back the sleeve of his jacket.

My breath catches when I see it. A deep gash stretches across his forearm, rimmed with irritation and dried blood. I have no idea how or when he got it, but it's painfully clear that for whatever reason, he hasn't bothered so much as to slap a bandage over it. "Wow," I breathe.

"It's fine," he says quickly, pulling back again. "It doesn't even hurt."

Instinctively, I reach out to take hold of his arm and bring it closer to myself, purposeful but gentle enough to avoid disturbing the wound any further. "Yeah, right." Plotting out my course of action, I pick up the damp washcloth that I brought out.

Atlas eyes me skeptically. "Do you even know what you're doing?"

"Of course. Roller skates, remember?" I say, flashing back to my disastrous second-grade phase. Our parents made the choice to get me roller skates for my birthday, and instantly paid the price. I was constantly covered in bruises, and they had to help me patch up skinned knees on the daily. Eventually they got so tired of playing doctor all day long that they just decided to teach me how to clean the wounds myself.

For a second my hand hovers above Atlas's cut, then I press the cold cloth to his arm. He flinches a bit, and something tells me it's not out of pain. "How did you get this?" I ask tentatively.

"Not sure," he says, his voice barely above a mumble. "It was sometime between the bakery and the mall and the train."

"You need to be more careful," I tell him, dabbing around the edges of the cut. "You can't just sit there when someone's aiming a loaded gun at your head or put yourself in these dangerous spots expecting your powers to bail you out every time. One of these days, it's going to get you killed."

There's quiet for a few ticks before he speaks again. "You sound like Mom."

That one takes the wind out of my sails. I freeze for a split second, then breathe out a laugh. "I kind of do, don't I?"

He watches while I work, silently feuding with myself over whether it's worth it to ask risky questions. This moment feels fragile, like one shift in the wrong direction could cause it to shatter. "Do you ever think about her anymore?" I ask, the question falling from my mouth before I can think about it too much.

"Not really," he replies shortly. "It was always easier not to. It was easier just to assume that everyone I loved was gone from my life forever. Up until a couple days ago, I was fully convinced that I'd never see you again."

His attempt to sound casual might've fooled me if I hadn't paid attention to what he just said. But I did, and those words are gutting. Based solely on the chaos of the past couple of days, I've already come to the conclusion that being a Rainloft escapee isn't for me. I haven't fully thought about what things must have been like for Atlas, living that life for the past *two years*. "What was it like?" I ask carefully. "When you escaped. What was it like?"

His mouth twists, and for a second I'm sure I've ruined it. "It wasn't easy. That's for sure," he says with a forced laugh, looking off into the distant city. "For the first year, I never stayed in the same place for more than a night. I couldn't go anywhere without anyone recognizing me, so I was constantly on the run. It didn't help that Alumni were always on my case. I was lucky to go a day without them finding me."

"Wow." Thinking, I replace the washcloth in my hand with a bottle of antiseptic and use it to wet a different cloth. "I don't understand, though," I say, choosing my words. "Even if people *did* recognize you, couldn't you just use your powers on them? Mind-control them into thinking you're someone else?"

A shadow crosses his face. "That's what I ended up doing," he says, his voice low, "but only because I had no other option. I avoided using my powers on innocent people for as long as possible."

"Why?" I ask, something in my brain refusing to add up. "If I had your power, I feel like I would use it for everything. I mean, you could get the owner of a hotel to let you stay there forever or tell some billionaire to give you their mansion. You could tell everyone to forget you ever existed or, really, couldn't you just take over the world?"

"Just because I can doesn't mean I want to," he says, a slight edge to his tone that wasn't there before. "I've never wanted to. I've never wanted the power I have. You know, you could end up with all the power in the world but that doesn't always mean you asked for it in the first place."

I just nod because I can't think of anything to say to that. Choice is something that Rainloft students have never had the luxury of—once you're selected, the rest of your life is instantly plotted out for you: you're given a random set of powers, you train said powers for eight years, then you spend the remainder of your days as an Alumnus. If you don't like it, then, well, that sucks for you. But the way Atlas says it makes me think that maybe it's more than just that. "What was so awful about mind-controlling innocent people?" I ask, dabbing antiseptic onto his cut as I speak. "Getting someone to do you a small favor like letting you stay in their hotel for a while really wouldn't hurt anything, would it?"

Based on personal experience, I know that antiseptic on an open wound stings like a thousand bees at the same time, but his jaw doesn't tighten until I ask the question. "It wasn't that," he says after a beat of silence. "I realize now that it was stupid, but after I escaped, I thought I wouldn't have to use my powers at all. I thought if I avoided using them on people who hadn't done anything wrong then I could gain their trust. Make them forget about the corruptive monster Avalon made me out to be and trust me. I thought that way, I could make allies—*friends*—without forcing their opinions. Because, really, if you have to brainwash someone to get them to trust you, then they're not your friend."

He gives a bitter laugh. "I thought that even if I had just committed the most unforgivable crime there was, there were still people who would see my side. It was my voice against Avalon's, and for a while I really thought I could win." His voice drops. "Eventually I came to my senses and realized they'd already made up their minds about me."

I could've assumed that was where it was going, but my heart still sinks when he says it. "So then you lost your faith in them." I fill in the blanks. "You gave up on trying to get them on your side and started putting yourself first—even if it meant using your powers on people you knew didn't deserve it."

"Bingo," he says, weariness in his voice. "I went back to our old house. Turns out we don't live there anymore, so I told the family who does that I was their long-lost son and they let me stay."

The fact that our house isn't ours anymore barely even fazes me. "I can't imagine what it was like," I murmur. "I mean, I escaped, but I have you and Ryn and Grayson. You were completely alone for *two years*."

"Yeah," he says. "That about sums it up."

The part of me that was already fractured shatters completely. I switch out the antiseptic in my hand for a roll of bandage and start wrapping it carefully around my brother's arm. "Well, you're not alone anymore," I tell him decisively. "You've got me and Ryn and Grayson, and we're not going anywhere. No matter how badly you might want to, you're not getting rid of us."

"Wow," he says with an exaggerated sigh. "Is that supposed to be comforting?"

His tone is all sarcasm, but that doesn't stop me from picking up on the telltale notes beneath it: *that landed.*

I finish wrapping his cut with gauze and seal it shut with tape. "Alright," I say, sitting back on the cold balcony floor. "You're all patched up. You'll need stitches eventually, but seeing as we're wanted criminals, that'll have to wait."

He nods, the faintest hint of a smile crossing his lips. "Thanks."

"No problem."

Shoving all the medical supplies off to the side, I get to my feet and lean over the railing. It doesn't take long for Atlas to join me. The sharp scent of antiseptic still hangs in the fresh night air, and somehow the view is even more incredible than it was ten minutes ago. For a second I just soak it in, but then my gaze lands on a shorter building wedged between two skyscrapers and I can't help but gasp. "Atlas, look," I say, pointing it out.

"At what?"

"That building."

He narrows his eyes at the nondescript black letters that stretch across the building's face. "Lebanon City High School?"

"Uh-huh."

"It… looks like a high school."

"You don't understand," I say, shaking my head. "That could be *our* high school. Once this whole thing is over, that could be *our school.* The place we go to learn things every day."

He looks at me like I have two heads. "But we don't live here."

"That's not the point," I say, my mind swirling with fantasies and dreams for the future. "Once the Rainloft comes down, we'll be *normal teenagers.* We'll do normal teenager things, like take math tests and go to football games and—oh, we'll get to go to *dances.*" I pry my gaze from the school and turn to Atlas, hardly able to contain my excitement. "We'll find some great people to go with, then we'll get all dressed up and Dad will make us stand in front of the house for those awkward pictures that parents love taking… There will be a giant table with all kinds of dessert, and there'll be slow dancing and not-slow dancing—whatever that's called. Doesn't that just sound *amazing*?"

He stares at me. "I'd rather be shot out of a cannon."

I shove him and sigh, but I can't help but grin. "There is something seriously wrong with you."

"Yeah, well, there's something wrong with both of us."

I set my alarm for a ridiculous hour. The helicopters don't leave for the Rainloft until eight, but Atlas insisted that we all need to be up and ready to go before six so that even if all the elevators break down and all the staircases collapse, we'll still have time to get up there. I'm not happy about it, but it's still not nearly as early as I had to get up every day at the Rainloft, so I don't argue too much.

I fall onto my feather-soft down comforter and immediately sink into the best sleep I've had in years. I'm pulled out of it not three seconds later by the shrieking of my alarm. Immediately in a mood, I fumble around for my clock with every intention of chucking it through the window when I look outside and freeze. The moon still hangs high in the inky-black sky, and that's the first thing that clues me in to the fact that *something's wrong.*

That's not my alarm. The tiny clock sits soundly on my nightstand, displaying the time: 1:18 AM. It takes me a second to register that the blaring is coming from outside my room.

Barefoot and bleary-eyed, I leave my room to discover that I'm the last person awake. Above the main door, a blinding white indicator light flashes wildly, lighting up the otherwise pitch-dark suite.

"What's going on?" Ryn shouts over the shrieking alarm, her brows knit. She and Grayson are both standing in front of their bedroom doors, looking equally as confused and bewildered as I feel. Atlas, however, is in the kitchen with his back turned, rummaging through the silverware drawer.

"Atlas?" I say, because he's clearly the only one of us with any clue what's happening.

He turns around, a dead-serious look in his eyes and a scary-looking kitchen knife in his hand. "It's them," he says finally. "They know we're here."

Chapter Eight

All my grogginess evaporates as the panic sets in. "What? How?" I ask, aiming the question at my brother. "I thought you told that receptionist lady not to say anything, how do the Alumni know we're here?"

"I don't know," he says, studying the monstrous knife in his hands. "All I know is that we need to get out of here."

"What's the knife for?" Ryn asks uneasily.

"It's just a precaution."

Before anyone can ask any further questions, there's a knock at the door. My heart jumps into my throat. "Don't do anything stupid," Atlas warns us all. Blade in hand, he strides up to the entrance and pulls open the door.

Standing on the other side is an Alumnus. His bald forehead is creased and his hand is braced around the Sim gun at his side. "Winters," he says immediately, whipping out the gun and aiming it at Atlas. "So the rumors are true."

His placid tone is completely at odds with his stance. "So they are," Atlas says loftily. "Are you surprised?"

"I wish I could say I am. Hand over the knife," the Alumnus grunts.

All the rest of us can do is stand in the background and watch this play out. "As you wish," Atlas shrugs, then obediently gives the blade to the Alumnus. For a second I think the Alumnus might be a Type Two, but then I see the flash of regret across his features.

"You know, there was this other rumor floating around," Atlas says slowly, the smirk on his face met by pure terror on the Alumnus's. "People are saying you stabbed yourself."

I turn my head in time to avoid the sight, but the sound of the Alumnus's uniform tearing as the knife penetrates his abdomen still causes me to wince. I turn around to see him stagger backward and slam into the opposite wall of the hallway. It happens in slow motion: he sinks to his knees and falls limply to the floor, blood pooling on the tile beneath him.

Altas turns back to look at the rest of us before leaving the room, and I take that as our cue to follow. Somehow I suppress the urge to throw up and join everyone else in the hallway.

The blaring alarm is even louder out here, and its blinding flashes light up the eerily dark area every other second. "The elevator is that way," I yell, pointing toward the end of the ominous corridor.

"The elevator?" Ryn repeats. "We should take the stairs—they're safer."

"No, they're not," I protest. "There are probably tons of Alumni blocking the stairwells. As long as there aren't any in the elevator, it'll be safe all the way—"

"We'll split up," Atlas cuts in. "Ryn and I will take the stairs and you two can take the elevator."

"Fine." Driven by the overwhelming urge to get away from the shrill shriek of the alarm as well as the dead body at my feet, I grab Grayson by the wrist and drag him with me to the elevators. Once we make it there I practically body-slam the *down* button.

Seconds later, there's a *ding* and the doors slide open to reveal a completely-empty elevator. Grayson and I step inside and I mash the button that will take us down to the first floor. I position myself as close as possible to the exit and wait as we inch down millions of stories. Grainy, obnoxiously-peppy music plays through a tiny speaker above the array of buttons, joining with the muffled alarm outside to fill the silence.

"Come on, come on," I mutter, willing the elevator to move faster.

In the reflective metal doors, a green flash of light catches my eye. I don't register what that means until I hear a *click*.

I whirl to find myself looking straight down the barrel of a Sim gun. My breath catches and I stumble backward into the wall of buttons. The gun's wielder is a blue-haired Alumna with a sinister grin on her face—a Type Four.

"Don't move," she snarls, using one hand to unhook a set of handcuffs from her belt while using the other to keep the gun pointed steadily at my head. "I've got you now."

Keeping my hands in the air I catch Grayson's eye, silently asking for his approval of what I'm about to do. He gives a subtle nod. Before I can think twice I seize the Alumna's arm, thrusting it upward and redirecting the gun's aim to the ceiling. There's an earsplitting *bang* and a bullet blasts a hole in the wall.

I manage to dive out of her reach, scrambling to the opposite side of the claustrophobic metal box where Grayson is standing. Immediately, the Alumna spins around and sets her aim on me. "That wasn't funny," she spits, closing the short distance between us.

There's a flash of light on my side and then Grayson appears behind her. He shoves her—*hard*—causing her to lose her balance and slam into the wall inches away from me. Her gun clatters to the ground and I seize the opportunity, stooping to grab it and pointing it directly at her head.

"Don't move," I say fiercely. The gun feels balanced and comfortable in my hands, but at the same time it feels so wrong to be the one holding it. "I'll shoot."

The second she flinches, I pull the trigger. The bullet disappears as soon as it hits her forehead, but her reaction is exactly as if she were just shot by a real gun: her head snaps back and she crumbles to the ground, sliding down the metal wall. She instantly goes unconscious.

The gun's recoil makes me drop it, and I don't pick it up. Real gun or not, *I just shot someone.* I'm just as shocked as Grayson looks. "Nice shot," he murmurs.

Two seconds later, the elevator doors slide open, depositing us in the lobby right next to the random kids' painting I'd noted earlier. The alarm light strobes across the room and makes it look like some sort of rave is going on, but as far as I can tell it's deserted.

"What do we do now?" I ask. Outside the giant windows there's a group of employees gathered, all of them looking grouchy and mildly disturbed, like being forced to evacuate the building because of dangerous criminals in the dead of night is a semi-regular occurrence. Ryn and Atlas are nowhere to be seen. "We can't go out there, but we can't stay in here either."

"I don't know," says Grayson. "Should we be worried that Ryn and Atlas aren't down here yet?"

I open my mouth to respond, but the framed kids' painting catches my eye. Without thinking, I move closer to it. I'd seen it before, but I haven't gotten a good look at it until now. Something about it feels strangely familiar, almost like I've seen it before—and not just earlier today—even before then.

"June?"

I squint at it for a second, racking my brain. The realization hits me like a ton of bricks. "I painted this."

"What?"

"I painted this picture," I repeat, more definitively this time. Up close, it's clearly a roller skate—I specifically remember sitting down to make it on my birthday after my parents gave me the gift. I gave them the painting as a thank-you for the skates. "So what is it doing *here*?"

"Are you sure that's your painting?" Grayson asks skeptically. "It's not just some staff member's kid that made it?"

"No, this is mine." Against my better judgement, I lift it off the wall and pop off the back of the frame, uncovering the back of the painting. The sloppy handwriting at the corner of the paper settles it for me: *June Winters, age seven.*

"Uh, June?"

"I can't believe it," I murmur. All that my mind will let me do is stare at the painting. No matter what I do, I can't get the dots to connect. *I gave this to my parents. This should be at our house. Why is it hanging up here, of all places?*

Grayson's voice jars me back into reality. "June, *turn around.*"

I do, and then I freeze. Positioned around the lobby are three different Alumni. Each one of them looks angrier than the last. All of them are armed, their Sim guns aimed steadily at the two of us.

"Don't shoot," I say hastily, my painting still hanging from my hands. "You'll—you'll regret it."

I curse myself as soon as the words have left my mouth. The Alumnus in the center chuckles softly, unflinching. "That's cute," he remarks. "Don't worry, we won't shoot unless you give us reason to. I just need you to come with us, can you do that?"

Grayson and I exchange a glance. There really isn't any way out of this: if we make a break for it, with three different Alumni, there's a dangerously low chance we'll escape without catching at least one bullet. They might not be real guns, but I saw what happened to the Alumna when I shot her in the elevator. I'll pass out and end up back at the Rainloft anyway.

There's a flash of light next to me. Before I can blink, Grayson is standing behind the row of Alumni. They all spin around and the burst of several gunshots at once forces my feet into motion. Still clutching my painting, I drop down behind the front desk, just out of the Alumni's eyeline.

The flurry of shots stops abruptly, and now the only sounds are the frantic alarm and my heart pounding in my ears. "Got him?" one of the Alumni asks gruffly.

A wave of dread crashes over me. "Yeah—hold up. Where's the girl?" asks a second voice, anger rising in her tone.

I creep around to the opposite side of the desk, resorting to what is probably the worst idea I've ever had but also my only option. I wait until all three of their backs are turned, then leap out from behind the counter and swing the framed picture with full force into an Alumnus's back.

That goes over about as well as I expected it to—the Alumnus barely stumbles forward an inch, but the painting flies out of my sweaty hands and the glass shatters when it hits the floor. I step backward and run straight into an Alumna.

Before she has the chance to act, I do. I whirl to face her, pull back my arm and let my fist fly, catching her right in the mouth.

That gets me nowhere. "You *stupid* girl," she rasps, swiping a trickle of blood off her face. With a grunt of pure fury she shoves me backward, hard enough that I lose my balance and fall back into the patch of shattered glass.

They don't even give me a chance to register the pain of thousands of glass shards digging into my palms. From behind me, a pair of hands clamps around my arms and hoists me to my feet.

"Try that again and I *will* shoot you," the Alumnus growls in my ear, using one hand to keep my arms pinned behind my back. The other brings the point of his Sim gun up to my temple.

This is it. This is the end of the road for me.

Not half a second after those words enter my mind, I feel the Alumnus's grip leave my wrists. There's a deafening *crash* to my right. I whip my head in that direction to see him pressed against the wall, writhing wildly and choking on air.

"Hi there." Ryn stands at the foot of the stairwell, her eyes locked on the Alumnus. My mind instantly floods with relief. Atlas is already by the Alumna holding Grayson hostage, telling her something barely audible beneath the alarm's screeching. It's almost like he hits the *power off* button on the Alumna: her expression goes blank and her arms drop to her sides, letting Grayson go.

I grin, catching a whiff of something other than the linen-scented air freshener—sweet victory.

But amid all the chaos, what I fail to remember is that the two Alumni in my field of vision right now aren't the only ones in the room. I turn to see the third Alumnus half a pace away from me, gun just inches from my nose.

Before he can pull the trigger I seize his hands and smash the weapon into his face. He starts to stand again before he even hits the ground, but doesn't get far.

"You can't move," Atlas tells him from beside me. "You don't remember how."

At our feet, the Alumnus goes completely still, every limb locking into place. Across the room, the other Alumna is frozen in the same position. Atlas turns to me. "We really can't leave you alone for five minutes."

"Guess not," I manage.

There's a *slam* and a strangled gasp from the opposite side of the lobby. My gaze snaps in that direction to find that the roles have reversed—the remaining Alumnus, clearly a Type One, has Ryn telekinetically pinned to the wall and points his gun at her with an unsteady hold.

I act before anyone else can. In one liquid motion I swoop down to pull the Sim gun off the body at my feet, target the Alumnus and pull the trigger. Two shots ring out at once—one from my gun and the other from his. He and Ryn both drop to the floor at the same time. He reaches for his gun, but Ryn is faster. She shakily gets to her feet and throws her hand out in his direction. Like an out-of-control baseball, his feet leave the ground and he's launched straight through the massive window. A shower of shattered glass rains down over the group of people gathered outside and he lands with an earthquaking *thud* in the middle of the crowd, sending all of them into a frenzied panic.

Ryn sinks to the ground, clutching her ankle. I'm over there before I even register that I've moved. "Are you okay?" I demand. "Did he hit you?"

She nods, drawing in a shaky breath. "Yeah," she says through gritted teeth. The bullet blasted a hole straight through her bedazzled sneaker, but still, it left no blood or any evidence to suggest that she was just shot. "Wow, they really weren't kidding when they said that hurts as much as a real gunshot."

"Guys, we have to go," Atlas interjects.

"Hold on," I tell him. "We can wait—"

"No, we can't," he hisses, and then I hear it, too. Voices, coming from the stairwell and getting louder as the Alumni descend the steps. "We have to leave, *now.*"

"But where will we *go*?" I ask, talking fast. "The helicopter idea was a bust. We won't be able to get to the Rainloft through this place, definitely not after *this*." I sweep an arm around the trashed lobby and the three incapacitated Alumni. "What do we do now? What's our Plan B?"

The prolonged silence that follows causes all my remaining hope to dissipate. "Come on. We can't just give up," says Ryn, her tone tinted with doubt. "We can't just let them find us. There has to be some place in the city, like a hotel or something, where we can hide and regroup."

Another beat of silence. Then Grayson speaks up. "I think I know a place," he says hesitantly. "My family has this cabin—or at least they *had* it before I was taken to the Rainloft. It's in Lebanon, somewhere in the woods right outside the city."

"Great," Atlas says briefly, heading for the exit without wasting a second. "We'll go there."

The amplifying shouts coming from the stairwell push me into action. I help Ryn to her feet and support her through the doorway, stepping out into the town plaza. The cool, misty night air washes over me like a wave of refreshment and some of the night's chaos slides off my back.

We don't stop long to enjoy it, though. Gunshots still echo faintly in my memory as we shove through the dense crowd of people. Most of them are too focused on the Alumnus lying unconscious in the shattered window's remains to notice us, but when they do, Atlas turns them around easily.

Before long, we break loose of the mass of people and make it to a road lined with massive buildings all jammed together along the sidewalk. The neon billboards that stretch across the faces of skyscrapers are reflected in the puddles of freshly-fallen rain beneath our feet. "So this cabin," Atlas starts. He cranes his neck to get a better view of the street ahead, aiming the question at Grayson. "Do you think you could get us there from where we are now?"

"I think so," Grayson shrugs. "My family used to go there all the time on vacation, I'm sure the directions will come back to me."

A second of quiet allows me to pick up on a sound I hadn't heard before. *Sirens.* My pace slows and I listen for a moment. I can't tell which direction they're coming from but they're definitely getting louder. "They're after us," I breathe out.

"Did you expect them to let us get away?" asks Atlas, pressing forward. "We'll take a taxi to the cabin. If the cops catch up to us, when we get there, I can turn them all around. That should at least buy us some time."

"Seriously?" I ask, tuning back into the sirens. "That sounds like a whole *drove* of cops. They'll probably bring some Alumni with them and there's no way you'll be able to take on that many at once. We barely got out with our *lives* back there, and that was only three of them."

"That's a bit melodramatic, seeing as we're still walking but all three of those Alumni are currently lying immoble in pools of their own blood," says Atlas. "Believe me, this will work."

"Okay, first of all, I'm *barely* able to walk," says Ryn, wincing every time her bad foot touches the ground, "and second of all, *you're crazy.*"

"They probably won't even catch up to us," Atlas says.

I sigh. "In case you haven't noticed, nobody agrees with you."

"In case you haven't noticed, I don't care. *Taxi!*" He waves down a beat-up blue car with a 'taxi' sign atop the roof cruising down the road to our left. Its tires glide through a puddle as it slows to a halt, spraying us with a refreshing mist as we approach it.

The driver—a middle-aged woman with huge glasses and silvery streaks through her dark hair—rolls down the window. The second she sees us, she reacts the exact same way that everyone else has so far: the blood drains from her face and her frown flips to an expression of pure bewilderment. She makes to close the window, but right on cue, Atlas stops her in her tracks.

"Hi there," he says, flashing her a cheery grin. "We need a ride out to the woods just outside the city. Can you do that for us?"

"B-but you're—"

"I know who I am," says Atlas, "but you don't. So you're going to take us where we need to go and stay silent for the entire drive there. Got it?"

A vacant expression settles over the driver's face. She nods. "Great."

Atlas sweeps past the rest of us and pops open the backseat door. I linger around the window for a second, manage an awkward "thanks" to the driver and follow him into the car.

Grayson claims shotgun and Ryn, Atlas and I cram into the backseat. I end up in the middle between the two of them. An overpowering detergent-scented air freshener fills up the claustrophobic airspace, almost covering up the faint stench of garlic.

Atlas meets the driver's blank gaze in the rearview mirror. "Listen to his directions," he orders, nodding toward Grayson in the passenger seat. "And drive fast."

The driver turns her head, her eerie gaze falling on Grayson. "Um," he says uncertainly. "We need to go to the, uh, Willowood Forest? I think that's the name?"

Without any sort of warning, she slams down on the gas and I'm thrown backward. The car rockets down the street, fast enough to break the law as well as several rules of physics. The city outside whizzes by in a blur of neon lights and shadowy storefronts.

"Oh my *gosh—slow down,*" Ryn shouts frantically. The car hurtles around a corner and we're all thrown to the left. The driver ignores Ryn completely and keeps flying down the road at breakneck speed. If I wasn't fully awake before, then I definitely am now.

My back stays glued to the leather seat and I maintain a death grip around my seatbelt, but after a bit the sense of imminent death starts to dissipate. In a matter of minutes, the endless line of skyscrapers fades into a slightly less urban area with a scattering of buildings and stores.

On my right, Ryn still clutches her ankle, her mouth twisted in pain. "Does it still hurt?" I ask.

"Oh, it's not that bad," she replies in a deadpan. "It only feels like someone stuck a knife through my ankle, set it on fire and then told me to jump off a cliff and land flat on that foot."

I stare at her, then attempt to translate that ridiculous sentence. "It still hurts?"

"Yeah, June. It still hurts."

"That'll last a while," Atlas chimes in from my other side, staring straight ahead. "Give it a couple days and it'll wear   off."

There are so many layers behind that sentence, but before I can even begin to untangle them, the car makes a razor-sharp turn and we're all launched to the side again.

Before long we drive out onto a gravel road that snakes between bunches of pine trees. "I think you just go straight here," Grayson says questionably.

We bump down the winding path in silence, diving deeper into the woods by the minute. Random buildings start to pop up along the road—rustic-looking bungalows and fairytale cottages alike pique my curiosity. Images of the mystery cabin where we might be staying appear in my head before I can stop them. *Don't get your hopes up,* I remind myself, eyeing Grayson's unsure expression. *This place might not even exist.*

"Turn right," Grayson says abruptly not half a second after that thought enters my mind. The road continues straight ahead but the driver obliges anyway, swerving off the gravel path and into the thick of the woods. We hug several trees and long branches scrape the metallic paint off the side of the car. The complete darkness makes it feel like a horror movie—any second now the pines are going to come to life and smash open our windows.

But then—*light.* The trees start to thin out and in the middle of a clearing is a cabin. I lean forward to get a good look at it through the front windshield.

The mystery cabin in question turns out to be a quaint little bungalow with a charming white board-and-batten exterior and rustic wood accents. A dim porch light illuminates the surrounding area, revealing a row of overgrown plants out front and a beat-up stone firepit a few paces away from the cabin.

I slide out of the car after Ryn. It's cooler here than it was in the city—and infinitely quieter. The constant rumble of traffic and herds of people is replaced by the chirp of cicadas and the burbling of a creek somewhere in the distance. Instead of fast food joints and cigarette smoke and about a million other pungent aromas at once, the only smells I detect when I inhale are pine needles and flowers. The pure freshness of this place almost makes me forget about all the chaos of tonight and our increasingly dire predicament.

Almost.

Atlas sends the driver away and our taxi disappears into the trees, leaving us stranded smack dab in the middle of nowhere. "Holy cow," Grayson murmurs, staring at the cabin in awe. "I actually remembered how to get here. I really navigated the city and this forest and got us here."

"Congrats, Columbus," says Atlas, striding up to the rickety front porch and trying the doorknob. "Any idea how to get us inside?"

"There's a spare key around here somewhere," Grayson says.

I take that as my cue to search. I scan the area, then drop to my knees next to the bushes that are in dire need of a haircut. I lift the first out-of-place rock that I find. "Eureka," I exclaim, holding up the key.

Everyone gathers around and I unlock the front door. I push it open and switch on a light to reveal a very antique-looking interior: the wallpaper is a strange red pattern that I can't quite make out, and the floors as well as the kitchen cabinets are all made of natural wood. I can see almost the entirety of the cabin from where I stand now—a large loft overlooks the kitchen, dining area and living space, which are all one big room. Everything is covered in a layer of dust. Two brown leather couches are positioned around the fireplace—a rusted old iron thing that I'd only use if I were a crazed lunatic with the urge to start a forest fire.

Ironically, the only one of us who doesn't immediately make themself at home is Grayson. Atlas and I head for the kitchen while Ryn flops down on one of the couches, sending up a cloud of dust. Grayson hovers awkwardly around the entrance looking almost like he just wandered into a stranger's house by accident, even though the dozens of childhood photos littered around the cabin instantly disprove that theory.

"So," Ryn says from the couch, staring at the ceiling. "How are we going to get the Rainloft down now?"

Atlas starts pacing. "Let's see," he starts, not a trace of optimism in his tone. "The RMF helicopters are the only way to get up there from the ground. That plan crashed and burned on the first go so there's no shot it will work the second try."

"Are the helicopters seriously the only way up?" asks Ryn.

"Unless you've got wings."

"Ryn, your powers got us *down* from the Rainloft," Grayson points out, still lingering by the door. "Couldn't they get us back up there?"

Ryn thinks for a second. "That would be too risky," she decides. "Carrying four people up zillions of feet is an entirely different thing than bringing three down."

I stare down at the kitchen island, racking my brain for ideas but drawing a blank.

Until it hits me. "Guys," I blurt out. "We're thinking about this all wrong. We need to *let them capture us.*"

That one sentence sucks all the air from the room. Everyone looks at me like I just announced an intention to perform an interpretive dance right there in front of them. So I elaborate. "See, what are the Alumni going to do if they catch us?" I say. "Avalon doesn't want us dead. She wants us back at the Rainloft. If we let them bring us up, then we can bring it down."

Ryn sits bolt upright. "But that's crazy," she says, shaking her head. "I mean, what if we get stuck up there again? If they know we're back, they'll have all eyes on us and there's no way we'll make it into the control room without getting caught by security. Then we'd be students again—*permanently*."

"June is right." Atlas's voice comes out sounding like he just swallowed arsenic. He stands eerily still in the middle of the room, arms folded. "It's a risk but at this point it's our only option."

Ryn opens her mouth to protest, then shuts it again. She heaves a sigh of resignation and falls back onto the sofa. "So what, do we just sit around here until they come to kidnap us? It could take them *forever* to find this place."

"It won't," Atlas says shortly. "Give them twenty-four hours, max. They'll be here."

"Until then," says Grayson, "we might as well get comfortable."

*   *   *

Seeing as it's still the dead of night, Grayson directs us to four modest sleeping areas (two of them being couches). I claim a long sofa by a scenic window at the back of the loft and drift off, hoping for one full night of sleep.

Surprisingly, that wish is granted. I wake up in the morning not to alarm bells or a claustrophobic bedroom, but to birds chirping merrily outside and a fairytale view from my window. The soft morning sun glitters in the waters of a shockingly-blue creek that stretches for what seems like miles into the distance, surrounded by crowds of towering pine trees.

Given it's been roughly half a decade since I've had a semi-decent sleep, I've almost completely forgotten what that feels like. But every once in a blue moon, when I miraculously pull off a whopping eight hours of rest, I'm able to leap out of bed with the energy of a sugared-up kindergarten class. And I do just that, practically skipping down the stairs and into the kitchen.

Shockingly enough, I'm the only one awake. An old clock on the wall tells me that it's seven in the morning, but judging the state of all the other electronics in this house, there's a fifty-fifty shot that it stopped working five years ago—or whenever the last time was that someone stayed here.

I come up with the theory that maybe Grayson's family stopped coming here after the Rainloft drilled that hole in their lives. A picture rested on the counter with a twig frame—possibly homemade—catches my eye. In it, a family clad in all forms of denim and flannel beams back at me. I'm easily able to pinpoint Grayson in the center sporting a gap-toothed grin, obviously younger but otherwise not much different. A teenage girl stands next to him with her arm slung around his shoulders—clearly his sister, based on the dirty-blonde hair and freckles that the two of them share. Behind them are their parents, whose smiles just radiate warmth, even through the picture's dusty glass.

One perfect, happy family, torn apart by the Rainloft. *Because that's just what the Rainloft does*, I tell myself. *It ruins lives for the sole purpose of ruining lives. Avalon is vile and cruel and destroys families for the fun of it.*

But maybe there's more to it than that.

The thought pops into my head before I can shove it out, and I immediately curse my brain for having the audacity to think it at all. There's no reason whatsoever that I should be willing to see Avalon's side. I've never supported the Rainloft, not even before I became subject to its torture myself. I've spent the last four years of my life hating it with a passion and the last few days actively trying to end its existence. *So why does the idea of bringing it down feel so wrong all of a sudden?*

This is the exact same feeling I had back on the train, only stronger. That time, I managed to distract myself with food or something and allowed myself to forget about it for a couple days, so I decide to do just that. A quick scan of the several glass-fronted cabinets tells me that food is off the table, so I try to find something else to do.

I'm magnetically drawn to an antique wooden bookshelf at the side of the living room. Next to it stands a rusted newspaper rack stocked full of issues that are almost comically outdated. Instead of the much more sensible decision to choose a book and get lost in a fantasy world, I opt for a newspaper.

I grab the first one I see, sit down right there on the floor and blow a layer of dust off the top. The headline instantly jumps out at me: *Local Scientist Saves the World.*

I'm well aware that this will do nothing to distract me from my thoughts, but curiosity gets the better of me and I read on.

```
Local Scientist Saves the World
Over    the    past    decade,    Lavon    has
experienced a sharp increase in crime, with
robbery  rates  reaching  alarming  levels.
Experts attribute this surge to the city's
inability  to  keep  pace  with  its  rapidly
```

growing population, leaving law enforcement agencies overwhelmed and outnumbered. As a result, public trust in the rule of law has steadily declined, with many citizens increasingly questioning the effectiveness of traditional policing methods.

The situation reached a tipping point when President Cosmo McAuley resigned after his family's home was violently invaded by armed intruders. His departure has further fueled the perception that the government is failing to protect its citizens.

Amid this growing crisis, a breakthrough has emerged from an unlikely source: Avalon Lockhart, a 35-year-old scientist at the Lebanon Innovation and Technology Lab. After 19 years of research, Lockhart has developed a groundbreaking serum capable of transforming ordinary humans into individuals with superhuman abilities. The serum, which contains a mix of various ingredients—most notably, gemstones—has the potential to reshape the city's future.

Lockhart's discovery has paved the way for The Rainloft Academy, a visionary initiative designed to train new generations of heroes. A select group of 100 ten-year-olds will be chosen at random each year to receive the serum and gain the responsibility of protecting Lavon from crime. These children will become the defenders the city has long needed, fighting to restore peace and stability to a society that has grown weary of fear and violence.

The news has sent shockwaves through the world, marking the dawn of a new era for Lavon. Gone are the days of uncertainty and lawlessness; the city's citizens can now look forward to a future where safety is guaranteed, all thanks to Lockhart's groundbreaking invention.

The cost of this new era, however, is a modest one: 100 children will bear the honor of becoming the first super-powered crime-fighters in Lavon's history. While some may question the ethics of such a selection, the overwhelming consensus is that 100 kids is a small price to pay for the common good. After all, these children will be providing a service to their community that most will never have the chance to experience—a legacy of protection and hope for generations to come.

100 kids is a small price to pay for the common good. Those words sink into my mind and marinate there for the longest time. In the grand scheme of things, a hundred people doesn't even come close to putting a dent in Lavon's population. If you think about it, the odds of being chosen are literally one in a billion. The vast majority of people never end up having anything to do with the Rainloft. I just so happen to be part of the unlucky bunch who do.

I turn the page to another article about Avalon, detailing her plans for the Rainloft and before I know it I've gone through almost every newspaper on the rack. Some of them are from before Avalon's plans were set into motion and some are from many years after. No matter the date, every single article paints Avalon in a positive light, portraying her as this godlike savior of Lavon and all its people.

Apparently, perspective changes *everything*. I'm one of the few who's had the great misfortune of being subject to Avalon's other side, and sometimes I've just assumed that's how everyone sees her. Sure, she basically saved the world, but because her solution came at the cost of a handful of kids' lives, in my head it was completely, wholly vile.

But maybe I was wrong. The mind-blowing, earth-shattering conclusion that my dangerous train of thought arrives at is that there will never be a perfect solution. There's always going to be *someone* who's unhappy, and in this case, maybe Avalon was just doing what she thought was the most right. Maybe she's *not* the ruthless monster I've made her out to be in my head. Maybe all she was doing was trying to come up with a solution that would satisfy as many people as possible, because she knew she couldn't make everyone happy and that no matter what there was going to be someone who suffered. Just because I ended up with the losing ticket in a lottery where everyone wins a prize doesn't automatically mean Avalon is to blame. Maybe she was just doing the best she could to solve an unsolvable problem.

I'm so busy drowning in my own thoughts that I fail to realize that there's another human being in the room. "What are you doing?" Atlas asks skeptically from the kitchen. "You look like you just saw every conceivable version of the apocalypse at once."

I pry my gaze from the newspaper and meet his eyes, trying and failing to change my expression to something a little less petrified. I know for a fact that I can't tell him about my epiphany—if I do, everything will blow up right in my face. *I'll lose my brother again.*

"Nothing," I answer finally, adopting the most realistic smile I can manage at the moment and shoving my stack of newspapers back into their stand. "I'm doing nothing. Those were just some old papers from, er, the 1350s. Some really crazy stuff was going on back then, you know?"

He lifts an eyebrow but decides not to press. And thank goodness for that.

*   *   *

I'm wrong. I am. I have to be.

I try my best to engrave those words into my brain, cement them into a wall to block out any stupid irrational thoughts. Because I'm being irrational. Even though I just emerged from the best sleep I've had in years, I'm not thinking clearly. *There's no way I'm thinking clearly.*

Somehow, the day flies. Before long I find myself out in the backyard, sitting in a faded zigzag-patterned lawn chair in front of the beat-up stone firepit. I hug my knees to my chest and stare into the sad little flame that took us way too long to build, breathing in the oddly homey smell of campfire smoke.

A little ways off into the distance there's a still creek flanked by a long stretch of pines, all dappled in gold as the sun sinks lower into the sky. Faint bird caws echo in the distance, and fireflies blink in and out of existence around us.

It's a gorgeous view and I'm surrounded by my favorite people, but I can't shake the feeling that I'm completely, utterly alone right now.

The screen door slides open behind me and Grayson steps outside, his arms full of all the boxed ingredients to make s'mores. "Okay, the good news is that we have food," he says, dumping everything onto a small folding table by the firepit. "The bad news is that most of it expired four years ago. But we need to eat something, so this will have to do."

From the lawn chair directly next to the table, Ryn reaches out to pull a graham cracker out of the box and bites into it. Immediately, her expression goes sour and she spits it out into the gravel. "Yeah, I think I'll survive another few hours."

"How long will it be, anyway?" I finally find my voice, aiming the question at nobody in particular. "What if our hiding spot is just too good and the Alumni never find us?"

"That's entirely out of the question," says Atlas with a bitter laugh. "They'll be here within the hour, I'm calling it now."

And then they'll take us back up to the Rainloft. And then we're going to bring it down, for good. *Which I am happy about,* I tell myself, willing that to become true again.

"I guess we'd better make the most of our last hour on land, then," Grayson suggests, dropping into the folding chair on my right. "In case things go haywire up there."

Ryn looks over her shoulder at the glittering creek, then gasps and clasps her hands together. "I know what we need to do," she says giddily. "We're going to skip stones."

"Skip stones?" Atlas repeats, narrowing his eyes at her.

"Yes, *skip stones,*" Ryn says firmly, looking at him with genuine concern. "*Please* tell me you've skipped stones before."

"What?"

Ryn's jaw drops. "Did you *have* a childhood?"

"Um. No."

She rolls her eyes and stands up. "Unacceptable," she says, grabbing Atlas by the wrist and yanking him out of his seat. "You're coming with me."

Ryn drags him out to the edge of the creek, and I watch for a while as she teaches him how to skip stones across the water. Hers skim gracefully across the creek's surface, and Atlas's plummet to the bottom instantaneously.

"In a shocking turn of events," Grayson remarks, referring to the two of them actually getting along for once in their lives. I nod.

Ryn's laugh and my brother's halfhearted complaints echoing off the water is almost enough to make me forget about my little crisis.

And now I'm thinking about it again.

"So what's it like being back here?" I ask Grayson out of nowhere, in a hasty attempt to distract myself. "It has to be kind of weird, right?"

If it were any other person, the way I just randomly blurted that out probably would've scared them a little, but Grayson hardly flinches. "Well, yeah, definitely," he responds with a laugh. "My sister and I used to love this place. Sometimes our parents would surprise us when they picked us up after school with a weekend trip here. We loved telling scary stories by the firepit and going for night swims in the creek." He sighs. "Those were the days."

"I get it," I say. "That's exactly how I felt seeing my old neighborhood again the other day. It's bittersweet, because it brings back so many good memories, but at the same   time…"

"You know that nothing will ever be the same again," he finishes for me.

"Exactly." *Nothing will ever be the same. Even if we bring down the Rainloft, nothing will ever go back to the way it was before.*

"I have to tell you something." Those words leave my mouth before I realize I've said them, and I keep talking before I have the chance to think twice. "You're going to hate me for it."

Grayson's green eyes fix on mine and concern settles over his features. "What is it?"

"Well. Um." It takes me a second to work up the nerve, but once I start talking, the entire confession falls from my mouth at once. "I read all those newspapers in the living room. They were all about how the world was basically in shambles and how Avalon came in and started the Rainloft and saved Lavon from total doom and all. There wasn't one single newspaper that made her seem like a bad person, and it's sort of been on my mind lately too, but I think maybe it's because *Avalon's not a bad person at all.* She was trying to help as many people as she could by founding the Rainloft. Only a hundred of us every year have to live through the consequences, and that really really sucks for us, but isn't it worth it if the rest of the world gets to be happy and live in peace? A hundred casualties is *nothing* compared to the number of people that benefit, and I really don't like it but I think bringing down the Rainloft would be a *huge* mistake."

I take a deep breath. Grayson is quiet for a painfully long time. I can see the gears gnashing in his head as he starts assembling a s'more, wordlessly handing me my own set of ingredients—crackers, chocolate and a pastel green marshmallow. He takes a pink marshmallow out of the same bag for himself.

I hesitate. "You hate me now, don't you?"

"Of course I hate you," he says. "Can't you tell? I kept the obviously superior strawberry marshmallow for myself and gave you—" he shudders "—the *apple-*flavored one."

That cracks a smile out of me. "I like apple just fine, thank you," I joke. "Seriously, though. You don't think I'm a terrible person?"

He looks at me strangely. "Why would I think you're a terrible person?"

"For starters, we all hate Avalon to a point where we're literally trying to knock the Rainloft out of the sky. And, well, we all have good reason to," I explain. I nod toward Ryn and Atlas pitching stones into the creek. "Especially them. I mean, Avalon *killed* Ryn's parents over a peaceful protest. And my brother?" I shake my head in disbelief, recalling the conversation I had with Atlas on the balcony the other night. "The Rainloft has *really* messed him up."

Grayson nods along, sticking his strawberry marshmallow on a tree branch and roasting it over the fire. I do the same with mine, stabbing a stick through the marshmallow and thrusting it out over the flame with an unintended air of frustration as I talk. "I'm a terrible person." I give a blunt, humorless laugh. "Avalon does all these horrible things—she single-handedly *robbed* one of my best friends of her parents and destroyed my brother's *entire* life and I *still* feel sympathy for her. All because of some newspapers."

"Maybe it's not *all* because of some newspapers," Grayson says with a shrug, rotating his marshmallow over the firepit. "There's no way you had a total change of heart right there just because of what some old reporters had to say. You've known all that about Avalon all along, haven't you?"

I let out a breath of air because he's right and I hate it. "Maybe I've always known deep down," I murmur, more to myself than to Grayson. Then I whip around to face him. "Wait. Do you agree with me?"

"I don't disagree with you," he says after a pause. "I agree that Avalon had good intentions and she probably didn't mean for things to get to this point. But then again…" he motions toward Ryn and Atlas and lets the gesture say the rest.

"She killed Ryn's parents," I say faintly, my voice sounding distant and strange. Suddenly, in my brain, something finally clicks into place. "She killed *all* those people. They were one hundred percent innocent, every last one of them, and Avalon dropped a nuclear bomb on them."

"Exactly," Grayson says grimly, watching the flames lick at our marshmallows and turn them golden. "I don't know about you, but in my book, doing something like *that* is more than enough to get you crossed off of Santa's nice list."

The knot of dread in my stomach starts to loosen. *Avalon isn't a good person. She shouldn't be in charge of all of Lavon—she should be in prison.* It's a greater relief than I would've imagined knowing that what we're about to do isn't totally wrong. It's not going to destroy the world—*it's going to save it.*

Right?

I don't get a chance to think or say anything else, because at that moment, my marshmallow catches on fire. I gasp and yank my stick away from the firepit, and blow it out with a huge lungful of air.

I stare at my scorched, blackened marshmallow for a second then glance at Grayson. We both crack up. "Just like old times," he laughs.

Grinning, I smash my charred apple-flavored blob of a marshmallow between a pair of graham crackers. Grayson does the same with his and I hold mine up high. "Cheers," I say, and we bump our s'mores together and take a bite at the same time.

Not one-tenth of a second later we're both spitting them out onto the gravel. "*Wow,* that's bad," I choke out.

Then I hear Grayson say my name. I look up at him and ask "What?"

But he cocks his head at me with confusion across his features. "Huh?"

"You said my name."

"No, I didn't."

"Really?" I shrug and look back to the fire. "Huh. I could've sworn I just heard someone say my name."

At that moment, a pinecone comes flying out of absolutely nowhere and smacks me straight in the head. "Ow!" I yelp. I whip my head back and forth, searching for the culprit. Instead I find someone completely different.

A shadowy figure emerges from around the side of the house, stalking ominously towards us like a monster out of the shadows. I have to squint to make out her facial features in the fast-approaching dusk. It takes me a second, but as soon as she steps out of the house's shadow and into the setting sun's warm orange rays, it hits me.

"Hey, that's Linda," I murmur.

"Who?"

"The Alumna from the bakery," I clarify, my unease seeping into my tone. "The one Atlas stabbed. Which... wait..."

I get to my feet while she's still a safe distance away from us, and Grayson follows suit. Linda's gait reminds me vaguely of a zombie's—which isn't a thing I've ever seen in an Alumnus—and she sways strangely in the breeze. It's almost like she's drunk or something, but her expression is dead-serious. When the light hits her right I can see a splash of dried blood against the back of her neck, stuck in her uncharacteristically messy hair. The fact that she doesn't have a whole entourage of teammates at her heels sets me even further on edge.

I toss my disaster s'more into the firepit and lick the gooey marshmallow guts off my fingers as I make my way over to the Alumna. Her lips are pursed into a thin line and she looks like she's trying to shoot lasers at us with her eyes as we step up in front of her.

"Um, hi," I manage, pushing on with our original plan and trying to keep my cool under her death stare. "Are you...here to take us up to the Rainloft?"

Out the corner of my eye I see Ryn and Atlas heading up from the creek, and I silently will them to walk faster. Linda ignores my question entirely. "Where is he?" she demands. Her tone is even enough, but the wild look in her eyes is that of a rabid animal.

I assume that the *he* in question is the one who stabbed her in the back and left her to die a few days ago, but since he's clearly within her line of sight at this very moment, the question throws me off. "Um."

"Linda," Atlas says loftily, strolling into her immediate view. Her head jerks violently in his direction, causing both him and Ryn to step back a bit. "*Jeez*. What happened to *you*?"

"You did," the Alumna accuses, sounding out of breath, almost like she just finished running a marathon. "*You* happened."

She takes a step towards the two of them, but then Ryn throws her hands in the air guiltily. "Okay, okay, you win," she sighs, hanging her head. "We give up. You can take us back to the Rainloft now."

Linda doesn't move. Her wild eyes stay locked on Atlas and her fingers curl into fists by her sides.

"Um, Linda?" I venture, taking a tentative step closer to her. "Did you hear that? We're done running. We're done hiding. *We're giving up.*"

She whips back in my direction and my heart skips a beat. "I don't *want* that," she growls, then swings her gaze back to my brother. "*You.* It's you I want."

"Well, you can't just have one of us," Ryn protests. "Either all of us are going up or none of us—"

"*No.* You misunderstand," the Alumna seethes. Atlas stays put with his hands in his pockets, and that only seems to upset her more. "Winters, I am through with this wild goose chase. These last two years, I have devoted my *entire life* to tracking you down only to end up maimed or manipulated each time in a new way that I didn't even think was possible. "

"Linda," I interject, panic rising up in my throat. "We're turning ourselves in, and that includes…"

I trail off when I realize she's no longer looking at me. Her gaze is fixed on something past my shoulder.

The firepit. And of course, the flames chose this moment to grow up.

"Hold on, hold on," Grayson says hastily, but at this point Linda is beyond reason. She raises her palm, writing with fury, zeroed in on the firepit. The flames glint in her wild eyes as they grow to a nightmarish size. Thick smoke billows up into the darkening sky and the fire spits sparks and embers over everything within a five-mile radius.

Linda lets the flames reach a height of at least twenty feet before she throws her hand toward a copse of near-dead pines. I stand there, petrified, as a glob of flames goes flying through the air and hits the dry grass with a *whoosh*. A monstrous fire blazes up from the ground, snapping and crackling like a bowl of rice cereal over a supersized speaker.

I expect Atlas to intervene, but all he says is "We have to go. Now."

The scene unpauses and all four of us burst into motion at once. We swerve around the side of the cabin, heading for the front yard and the way out of this forest. I run as fast as my feet will carry me, gaining momentum with every step.

Flames rip through the trees to my right. They scorch everything in their path and spread at the speed of light, a thousand times faster than they would if they weren't being controlled by the Alumna. By the time we've reached the front yard they've already consumed what seems like half the forest. No matter how fast I run I can't escape the thoughts racing through my mind. *We're gonna die. We're all gonna die.*

I'm already out of breath by the time we skid to a halt on the dirt driveway. "Grayson, do you know the way back to the city?" Ryn asks urgently.

"I—kind of," he says. "I could try to—"

"Whatever. *Let's go,* Magellan!"

Grayson hesitates for a second, then makes for the start of the deep forest in front of us. We follow him and the fire follows us. I don't see Linda anymore but the flames carry on without her. They ravage the woods around us, turning grass to ash and snapping sturdy pines in half like twigs.

Don't think, just run. The fire swallows the forest whole and chases after us like a roaring monster with an insatiable appetite. I can't breathe and there's a stabbing pain in my side. Thick smoke claws at my lungs, burning down my throat as I gasp for breath. Inescapable heat radiates off the trees and makes me feel like I'm being boiled alive even though the fire hasn't touched me yet. My legs beg for a break and my muscles burn but I urge myself to *go, go, go.*

Each step I take is even less steady than the last. Trees crash to the ground and we have to curve around them. It's near impossible to keep track of everyone else in front of me through the smoke and haze. I see Grayson and I see Atlas up ahead. But something's wrong.

"Guys!" I scream, smoke straining my voice. "Where's Ryn?"

They both turn around and scan the area around us. The blood drains from Atlas's face and he swears. "Her foot," he says. "She must've fallen behind."

"We have to go back," I choke out, turning back around even though there's a wall of flames mere inches away from me. I don't care. "We can't leave her here."

"I'll go," Grayson shouts firmly. "I'll go back for Ryn, you two get out of here."

"No," I say immediately. "You'll die."

"I'm not going to die," he assures me, taking a step in my direction. "I know this forest. Plus—powers, remember?"

That hardly makes me feel any better, but it's literally our only option at this point so I force myself to nod. "Please be careful," I manage. He gives me a quick salute and disappears into the wall of fire, leaving Atlas and I to fend for ourselves.

Smoke and overwhelm bring tears to my eyes as I meet my brother's gaze. I nod again, and we both make a break for the end of the forest.

The trees seem to stretch on forever. I'm dizzy and smoke blurs my vision so that now I can barely make out where the trees end and the ground begins. I push forward blindly. My throat is raw and each breath feels like I'm swallowing flames. Two words echo in my mind over and over again, *keep going, keep going.*

Up ahead, the trees start to part. Light streams in through the gap way up ahead and a faint sound cuts through the fire's roar. *Sirens. Fire trucks. They're here.*

One last push and we're there. Atlas and I burst through the final line of trees and stumble out onto a wide field. My knees give out and I drop to the ground, drinking up gallons of fresh air faster than my lungs can take it in.

It takes a second for the fog to clear before I register my surroundings. At least six fire trucks have already made it to the scene. Herds of shouting firefighters stampede straight past Atlas and me, stopping the fire at the forest's boundary by blasting it with an ocean's worth of water.

"You good?" Atlas asks me breathlessly. Ash is streaked across his face and his hair is plastered to his forehead with sweat.

"Yeah," I say, shakily getting to my feet. A wave of dread crashes over me when suddenly, reality sets in. "Ryn and Grayson. They—they're still back there, we have to do something."

I spot a pair of firefighters standing by a truck and don't waste a second, staggering pitifully in their direction before I can think twice. "Officers!" I wave them down and that's all it takes to get their attention.

They rush over to me, concern written all across both of their faces. One of them starts, "Were you in the—"

"Yes," I say hoarsely. "W-We just came from the fire, but two of our friends are still back there, I think they're trapped and you need to go help them ASAP..."

I trail off when neither of them says anything. I watch as simultaneously, both of their expressions fade from worry to disbelief. "Wait," one of them says, his brow furrowed and his eyes wide. "You're—you're those kids who escaped. You're the—"

"*No,* you idiots," Atlas says impatiently. "*We're not. And that should be the least of your concerns, because right now there are people burning alive in those woods and without help, they're all going to die. So I'd highly recommend you do your job.*"

I can't tell whether that was mind-control or not, but the firemen get moving without a single complaint. They grab their gear and join the herd of first-responders pouring into the forest.

Atlas and I cop a seat in the grass nearby and wait for a small eternity. A massive cloud of smoky steam billows up from the woods as the firefighters go to work on the flames. Dozens of people are evacuated, all of them soot-covered and shaken to their cores, but none of them are

Ryn or Grayson. What little hope I have left is halved with every minute that passes.

Both of us are silent for the better part of an hour. But then out of the blue, Atlas narrows his eyes at something off in the distance. "What is it?" I ask hopefully, my heart lifting a bit. I follow his gaze to one of the fire trucks, but there's nobody there.

"Hold on—I just saw…" he murmurs, then he trails off and shakes his head. "Nevermind. It was nothing."

Just like that, all hope goes back out the window. We go back to waiting in a buzzing, anxiety-fueled quiet. On the very edge of giving up, I fall back into the grass and stare up at the sky. Dark smoke blocks out most of the stars, but there are certain ones that shine right through it. There's one in particular that grabs my attention. It's the only visible light from here, save for those of the distant city and the red and blue ones flashing atop the fire trucks. It's brighter than the moon itself, and somehow, it only seems to be getting brighter. And closer.

Until I realize that's not a star at all. I sit bolt upright, squinting up at it. "Is that—?"

"A Rainloft helicopter," Atlas finishes for me, swallowing hard. "Yeah."

I whip around to face him. "What do we do? Do we just keep going with our plan and let them take us up?" It pains me to say that, knowing we might have to carry on without Ryn and Grayson.

"Well, we could try," says Atlas, a strange uncertainty in his tone. "It would be risky."

"We can't do it without them," I murmur. That's not an easy pill to swallow. This whole time we'd planned to take down the Rainloft, and we'd planned on doing it together. Because that's the only way it could've been even remotely possible—if we did it together, the four of us as a team. As incredible as Atlas's powers are, even he wouldn't be able to do it alone. Not with Avalon and the entire body of Rainloft Alumni to stand in his way.

Now, our party has been chopped in half and Ryn and Grayson are—I force the thought out of my mind. The rational part of me knows that by this point, their odds of survival are probably in the negatives. But thinking it makes it even more real and reality just isn't something I can face right now.

"So what do we do?" I can't keep the defeat from weighing down my tone. "Accept our fate? Become Rainloft students again and let the Rainloft live on?"

Maybe that wouldn't be the worst thing ever. The thought comes before I can suppress it.

"No," says Atlas. "We run."

He gets to his feet and starts strolling across the field without checking to make sure I'm following. Of course I do, though. "Wait, what?" I ask, jogging to catch up with him. "What do you mean, 'we run'?"

"I mean, we leave," he says simply. "If we're still here when the Alumni touch down, they're taking us up there and then it's game over. Being an escapee is no walk in the park, and I don't know about you, but I think I'd rather die than submit to a life as someone's playing pawn. Least of all Avalon's."

I'm silent for a second, digesting all that. "But where will we go?" I ask.

"Not sure."

We weave past fire trucks and dodge paramedics and their shaken patients, headed for a worn-down road that leads into the distant city. I'm not entirely sure whether I agree or not—sure, the idea of spending the rest of my life at the Rainloft sounds like a living nightmare, but if my sacrifice is to the rest of the world's benefit, wouldn't I rather stick it out than die entirely? Would it be worth it, even if it means giving Avalon that satisfaction?

We walk in quiet down the deserted road, putting more distance between us and the scorched forest every second. We keep getting further from the scene, yet everything that just happened only becomes more and more real in my head. *We just burned down a forest. Ryn and Grayson are dead.* Those thoughts are inescapable now. They're like a whirlwind in my mind, overwhelming me and robbing me of my ability to think straight.

On either side of the road is an endless expanse of nothingness—dry grass and random scatterings of trees. But soon we come up on an oddly-placed structure by the side of the road. "Is that a playground?" I ask.

Atlas opens his mouth to reply, but then closes it again and slows to a stop in the middle of the road. "Sirens." As soon as he says it, I hear them too. *Great. Just what we need right now.*

"We can hide there," I say, gesturing to the playground up ahead. We head over there, cross the sad patch of mulch and duck behind a wide blue tube slide. Shards of mulch dig into my knees as I peer out from behind the sky-colored plastic. I wait, staying as still as I can manage, my breath forming frosty clouds in the cool air in front of me.

A sleek black SUV—clearly a Rainloft vehicle—comes into view down the road. And then it cruises right past us. It's gone as soon as it came.

Once I'm sure the coast is clear, I get to my feet and walk out from behind the slide. I remember that I don't know where I'm going so I come to a stop around the center of the mulch.

"That was close," I say, forcing a laugh as I look around the silent playground. Suddenly, I'm overcome by a wave of emotions. Last time we did this, last time we narrowly evaded capture by Alumni, Ryn and Grayson were with us. *Last time we did this, Ryn and Grayson were alive.*

My heart settles in the pit of my stomach. It feels like everything that could possibly be going wrong is going wrong. Wasn't it just yesterday that we were full of optimism, fantasizing over how incredible life would be when we brought down the Rainloft? Yesterday, it wasn't an *if* to whether we would do it or not—there wasn't a doubt in any of our minds that we'd pull it off. I thought it would be easy.

Now my two best friends are gone for good. There's no chance of achieving our goal now, and the worst part is that I don't even know whether I even want there to be.

Truth be told, I have *no idea* what I want anymore. In my head the line between right and wrong has blurred to the point where I can hardly tell one from the other. And that's *terrifying*.

I can't deal with this right now, so I don't. I take all my emotions, stuff them in a box and punt that box to the very back of my head.

Then I whirl to face Atlas. "Remember Superman?" I ask, grinning.

He stares at me. "What?"

I jog over to the swingset, my smile threatening to split my face in two. This was our favorite thing to do as kids. Whenever we'd go to playgrounds, the second we got out of the car we'd sprint to the swings and beg our mother to do Superman. It was her special thing she loved to do with us—our dad partook too, occasionally, but it just wasn't the same. Superman was Mom's thing, and everyone knew it.

The sudden burst of memory gives me a burst of adrenaline and I feel *alive*. I drop into one of the swings, which hangs down so low that I have to bring my knees close to my chest. The rusted metal chains are cold under my hands and they're in dire need of some WD-40.

Atlas watches me from a distance away with his arms folded, looking utterly bemused. "What are you doing?"

"Push me," I say.

"You're insane."

"I know," I grin. "Come on. For old times' sake."

He sighs, then walks around the other side of the swingset. I kick off the mulch and when I swing back, he pushes me. It's been so long since I've been on a swing that I completely forgot why I used to love it—the whizz of air past my ears, the fleeting moment of weightlessness when I hit the highest point. If I were allowing myself to feel stress right now, this would be a great way to relieve it.

A second later I'm as high as I can go without flipping over the swingset completely. "You have to count down!" I shout over the wind in my face.

Atlas sighs again, but I can tell he's smiling. "Metropolis will be destroyed in three... two... one—"

"Superman!" I fling myself off the swing, pumping my fist in the air as gravity yanks me back down. I actually land on my feet, but the impact sends shockwaves through my already-sore legs and I fall flat on my back in the mulch.

"Wow," says Atlas, striding over to where I lay now. "I'm no expert, but I'd say that performance deserves a gold star and a juice box."

I snort and reach my arm out for him to help me up. "Your countdown wasn't so bad either," I say as he hoists me to my feet. "Mom would be proud."

A faint smile tugs at the corners of his lips. There's a beat of silence, and then I hesitate. "Thank you. I know it's stupid, but I kind of needed that."

A faint smile tugs at the corners of his lips. Neither of us says anything after that—partially because we don't need to, but also because there's a *thud* to my left that successfully steals both of our attention.

I spin to face the source of the sound and find a blindingly sparkly object sitting at the center of a crater in the mulch. I stoop to grab it and hold it up, my eyes wide.

"Is that Ryn's shoe?" asks Atlas.

There's no mistaking it. Its purple rhinestones glitter like a disco ball in the moonlight. The sole is covered in mud, and there's a blackened hole blasted in the side—the spot where she was hit by a Sim bullet.

Before I can say anything else, the shoe lifts up out of my hand and hovers in the air for a second. Then it goes flying straight into the road, where it's flattened beneath the tires of a huge black SUV. *A Rainloft van.*

"We need to go," I say hastily, then whirl and scan the playground for hiding places. My eyes land on a wide blue plastic tube that connects two jungle gym platforms, and I make for the ladder that leads up there.

It takes me a second to realize that Atlas isn't following. "Atlas, we have to hide," I tell him urgently, but his feet remain planted firmly on the ground.

"You hide," he says without meeting my gaze. "I'll turn them around."

"What?!" I blurt out. "No! There's probably a whole *pack* of Alumni in that car, you can't take them all—"

"June, I've been doing this for the past two years," he says harshly, looking me straight in the eye. "This time won't be any different."

I open my mouth to object, but he lifts an eyebrow at me and I know that it's hopeless. I scurry up the jungle gym and dive headfirst into the blue tube.

The static electricity makes my hair stand on end. I don't dare move a muscle. For a second I can pretend I'm six again, playing hide-and-seek with my friends during recess. But then—*gunshots.*

A hundred consecutive shots ring out within the same millisecond and shatter the quiet of the night. I clasp a hand over my mouth and squeeze my eyes shut, forcing myself to stay put when everything in me wants to go out there and intervene.

The Sim guns fire rapidly, zero breathing room whatsoever in between their deafening pops. And then, nothing. All at once, the gunfire stops. It's almost like the night came to life and swallowed everyone out there whole.

I wait a long moment before I crawl out of the plastic tube, then shakily get to my feet. The Alumni are all gone, and so is Atlas. The playground is eerily quiet—the swings sway gently in the breeze and if it weren't for the bullet holes in the jungle gym, I'd believe I just imagined everything that just happened.

Until I realize: *I'm not alone.*

Her shadowy silhouette blends in seamlessly against the sky's obsidian backdrop. She stands dead still at the center of the mulch with her back turned to me, her long black dress billowing lightly behind her.

"Hello, June," Avalon drawls. "Join me."

I drop off the jungle gym and storm up to her, boiling anger rising up in my chest. "What did you do with my brother?" I demand.

She turns, peering at me from behind her feathery black mask. "Why, it depends," she says calmly, and leaves it at that.

"Wh—*it depends?!*" I sputter. I don't have the patience to deal with her pointless riddles, so I raise my voice. "I can't *believe* you. I can't believe I ever thought you were a *good person.* You killed my best friends and you kidnapped my brother! You're heartless and cruel and that's all you *ever* will be."

"What if I told you there's a way to get them back?" Avalon says levelly.

My thoughts grind to a halt right there. "What?"

"I can help you get your friends back."

I don't know what I was expecting her to say, but it definitely wasn't that. "What's the catch?" I ask skeptically.

She extends her hand to me, palm-up. "I require your trust."

The knot in my stomach tightens. I'm hit with a flash of déjà vu—this scene is a mirror image of what happened back on the train. Avalon had asked for my trust, and I'd declined without an ounce of hesitation. Only then, there weren't any stakes. Now everything is on the line—as little faith as I have in Avalon, this could be my only chance to get my friends back. If I don't take it, they could be lost forever.

All my fury evaporates and it's replaced by this overpowering drive to save my friends. "Okay," I breathe. And I place my hand in hers.

There's a strange *whizz* past my ears. I blink, and when I open my eyes I'm no longer standing at the center of a deserted playground.

Intense sunlight beats down on me, even though it was nighttime merely three seconds ago. I use my hand as a visor and scan my surroundings. I'm standing in a bustling town square, surrounded by skyscrapers and droves of people who barely even notice the fact that I just materialized out of thin air. There's a giant, burbling fountain a few feet away from me with a stone dolphin perched at the top.

The Lebanon city plaza, I realize.

This is a feeling I know all too well. "Excuse me?" I ask the first person to my right—an older lady in a floppy hat. "Do you happen to know what year it is?"

She looks at me like I've lost my mind, but tells me anyway.

It's the same day. Just thirty years ago.

Time travel.

The pieces start to fall together: Avalon, a Type Five, mimicked my power and used it to send me thirty years into the past. *But why am I here, of all places?*

There's no sign of Avalon anywhere. I start to wander aimlessly around the square, bumping into people left and right. None of them seem to know who I am. But why would they? I haven't escaped yet. I don't even *exist* yet, for that matter. And neither does the Rainloft.

Suddenly, I have a hunch. The Rainloft Management Facility is directly in front of me. My eyes travel up the skyscraper, only to find that I'm wrong—it's the same building as the present-day RMF, but the sign reads *The Lebanon Innovation and Technology Laboratory.*

That's where Avalon used to work, I realize, subconsciously recalling that newspaper I read this morning.

My feet move before I can tell them to and I find myself inside the building. It looks exactly the same inside—beige and boring.

And there's my roller skate painting, on display by the row of elevators. I do a double take. *Wait.* I squint at it, the dots refusing to connect. *I don't exist yet. How would I have painted that picture if I'm not even—*

"Can I help you, dear?" the receptionist asks sweetly, looking up at me from her computer.

I manage to regain my composure long enough to ask, "Could you, by chance, direct me to Avalon Lockhart's office?"

"Fifth floor, third door on your right," she says automatically. I thank her and I'm about to leave when she tilts her head at me. "You know, it's curious. You look so much like her."

Normally I'd find a comment like that odd, but I have bigger things to worry about right now so I smile and fly out of the room. I take the steps two at a time and I've reached the fifth floor within an instant.

Avalon's door has a small plaque hanging at the center, displaying her name in nondescript silver lettering. Her door looks exactly like all the other ones lining the corridor. If I weren't from the future, I never would have chosen this office as the one belonging to the woman who saves the world.

The door is propped open, so I push by it and barge in uninvited. Then I see her and I stop dead in my tracks.

A woman sits at the desk, hunched over a mountain of important-looking paperwork. Her long, dark hair is tied back in a loose ponytail and a pair of thick glasses slides down the bridge of her nose. She looks deep in focus, but when I walk in she tears her gaze from the documents and her eyes go wide.

This is the first time I've ever seen Avalon without her feathery masquerade mask. Except, this isn't Avalon.

It's my mother.

Chapter Nine

There was this day when I was a kid—maybe six or seven at the time—that's still weirdly vivid in my memory. Springfield had just been hit by the greatest blizzard of the century. Multiple feet of snow were piled up outside our door and all the roads were frozen over completely. I didn't mind, though, because A: I didn't have to drive on them and B: school was closed.

At first I was ecstatic—twenty-four hours of watching TV and building snowmen sounded like a dream come true—but the whole snow day thing got old fast. There was nothing good to watch, and Atlas was wrapped up in a video game and refused to play with me.

So naturally, I resorted to bugging my parents. I wandered into their bedroom to find my mother sitting at her vanity, putting on her makeup for the day.

"Mom?" I asked from the doorway. "Why are you doing your makeup? It's a snow day! You don't have to go to work, remember?"

She smiled. "I wish it worked that way," she said wistfully, then patted the surface of her vanity. "Come here. I'll do yours."

My face lit up and I scurried over there, perching at the edge of her desk like I always did. I just loved it when she did my makeup for me. I would beg her to do it on school mornings, but my dad claimed it made me look like I was on my way to the world's fanciest gala, which was apparently too much for second grade. So her offering to do my makeup wasn't really a usual occurrence.

Even though she was only halfway done with her own, my mother whipped out a palette of glittery eyeshadow and expertly swept some over my eyelids with the ball of her thumb.

"Mom, what's your job?" I asked out of the blue.

She didn't flinch and her expression didn't change, and I didn't know why it should have. "Well, I'm a scientist," she replied evenly.

"I know that," I said, giggling as she swiped powder blush across my cheeks. "But what type of science do you do?"

She answered that question the same way she did every time I asked it: with a smile and an annoyingly cryptic reply. "A type of science that's going to change the world someday."

"But how?"

"Honey, you're too young to understand that right now," she told me, which just ticked me off even more. "You'll understand someday. Just not yet."

"But I wanna know now," I protested, then held up seven fingers. "Mom, I'm seven now. I'll understand."

She just smiled again, like that sufficed as a response. She packed up her makeup supplies and left the room, and I trailed after her.

We ended up in the kitchen. My dad was standing at the counter with a steaming cup of coffee in his hands. Mom greeted him with a quick kiss. Then she grabbed her keys off the table and headed for the foyer, her high heels clicking on the tile floor.

"I'll be back before dinner tonight," she said vaguely. "Anyone need anything before I go?"

"I thought the lab was closed today," said Dad, nodding toward the huge drifts of snow out the window. "Those roads are a *disaster*."

My mom stopped in her tracks, and she hesitated before she spoke again. "I need to go in today, Frank. I think I'm on to something and I have to follow this lead."

Dad opened his mouth to protest, but evidently remembered who his wife was and realized that wasn't going to get him anywhere. "Just be careful," he told her.

That was the first time something like that happened, but it certainly wasn't the last. The number of hours she worked steadily ticked up, and before long, she was out of the house more often than Dad was—and seeing as he was a surgeon, that was a high bar. She started working twelve-hour shifts every day of the week, including weekends, pursuing this mysterious lead that none of us knew anything about.

Two years later, she was gone.

That's a day I remember just as well, if not better. Atlas and I had just gotten off the school bus. We were walking up the driveway to our house, and I was venting to him about this great Valentine's Day predicament I was having.

"I wanna make valentines for the whole class, except for Mike, because then he'll think I like him," I was saying. "He'll rub it in my face and tell everyone I have a crush on him, and I *don't*! But Miss Glass said we're not allowed to leave anyone out…"

Atlas nodded along, pretending to be interested. I kept complaining until we walked into the house and threw our backpacks on the ground. I knew the second I stepped into the kitchen that something was wrong.

Our dad was hunched over the counter, staring down his phone while peppy hold music blasted from the speakers. His brow was creased and he looked like he hadn't slept in weeks.

"Dad, what's wrong?" I asked.

His head snapped up like he hadn't noticed we'd walked into the room until that moment. "It's your mom," he said finally. "She's missing."

Just like that, my whole Valentine's Day dilemma dropped to the very bottom of my list of concerns. Its spot was taken by a problem much, much bigger.

I no longer had a mother.

This isn't happening.

This can not be happening.

I can't move. I can't think. It's like the order of the planets in the solar system has reversed, gravity just plain switched off, the earth has stopped spinning on its axis and my body has no idea how to process the change. I stand there and stare at my mother and my mother stares back at me. *My mother.*

Everything makes sense now. Yet at the same time, not one bit of it does.

"June?"

That makes a path through the fog just wide enough for one clear thought to squeeze through: *I need to get out of here.*

So I bolt. Next thing I know I'm halfway down the hallway, moving as fast as I can with no sort of destination in mind. I don't know where I'm going but I need to get there and that *there* is anywhere but here.

"June!"

My feet lock into place without my permission. *It's not her.* I force the thought into my mind. *That's not your mother. It's only Avalon, and she just so happens to look—and sound—exactly like her.*

I make myself turn around to face her, and those thoughts immediately fly out of my mind. *It's definitely her.*

I open my mouth to say something—though I have no idea *what*—but she beats me to the punch. "June," she breathes. "It's really you."

"*You're* Avalon?" I accuse, borderline shouting over the roar in my ears. "Wh—*how?* I can't—I don't understand, *how is that possible?*"

"It's—" she starts, but cuts herself off with a sigh. When she looks up at me, there's no mistaking the guilt in her storm-gray eyes. "How long has it been? Since I left?"

I pause. "Five years," I say. I hate how the longer I look at her, the more my tone softens. Part of me wants nothing more than to hug her. The other part has this overwhelming urge to slap her for leaving without any sort of warning.

"So let me get this straight," I say, pressing one hand against my forehead, centimeters away from utter hysteria. "Five years ago, you abandoned your husband and your nine-year-old children and practically your entire *life* to travel into the past and *become Avalon??*"

"There's more to it than that," she says hastily. "I couldn't even *begin* to tell you how sorry I am for what I did, but I had no other choice."

"What do you mean, you had no other choice?"

She sighs. "It's a really long story. One you'd probably never understand."

I fold my arms and shrug. "I've got time."

She opens her mouth to protest but closes it again, evidently remembering that I'm her daughter and I'm not going to budge. "Okay," she concedes. "But not here."

Twenty minutes later, I've followed my mother deep into downtown Lebanon, all the way to a tiny little ice cream parlor jammed between two skyscrapers. In the time between our departure from the RMF and our arrival at the ice cream shop's front window, she hasn't offered me any answers whatsoever. She's pointed out a pair of pigeons fighting over a french fry and noted how miserably hot the sun is today, but she hasn't given me anything even remotely helpful. It crosses my mind that back in the present, my friends are quite possibly fighting for their lives and I'm here taking a leisurely stroll through the city with my mom. I resolve to get the answers I need and return as soon as I can.

The line for the ice cream parlor goes by quickly. The striped pergola offers some much-needed shade and gives me a chance to read the menu, but when an employee comes to the window my mother orders for me. "Three scoops of mint chip on a waffle cone, please. One for each of us."

I would be mad, but that's exactly what I would've ordered anyway. The employee nods and disappears back into the kitchen.

The awkward silence instantly returns. I rock back and forth on my heels, pretending to be interested in my tragically mundane surroundings and avoiding my mother's eyes at all costs. Until I realize that she's staring at me. "What?"

"You've grown so much since I last saw you," she remarks. "You're a *teenager* now. I mean, you're almost as tall as *me*. When did *that* happen?"

That ticks me off a little but also scratches this inexplicable itch that I've had for the last five years. "I don't know."

The employee comes back to the window, one ice cream cone in each hand. My mother pays and we take our ice cream over to a nearby picnic table shaded by a crooked umbrella.

For a second we eat in silence. I have to balance all three scoops of ice cream, fighting to keep them from splatting onto the table, until it occurs to me why we're here. "So," I say over a mouthful of mint. "I believe I'm owed an explanation?"

She shakes her head. "Okay, let me just preface this by saying *you're not going to understand,*" she tells me, her brow creased. "Truthfully, I don't even understand it myself. It was all just a series of wildly improbable events that led to me doing something I never wanted to do, and that I never won't regret. You have to believe that."

"Okay."

She takes a deep breath. "It's hard to pinpoint exactly when it started, but I'd say it was a couple of years before I left. I was still working at the lab in Springfield, and one day, I stumbled across a news article about Avalon. At that point, I already knew how I felt about the Rainloft. As a mom, I knew how much it would break me to have you or your brother taken away from me and see you lose your entire childhood to someone like Avalon—"

"Wait, wait, wait," I cut in, my head already spinning. "So the Rainloft and everything—it all existed then, in the present, even though you hadn't created it? And you had no idea yet that *you* were Avalon?"

"Correct. I knew just as much as you or anyone else did at the time," she says, then keeps talking. "Anyway, I really didn't know of anyone who had the same opinions as me. That article I read was written by a journalist who saw the Rainloft the same way that I did. It changed something for me—it made me realize that I wasn't the only rational human being left in the world. I wasn't the only one who saw how cruel and inhumane the Rainloft was.

"That article sent me down a rabbit hole. I found all sorts of forums, reports and tragic firsthand accounts from parents whose kids were selected that really made me wonder: is the Rainloft really the best solution to this world's   problems?

"I didn't totally disagree with Avalon—as a scientist, I knew how incredible her whole miracle serum was. But the great fault in her system was the lack of choice, and that led me to an idea. I thought that if I could somehow recreate her serum, I could found a new Rainloft. One where people could apply *by choice* to become superpowered crime-fighters. Then, innocent children wouldn't have to lose their lives and innocent families wouldn't have to lose their children."

"A new Rainloft," I murmur. It makes a lot of sense. So much sense that I have to wonder: why hadn't anyone thought of it before her? "If that was your original plan, how did the Rainloft end up the way it is now?"

"I'm getting there," she assures me. "Anyways, I got to work. My regular shifts were jam-packed with projects for the lab, so I had to make time outside of my normal workday to work on the serum. Avalon never disclosed her recipe to the public—except for the main ingredient, which was gemstone. Knowing the key part of the tonic, I thought it would be easy to replicate. But I was sorely mistaken. Every time I thought I was close to the finish line, I'd hit a wall and have to start all over again.

"Before long I was obsessed," she frowns, shaking her head. "I went into the lab on my days off and stayed there well past the ends of my regular shifts. I kept chasing these intangible leads, positive every time that if I used a fraction of a percentage less of this ingredient or half a milliliter less of that then I'd have it. I'd have the miracle serum, the cure to all of this world's problems."

"So that's where you were," I say slowly, an unintended edge of resentment behind my tone. "Every time Atlas or I had a school art show or a class play, you were at the lab working on a fruitless pet project that nobody knew about."

"I know," she exhales heavily, hanging her head. "And I'm so, so sorry for that. I'm a terrible mother, and if I could somehow undo everything I did, believe me, I would. But I just had this *feeling*—as impossible as it seemed, something in me knew that my idea was going to work. That it wasn't just a 'pet project,' but something the world needed me to do. And sometimes you have to follow your gut, right?"

Even if that means ditching your entire family without so much as a heads-up, I think, but I don't say it out loud. I just lick my frozen toothpaste and nod.

"In this case, my gut turned out to be right," my mother shrugs with a humorless laugh. "I hate that with every ounce of my being, but it was right. Because, a couple years later, I had it.

"The day I figured it out, I knew. I had just finished a new prototype, and I was planning to test it out that morning. At that point, I'd botched it so many times that there was no reason to think this version wouldn't end up as another failure to add to the pile. But I just knew it. I knew that this serum would be the one."

She takes a breath. "I was *so* confident, in fact, that I decided to inject the serum into myself that day. I was alone in my office, sitting at my desk, and despite all the risks I stuck the needle into my arm.

"I immediately started to lose consciousness," she says. The further she gets into her explanation, the harder it seems to get for her to keep talking. "I panicked. I didn't know what was going to happen, if my serum had worked or if it was about to kill me. I grabbed on to the most important thing within my reach—a picture of a roller skate that you drew for me when you were really little.

"And then I was out." She swallows hard. "That was the last time I ever existed in the present. Because when I woke up, I'd traveled into the future."

"The future?" I repeat, trying to grasp the magnitude of what she's saying. "How far *into* the future, exactly?"

"I don't know," she says, a heavy weight behind her tone. "But that's not what mattered. Because, when I woke up, do you know what I saw?"

"What?"

"Ruin." She meets my gaze, a dead-serious look in her icy eyes. "Ruin, as far as the eye could see. I was standing with your drawing in a field of wreckage—buildings that had been turned to dust, fire and twisted metal all over the place. The sky was a horrendous swirl of smoke and there were so many people—*so many* people whose lives had been claimed by whatever awful disaster had taken place. It was the end of the world. There was no mistaking it."

My stomach twists. *That* took a turn. "It would be *really* nice to know how far in the future that happens."

"That's not all," she says uneasily. "You were in the middle of it."

My heart skips a beat. "Me?"

"Yeah. You and your brother. Somehow, you were both alive. And you were *helping* people. The two of you were helping survivors, getting them out of danger and guiding them to safety. It was incredible." She shakes her head in awe. "You were like a beacon of light in that dark sea of tragedy. I knew it, right then and there, that my kids would be the ones to save the world."

My head is spinning. The ice cream I'm holding is melting, dripping down the cone and past my fingers, but I'm in too much shock to do anything about it. "Wh—how? How old were we? What happened next?"

"I was too far away to determine exactly how old you were," she says with a frown. "As for what happened next, I wouldn't know. After a few moments, I regained my senses and everything I knew about time travel came back to me. Interacting with people from a time period other than your own tends to have catastrophic consequences. You just can't mess with time. It's like pulling a thread on an old sweater—one tug, and everything unravels. I knew I couldn't stay in the future, right in the middle of such a pivotal moment.

"So I closed my eyes and begged my new powers to bring me back to the past," she continues. "My wish was granted—but not in the way that I'd hoped. Instead of the present, where you and Atlas and your dad were, I ended up here. In Lebanon City, fifty-five years before then.

"As you may know, here, the Rainloft doesn't exist yet," she says, sweeping an arm around the bright, bustling downtown. "When I first arrived, the city was in a state of total chaos and disorder. I'd thought by then, there would at least be rumors of the Rainloft. Even if it hadn't been constructed yet, there would still be plans in place. But there weren't. Nobody had heard of it, and nobody at the Lebanon Innovation and Technology Lab— where Avalon was said to work—had even come up with the idea yet.

"That's when the dots started to connect," she says with a grimace. "It was around the time that news was *supposed* to break out of Avalon's great discovery, yet

Avalon was nowhere to be found. I had the recipe for the miracle serum. Take away the mask and the feathery statement dress and I looked exactly like present-day Avalon."

I really should've seen that coming, but that doesn't stop my jaw from dropping when she says it. This story has more twists and turns than any roller coaster I've ever been on.

"So I got a job at the LIT Lab. I hung up your drawing—the only piece of you guys that I'd brought with me—and got to work. I began retracing her footsteps, in a way, taking all the stories I'd heard about her in the present day and living them out myself. I changed my name from Lucy Winters to Avalon Lockhart. I made myself a mask just like the one I knew her to wear and now I put it on almost every time I go out in public, clinging to the number-one rule of time travel and ensuring that nobody sees my face. I carried on with perfecting my serum, only now in a different setting and without my family to go home to at the end of the day.

"That just about brings it to today," she exhales, the words heavy. "As of now, I've fully refined three of the five formulas. Plans for the Rainloft are in place, and construction is set to begin a little over a month from now.

I've already assembled a small army of test subjects to protect Lebanon for the time being until we get the Rainloft up and running."

For the first time in the strangest five minutes of my life, she's quiet. And so am I. There are so many questions running through my brain, but my mouth flat-out refuses to ask them. All I can do is stare at my ice cream cone, watching melted drops slide over my fingers and drip through the holes in our picnic table.

My mother tilts her head at me with a sympathetic smile. "You hanging in there, honey?"

"How did things end up the way they are?" I ask. The way she calls me *honey* and how it causes righteous anger and nostalgic longing to collide in my mind helps me find my voice. "If your original plan was to create a new, more humane Rainloft, then why didn't you? You had the *perfect* opportunity."

She sighs. "I wish it had been that simple. Believe me, I fought for it as much as I could. The idea of a choice-based Rainloft, where kids could apply voluntarily… It was everything I'd ever wanted. But the timeline simply didn't allow for that. The past can't be changed, not without horrible consequences. The way things needed to unfold for everything to stay intact, for you and Atlas and everybody else to get to where you are now—it had to happen exactly the way it's happening. The future relies entirely on certain events lining up in a specific order. If I'd tried to start a new version of the Rainloft, one that was so drastically different from the one we know in the present, it could have set off a chain of events that led to disaster."

She shakes her head slowly, a faraway look in her eyes. "The more I've learned about time travel, the more I've come to realize just how fragile everything is. Even a single, seemingly harmless decision could ripple outward and completely shift the future in unpredictable ways. I just couldn't risk it. No matter how much I wanted to do things differently, I had to respect the timeline, or else I might've erased the very future I was trying to protect."

"The future," I repeat skeptically. "You told me a minute ago that you *saw* the future. This timeline you're trying so hard to keep in place—the one with Bad Rainloft—it results in *the end of the world as we know it.* Why *wouldn't* you want to change that? Stop it from happening in the first place?"

"I don't know exactly what I saw," she elaborates. "It certainly looked like it was close, but the world hadn't yet *ended.* Whatever disaster had taken place, some people survived. *You* survived. When I saw you and Atlas there, in the future, helping the injured and guiding them through the wreckage—it was like something I'd never seen before. You two were like this incredible spark of hope in the middle of all the darkness and tragedy. I knew right then and there that you two were Lavon's only hope of rebuilding. That you'd be the ones to save the world."

A weight settles on my shoulders as I mull all that over in my head. "I have to save the world from some gigantic disaster that hasn't even happened yet," I murmur. "No pressure, right?"

"Don't get me wrong: I don't *want* all that to happen," she says hastily. "I'd never put you guys in a position like that if I didn't absolutely have to. But the problem is that *I just don't know.* Maybe the disaster is inevitable. Or maybe a shift in the timeline could stop it from happening altogether. But as I'm sure you've gathered by now, time is impossibly delicate. If I were to change something, sure, it's possible that I could delete this disaster from the course of history—but one misstep and I could wind up erasing *you guys* from the timeline. It's simply too risky. If the disaster still happens, but you two cease to exist, then all this world's hope is gone."

I close my eyes and press my free hand to my forehead, more overwhelmed than I would've thought possible ten minutes ago. It's like eating an entire five-tier birthday cake that looks delicious from the outside, but you don't realize until you've eaten the whole thing and you're full to the point of bursting that you don't actually like cake. Ever since my mother disappeared, all I wanted was an explanation. And now that I finally have it, I wish I'd never asked for it in the first place.

Now I know that the woman I've loathed for my entire life is my own mother. Now I know that she's never coming home. Now I know that it's up to me and the brother that I barely even know to save the world. I have all the knowledge I could possibly want and I really, really wish I didn't.

"You're Rainloft students now, aren't you?" My mother's voice jolts me back into reality. "You and Atlas?"

"Uh-huh."

"Ah," she nods, a shadow crossing her face. "So I *do* end up selecting you two."

My head snaps up. "Wait. You *picked* us? But it's supposed to be *random*! I thought—"

"Come on, June. You're smarter than that," she says, her cherry-red lips turned downward. "In a totally random selection of one hundred eleven-year-olds from a pool of *millions*, what are the odds of *both* of you being selected?"

I gape at her, positively dumbfounded. "Why would you *do* that? You obviously know how awful Rainloft students have it, and we're your own *children!*"

"You were wearing Rainloft uniforms," she cuts in evenly before I can say any more. "When I saw you in the future, saving the world, you were wearing Rainloft uniforms."

"Oh. So it was just another effort to protect the timeline," I say, filling in the blanks. "To get us to that exact version of the future."

Of all the things she's told me so far, this should rank as one of the very least surprising. But I have more of a problem with it than I would've expected. "I don't get it," I say with a bitter laugh. "You're willing to put your own family through *all of this*—you abandoned us all without bothering to tell us why, then sacrificed Atlas's and my entire childhoods just so that the world can end when it's supposed to?"

"June, I need you to believe me: I didn't do it to hurt you guys," she pleads, and the apology in her tone sounds genuine but I refuse to let myself believe it. "This is bigger than just our family. The fate of the *world* is at stake here. It's nothing personal."

"Really? Because it feels pretty personal to me," I snap. "I mean, Dad was a *mess* when you left. You only made it worse by robbing him of us, his only remaining family, *less than a year later*. As for me and Atlas? We have had it *impossibly* hard since we were taken to the Rainloft—*light years* harder than most students, if you can believe it. And that's why we escaped."

At that, all the blood drains from her face. "You did *what*?"

"We escaped," I repeat firmly. "Atlas a couple years back, and me just a few days ago."

"You have to go back," she says, her voice razor-sharp. "You have to let the Alumni bring you back up and you have to *stay there*."

"Why?" I ask. I try to keep my tone cool and even, but the unblinking stare she's giving me scares me a little. "I still don't see why you're so set on getting the timeline to play out in *this exact way*. I mean, it results in some giant disaster, and you don't even know what *triggers* that. What if the cause is the Rainloft you're creating? What if it's the two of us being students? By changing something, you could stop the disaster from happening in the first place *and* save thousands of kids' lives from being ruined!"

"It's just too risky," my mother says, her voice hard. "This is the way the universe intended the timeline to play out. Meddling with fate is equivalent to asking for disaster. And at least in this version of the timeline, the world itself doesn't end. If that's as good as it's going to get, we just have to accept that."

I open my mouth to protest, then close it again. As much as I hate it, she has a point. It's hard to argue with the universe itself. If this is the way nature intended for the timeline to happen—how everything would go down without time travelers interfering—shouldn't we leave well enough alone? Even if some deadly disaster leaves my brother and I with the fate of the world in our hands, wouldn't that be better than potentially ending all of life itself?

"June." My mother's tone is softer now. She reaches across the table and takes my free hand in her own, giving it a tight squeeze. "I need you to know that I am so, *so* sorry. For everything. If there were a way to undo all the awful things I've put you through without the rest of the world suffering the consequences, I would do it in a heartbeat."

"You did what you had to do," I hear myself saying, the fury melting off me. "It's for the greater good. If my sacrifice can save the rest of the world, why should *everyone* have to suffer?"

She gives me a sad smile. "I'm not asking you to understand, and I'm not asking you to forgive me. I just need you to know that I was never trying to hurt you. That was never, ever my intention. But knowing all that I do, I have to try everything in my ability to save as many people as I can from what's to come. Even if it's at your expense."

I nod. I don't say anything for the better part of a minute, letting the weight of it all sink in. "Everything you've done, that Avalon's done, even the things that hardly make any sense… it was all to preserve the timeline," I conclude. "All the pointless rules at the Rainloft, all the illegal crimes you're going to commit— like, say, dropping a nuclear weapon on a group of peaceful protesters—*all of it* is purely for the sake of the future?"

"Yes," my mother sighs, a sting of remorse in her tone. "The Lebanon Massacre… trust me, I'm not looking forward to it. But the timeline requires that the Rainloft stays in the sky, and I simply can't have anyone standing in the way.

"As for the Rainloft's rules—they're not pointless." She shoots me a pointed look. "For one, the rule about different types not being allowed to interact is to keep you guys from combining your abilities and becoming overly powerful—and eventually doing something bad. Like *escaping*."

I throw my hands up innocently. "Hey! If I had known that, then I wouldn't have done it!"

"I know," she chuckles. "It's not your fault. None of it is. I only ask that you consider going back up to the Rainloft. The fate of the world is at stake, after all."

I smile, but it instantly drops when it hits me. Something I'd neglected to remember up until this moment.

We didn't escape the Rainloft just for the purpose of escaping.

We were planning to bring it down.

Crap.

That's been the plan all along. As far as I know it's *still* the plan, at least for Atlas and Ryn and Grayson. But there's no way we could go through with it anymore. Not now.

Against my better judgement, I open my mouth to tell my mom. But she beats me to it.

"I love you, June," she says. "And I miss you so much. There hasn't been a moment since I left that I haven't, and there'll never be a moment that I won't. You have to know that. But you have to go."

"Yeah, I love you too," I say without thinking, "but—"

I cut myself off with a gasp when I feel a pair of ice-cold hands clamp over my shoulders. Before I realize what's happening they yank me backwards and I'm sent flying over the back of the picnic bench, my eyes squeezed shut and wind whizzing past my ears.

When I hit the ground, it's not the rock-hard cement of the ice cream parlor's patio. It's mulch. And when I open my eyes, I realize that I'm not in Lebanon anymore—I'm back at the deserted playground where Atlas and I ended up after we fled from the fire. *In the present day.*

The frosty night air is a shock to the system after the boiling heat of Lebanon City. It's not until after I've pushed myself into an upright position, sharp shards of mulch digging into my palms, that I realize she's standing right in front of me. Billowing black dress, feathery mask and all.

Not Avalon.

"You know, I remember that day," my mother says wistfully, face turned toward the moon. "It was such a joy getting to see you again. It had been two years since I'd left the present, and I truly believed I would never get to talk with you again. At least, not as myself."

I get to my feet, brushing the mulch off my back. For a minute, I don't say anything, and she doesn't prompt me to. Everything makes sense now. This playground is exactly as it was when I left it, yet for me, everything has changed. I have all the answers I've ever wanted—where my mother has been, who Avalon is, the motives behind the founding of the Rainloft. There are hardly any questions left in my mind. Except for one.

"Nineteen years," I say, shattering the silence between us. "That's how long you tell everyone it took you to perfect the serum. But according to your story, it didn't take you nearly that much time."

"Well, I started working on it one year and finished it six decades *before* then. It was simply easier to make up a number than try to explain that," she says shortly. She turns to look at me, silver eyes peering out from behind her mask. "I've always liked the number nineteen. It reminds me of my family."

"Nineteen seconds," I realize. "That's the age gap between me and Atlas."

"Ah, that was all you two would talk about in the days before I left," she reminisces. "You just loved to tease him about it. It was for that very reason that your father and I hadn't told you who was older before then."

I can't help but smile. For whatever reason, that was basically my favorite pastime as a kid—finding the most meaningless little things to make fun of my brother for.

My brother. "Speaking of Atlas," I start, "you said that if I trusted you, you would get my friends back. All of them."

"Is that what I said?" she asks breezily. "That I personally would retrieve them all for you?"

"Um, I think so, yeah," I say, my smile fading. "You *are* going to bring them back, right?"

She meets my eyes. "I think you know what to do," she tells me. "I will say: it doesn't look good for your friends. However, I believe that if the right measures are taken, they'll be just fine."

And then she turns on her heel and walks away. "Wait, where are you going?" I holler after her, the knot of dread in my stomach tightening. When she doesn't stop, I yell, "You *lied* to me! I can't believe I trusted you!"

She shoots a glance at a nearby tree and then vanishes in a burst of green light, leaving me standing at the center of the playground, completely and utterly alone.

"How could you?" I whisper to no one, looking around helplessly. "You said you would…"

And then it clicks.

You know what to do.

I'm hit with a sudden rush of adrenaline as I look up at the sky and try to gauge the time. The moon is high and the sun has long since set, so it has to be at least nine o'clock. *How long ago was the fire?* I think, racking my brain. I decide two hours is probably a safe bet.

Every single lesson I've ever had at the Rainloft comes flooding back to me as I close my eyes and try to center myself. Maybe my powers aren't totally useless after all. *Or maybe they'll be the very thing that blows everything up.*

I guess only time will tell.

Chapter Ten

You can't be seen.

The words of every teacher I've ever had at the Rainloft echo through my brain as I step up on top of a merry-go-round next to me to get a better view of the sky. I raise my right hand, palm-up, and bring my gaze to the stars.

Do what needs to be done and nothing more. Leave everything else untouched.

I take a breath, then concentrate. All at once, the world around me blurs into a whizz of colors and motion, but I keep my feet planted firmly on the ground and focus on what's above me.

Focus on the time alone. Don't get distracted.

The moon begins to shrink back behind the distant city, cowering in the face of the slowly rising sun. The darkness dissolves and stars start to fade. Around me, the shadows of trees and playground equipment begin to stretch across the ground, and the icy bite of the night air dies down to a gentle evening breeze.

Once the sun has reached a point that I estimate to be roughly two hours before the present, I snap my fist shut and everything locks into place. I hop off the merry-go-round and immediately turn to the forest. The massive pines are all intact, gilded in the sun's golden rays, and there isn't a trace of smoke. I take that to mean my friends and I are still at the cabin.

I don't have a second to waste, so I get moving. I set off down the deserted road that leads to the woods with a strange pep in my step. I've never managed a time jump that big before. The furthest I've gone into the past has been thirty minutes. And next to the six-decade leap that I just watched my mother pull off, two hours is pretty pathetic, but it's an achievement nonetheless. It's crazy how much motivation you get from having all three of your best friends' lives on the line.

Before long I've made it into the forest. *The forest that'll be burned to the ground in a matter of hours,* I think, walking a little faster. I follow the road for as long as I can, relying on my vaguely-familiar surroundings as waypoints until I reach the spot where we swerved into the trees. Faint tire tracks in the dirt guide me through the overgrown thicket—thorns and outstretched branches tear at my cheeks and snag at my sweatshirt until I finally stumble out into a clearing.

Grayson's family cabin stands before me, exactly as it was the last time I saw it. Except there's someone standing at the door.

"Linda," I call out to the Alumna, making sure to keep a safe distance between us. "What are you doing here?"

She jerks around to face me, and I instinctively take a step back. If she were to tell me now that she just rolled off a mountain and landed in a swamp somewhere before coming here, I would believe it—her eyes are bloodshot, there's dirt all over her uniform and blood is caked in her hair.

"You." She wrinkles her nose at me as if I'm something her dog just tracked in from the backyard rather than one of the very students she's supposed to be after. "Where's your brother?"

"My brother? Oh, he's not here," I say against my better judgement. "He's, uh, back in the city. And so are the others."

She narrows her eyes at me and I shrug, fighting to keep my cool. Of course, at that very moment, there's a loud burst of laughter from behind the cabin. The Alumna turns away from me and starts staggering around the side of the structure, hand braced around the Sim gun at her side.

Shoot. I immediately know that going after her won't do me any good so I round the opposite side of the cabin, coming to a screeching halt by its corner when I suddenly remember the number-one rule of time travel: *you can't be seen. Most definitely not by your own past self.*

I chance a peek beyond the wall to find two people by the fire pit—Grayson and *me*. Past Me has her back turned in my direction, and somehow there's marshmallow in her hair. Without thinking I touch my ponytail, only to find that it's still there. *Great.*

Then I remember I have bigger things to worry about right now. Linda is stalking ominously out of the shadows like an off-brand movie villain, yet neither Grayson or I seem to notice. We're too caught up in our s'mores to look up.

The way the Alumna still grips her weapon pushes me into action. "June!" I hiss in a desperate attempt to get my own attention. Past Me looks around a little bit but then just shrugs and turns back to the fire. So I choose violence. I scoop up the most throwable object within my reach, which comes in the form of a pinecone, and chuck it at my past self.

Sure enough, it conks her right in the head. "Ow!" she yelps, whipping her head around wildly. That's when she finally realizes that Linda's standing a few yards away, and she and Grayson get to their feet.

I grin, mentally high-fiving myself as I watch the scene play out exactly as I remember it: Grayson and me walk up to the Alumna while Ryn and Atlas head up from the creek. We start talking to her, which goes very wrong very fast—Linda swings her attention from my brother to the firepit, and within seconds, the flames have grown to the height of a small skyscraper. The Alumna hurls a giant fireball into a nearby copse of trees and it instantly starts spreading. After a second all of us leap into action, sprinting around the side of the cabin that Linda just emerged from and out of my sight.

I take that as my cue to move. I turn around and head for the front yard, stopping just before I cross into our past selves' field of vision. Flames tear straight through the woods around us as we pause to come up with a plan, then plunge headlong into a blazing world of fire.

My breath catches when I finally register that *I have to follow us.* Which means nearly—or quite possibly *actually* dying for the second time tonight. But I remind myself that if I don't move now, my friends are all doomed.

I take a breath and brace myself. *Here goes nothing,* I think, then launch into the burning woods.

The second I pass the treeline, a wall of flame closes off the forest behind me. *No going back now.* Smoke burns my already-raw throat and stings my eyes. Up ahead, through the fiery ember-filled haze I can see Ryn, starting to lag behind the rest of the group.

And then it happens. A massive, charred branch snaps off a tree and plummets. Ryn sees it coming and tries to dive out of the way, but the branch catches her foot and pulls her to the ground.

"Ryn!" I race to her side, dropping to my knees in the scorched grass. "Are you okay?"

She gapes at me. "Wait. June? But you just—I just saw you run *that* way, how—?"

"I did," I say, talking fast. "But I time-jumped from a merry-go-round and now there are two of me."

"*What?*"

"I'll explain later!" My eyes flit to the giant branch pinning her foot to the ground. "There's no way I'll be able to lift that alone, but Grayson should be getting here right about—"

"*June?*" Right on cue, Grayson bursts from the trees, winded and covered in ash. "What are you doing here? I thought—"

"Time travel," I say simply. It's a huge relief to see them both alive, but we're not off the hook yet. "Here, help me lift this branch—"

Each of us takes one end of the massive log, and together we hoist it off Ryn's foot, setting it down in the grass. "Can you walk?" I ask Ryn.

"Not a chance," she says hoarsely. "Not with a bullet wound *and* whatever that stupid branch did."

My hope fades a little but I don't let it show. I grab Ryn's hand and pull her to her feet, only to look up and realize *we're surrounded.* There's a glowing dome of fire on all sides of us, caving inward and threatening to boil us alive.

"*Shoot,*" I choke out, thinking fast but drawing a blank. The wall of flames three inches from my face blocks out all rational thoughts and replaces them with pure terror. "What do we do? I—"

"Here," says Ryn. Still leaning heavily on me for support, she thrusts a palm toward the blazing trees. The flames begin to spread outward from where we're standing and peel apart like curtains, opening up a clear path through the trees. The heat on my face immediately starts to fade.

"Let's go," Ryn says through gritted teeth, her voice strained. "I can't hold it for long."

And so we do. The three of us press forward, weaving between overcooked trees, the blackened grass crunching beneath our feet. Ryn keeps the flames at bay and clears them away from our path until finally we break free of the trees and stumble out into safe harbor.

I'm instantly hit with a flash of déjà vu. We're standing at the edge of a vast field, full to the brim with fire trucks and shouting first responders and hysterical fire escapees. Firefighters stampede past Ryn, Grayson and I, flooding the forest and causing a massive cloud of smoky steam to rise up above it.

My hands drop to my knees and I bend over, taking in as much fresh air as my lungs will hold. This feeling is too familiar. *Not very many people can say they survived the exact same forest fire twice in one day.*

"Holy cow," Grayson says breathlessly, dragging a hand across his sweaty brow. "Everyone alright?"

"Uh-huh," says Ryn, "but I'd prefer to never do that again if possible."

I breathe out a laugh. "I second that."

There's a beat of silence—and then I come to my senses. I stand bolt upright and scan the area, and sure enough, *there we are*. Past Me and Atlas, both of us looking like we just tried to battle some flaming trees and lost miserably.

"*Shoot,*" I mutter. We're a good fifty yards away, but I'm not taking any chances. I grab Ryn and Grayson by the wrists and drag them behind the nearest fire truck.

"Wh—? June, where are we going?" Ryn blurts loudly.

I whirl around to face her and Grayson once we're safely in the truck's shadow. "*We're* over there," I say, keeping my voice low. "Me and Atlas. We just got out of the fire."

They both stare at me like I have two heads. "June, you're right here," says Grayson, his eyebrows knitted in concern. "Are you sure you feel okay?"

"No—I'm fine. It's time travel," I whisper. "After Atlas and I left the two of you in the woods, we came out here. We'll wait to see if you turn up, but you never do. Then we see a Rainloft helicopter in the sky and we'll be forced to leave. We end up at this old abandoned playground, but eventually the Alumni catch up to us and they get Atlas. So after that, I decided to travel two hours back in time in hopes that I could save the three of you."

I peer around the edge of the fire truck. Past Me and Atlas walk away from a couple of firefighters and sit down in the grass, a little closer to us than I would prefer. Ryn and Grayson poke their heads out there next to me.

"Whoa," Grayson murmurs. "Now that's trippy."

"Be careful," I mutter. "We can't let them see us— under *any* circumstances."

"Why not?" asks Ryn, folding her arms. "If Atlas ends up getting caught by the Alumni, then why don't we just run out there and grab him right now?"

I turn to face her. "Ryn, who's that sitting next to him?"

"Um… you."

"Uh-huh," I say slowly. "And what do you think *you* would do if you looked up and saw *yourself* running towards you?"

"I would think it's some kind of mind-control illusion," she realizes with a frown. "And I might even try to hurt her somehow."

"Exactly," I say, returning my attention to my past self. "And even if *I* were to realize that it's time travel, there's no way Atlas would believe it. He'd never trust that enough to come with us if there were two of me right in front of him."

"Wow," Ryn grumbles. "Time travel is really annoying."

We watch in silence for the better part of half an hour. I didn't realize when I was living it through for the first time just how long Atlas and I waited before the Rainloft helicopter forced us to leave. Ryn leans back against the fire truck with her arms crossed, and Grayson and I keep an eye on Past Me and Atlas. A few times, first responders come by to shoot us strange looks or ask what we're doing, and I brush them off as quickly as possible so that they don't have time to register exactly who we are. If they did, without Atlas to send them away, we'd be pretty doomed.

Ryn looks around the edge of the truck, stepping a little too far out of its shadow for my comfort level. Then she pulls back with a sharp gasp, her eyes wide. "He saw me," she whispers. "Atlas saw me. I'm sorry, I didn't mean to—"

I press a finger to my lips and she falls silent. All three of us stand statue-still. Through the buzz of firefighters' shouts and steady streams of water pouring into the trees, I can very faintly pick up Atlas's voice. "Hold on—I just saw…" he starts. "Nevermind. It was nothing."

I breathe a sigh of relief. "It's okay. We're good."

A small eternity later, out of the blue, Grayson says "You're leaving."

Sure enough, we are. Atlas is headed for the worn-down road that leads to the abandoned playground and I'm jogging to catch up to him.

I take a step out from behind the firetruck, but then rethink it and pull back. "We can't just follow us," I say out loud, rifling through all my memories of this specific moment. "If I remember right, that road is silent. There's no way we wouldn't hear us coming."

For a second the two of them are quiet.

"I have an idea," Grayson hesitates, his tone full of uncertainty. "June, you said the two of you end up at a playground down that road, right?"

"Yep."

"How *far* down, exactly?"

"Um." I scrunch up my nose, racking my brain. "I don't know, maybe a mile or so?"

"Okay," he nods slowly, and I can see the gears grinding in his mind. "I think I can do that."

"Do what?"

He turns to face Ryn and I. "I've never done it before, and I can't promise it'll go well, but I *think* I can teleport all three of us over there. It's risky. I've seen my teachers at the Rainloft do it before, but I've never tried it myself."

Ryn shrugs indifferently. "We've already almost died about eleven billion different times in the last three days," she points out. "I'll take my chances."

I can't argue there. "Okay then," says Grayson, extending a hand to each of us. I take it. "Here goes nothing."

There's a blinding flash of green light. It's like I'm watching this happen on a movie screen because there's *no way* this is real life. The ground disappears beneath my feet, the wind stops blowing and suddenly I have no perception of space whatsoever. A dark vignette creeps up around the edges of my vision. It swallows all the green light whole and then—darkness.

I hover in nothingness for half a second. Then the world explodes into color and my feet slam into solid ground, sending shockwaves up my bones. I almost manage to stay upright but fall back into the mulch for what feels like the tenth time today.

"Oh my *gosh*," Ryn says a few feet to my right, but I can barely hear her over the ringing in my ears. The playground around me is humming and blindingly bright even though nightfall is mere minutes away.

"It can be disorienting the first time. I'm just glad you're both still alive," Grayson says lightly. "But, uh, we might want to move. Because you're right there, June."

I whip around to face the road. Past Me and Atlas are coming our way, and we're still safely out of their field of vision—but just barely. I scan the area, my eyes landing on a random clump of trees a ways away from the playground. "There," I say.

I'm still trying to reacquaint myself with gravity as I scrabble over there, Ryn and Grayson at my heels. We duck behind the trees' thick trunks and I peek out to watch the scene unfold.

It happens exactly as I remember it: Atlas and I stop in the middle of the road when we hear sirens, then head for the playground and hide behind the big blue tube slide. A Rainloft SUV cruises down the road and straight past us. A second later, Past Me walks out to the center of the mulch. I just stand there for a second, then my face lights up in memory and I make for the swingset.

"What are you doing?" Ryn whispers. "Are you *swinging?*"

I can't help but cringe at myself. "Um—yeah." Past Me drops onto one of the swings, grinning like a lunatic. Atlas just stares at me like I've lost my mind. Which, in hindsight, I most definitely have.

"Wow. You think Grayson and I just died, and now you're playing on a playground," Ryn whispers in amusement. "Glad to know that's how you feel about us."

"That's not—" I sigh. "Believe me, this…wasn't my finest moment."

Atlas reluctantly agrees to push Past Me on the swing. A few seconds later she flings herself into the air, shouting 'Superman' at the top of her lungs.

Part of me seriously wants to crawl into a hole and die of embarrassment. Ryn and Grayson just watch with unreadable expressions, and it doesn't seem like they're judging me but they have to be judging me. I know *I'm* judging myself.

Past Me totally wipes out in the mulch and Atlas comes around the swingset to make fun of me. Then he helps me up. We start talking, and I'm too far away to hear what we're saying, but I know what it is. I remember.

"Uh, June," Grayson says uneasily, pointing at something in the distance. I pry my gaze from the scene before me to see what it is, and then my heart skips a beat. *Another Rainloft SUV.* The one that takes Atlas.

But something's wrong. "We don't see it," I murmur, straining to remember what happens next. "We're supposed to see it, and we're supposed to hide, why are we still talking?"

"Here," says Ryn. She bends down and pulls off one of her sparkly purple shoes—the one with the singed hole blasted in the side.

I freeze. "Ryn, what are you doing?"

"I'm saving your lives."

"No, we'll *know*—"

But it's too late. She steps back and launches the shoe into the air. I watch in horror as It blasts a crater in the mulch, and both Atlas and me whip around to face it. Past Me picks it up, looking utterly bewildered.

With a flick of Ryn's wrist, the shoe starts levitating out of my hand. It rockets back across the playground and into the road, where it's flattened by one of the SUV's monstrous tires.

"No way," I laugh under my breath. "That actually worked."

"Let this be a lesson," Ryn says smugly. "Don't doubt me."

"I really should've learned that by now," I admit.

"Yeah. No kidding."

"What do we do next?" asks Grayson. When I look back at the playground, I'm nowhere to be found. *Hiding in the big blue tube,* I realize. Atlas stands there with his hands in his pockets, ready to greet the Alumni.

The SUV's doors pop open and two armed Alumni step out with their Sim guns raised, already aiming at Atlas. Avalon floats out of the car behind them. "Don't move," one of the Alumni spits.

"And now we move," I say.

Before I've fully thought it through, I fly out from behind the trees and make a break for the playground. Ryn and Grayson follow me. Immediately, both Alumni shift their aim to the three of us and open fire.

"Stop right there!" the Alumnus yells. I don't slow down. Ducking and dodging bullets left and right, I leap onto the playground and grab my brother.

"*What* the—" he starts before I yank him down behind a slide. Bullets *ting* off of metal structures and blast holes straight through the plastic slides—until all at once, they stop. I chance a look out into the open just in time to see both Alumni fly through the frosty air like frisbees and simultaneously hit the SUV with a deafening *crash.* The car skids halfway across the road under the impact. Obviously Ryn's doing.

Grayson dashes over to the heap of Alumni and car and for a second, I think he's about to help them up. But then he sets a hand on each of their shoulders and in a flash of green light, both of them have vanished. Gone like they'd never been there in the first place.

That just leaves Avalon. She stands eerily still at the center of the mulch, and she doesn't look fazed in the slightest. She's looking directly at me and it's hard to tell behind her mask, but I think she's smiling.

"Nicely done, June," she says in her buttery-smooth tone. "I knew you would pull it off. But I'd strongly advise you vacate the area." She gestures to the tube where Past Me is still hiding, then tilts her chin downward in what I assume is a more serious expression. "Goodbye for now—though hopefully not for long. I won't force you either way, but I trust you to make the right decision."

Now everyone's attention is on me. I swallow hard. "Yeah."

She walks to the edge of the playground and turns her face to the moon. I take that to mean it's time for us to leave. "Come on," I say to Atlas. "We have to hide."

He, Ryn and Grayson follow me back to the little copse of trees we just came from. As soon as I turn back around, Past Me emerges from the blue tube.

This is right about where the relief should start to sink in—the keyword being *should.* I've saved all three of my friends. We're all safe, at least for the moment. But the one thing that's thrown a wrench into it all, that's stopping me from jumping for joy and living happily ever after, is Avalon. *Not Avalon,* I remind myself.

I trust you to make the right decision. Those words sting. Because I know the 'right decision' that she's implying—or, rather, the choice that *she* thinks is right and that I'm starting to think is right myself—and I hate it with every ounce of my being. In some shadowy corner of my brain, I know that the truth of it all will have to come out eventually. I know that my friends—the friends that I've just spent a week actively trying to end the Rainloft's existence with, that have painfully valid reasons to do more than just hate Avalon—might just kill me for it.

"June, what are you doing now?" Grayson's voice calls me back to my senses. Past Me is standing in front of Avalon, my expression completely blank like a frozen computer screen. When Avalon extends her hand to me, I take it. And then we both disappear.

"It's—it's a long story. I, um—I couldn't even begin to explain it," I say, grappling for words that don't really seem to exist. I turn to Atlas, who looks more lost than I've seen him look in years. "I'm glad you're alive," I say. "I'm glad you're *all* alive. Really."

"Why wouldn't I be alive?" asks Atlas. He looks at Ryn and Grayson. "How are *they* alive? And how were there *two* of you?"

"It's time travel. Get with the program," says Ryn.

Atlas turns back to me, a hint of surprise in his expression. "Well done."

"Okay, so—next steps," says Grayson, clapping his hands together. "Before that… *minor* interruption… we were planning on letting the Alumni bring us back up to the Rainloft, right? So we could bring it down from there?"

"Uh-huh," Ryn grins. "After all this time, Avalon's reign of terror is coming to an end. We're finally going to bring it down."

There's a stretch of silence, and I see my opening. "I have something to tell you guys," I say through a long breath out. Now everyone's eyes are on me and I can't help but wish I could backtrack and tell them *ha-ha, that was a joke, gotcha there.* Instead, I force myself to face Atlas. "First of all, well, this won't be easy for you to hear. But I spoke with Avalon a couple of hours ago, and I got to see her without her mask on. And it turns out she's… um." I know exactly what I need to say: *Avalon is Mom.* It's only three words. It shouldn't be hard, but my mouth just flat-out refuses to say the words. "She's… well—"

A twig snaps behind me. When I spin around to see who's there I'm met by a blinding white light shining straight in my face.

"Put your hands in the air," says a gruff voice behind the light. I blink repeatedly to get my eyes to adjust and once they do, I have a clear view of the uniformed figure before me. *An Alumnus.* Not just one—a whole pack of them.

Past them, a few yards away, is a pair of Rainloft helicopters. It really is wild how quiet those things are.

"I *said,* put your hands in the air," the flashlight-holding Alumnus growls. It takes me a second to realize that *he's talking to me.* Ryn, Grayson and Atlas have all obeyed his order and they're watching me expectantly.

I know immediately that they're not surrendering—they're going through with our original plan. *If the Alumni take us up, then they're going to bring it down.*

I'm completely out of options. It's either give up and hope with all hope that they've revamped security at the Rainloft, or try to escape the Alumni and blatantly disobey my mother's orders to let them take me back up. With the hulking group of Alumni after me coupled with my utter lack of athleticism and coordination, the odds of the latter actually working are slim.

So that leaves me with no choice.

I put my hands in the air. All at once, the Alumni rush forward, each of them equipped with a set of handcuffs. In a matter of seconds my hands are locked behind my back and I'm being forcefully guided out from behind the trees and into the back of a helicopter next to Ryn.

An Alumnus slams the door shut behind me and climbs into the front seat. I don't even notice when we take off—if it weren't for the view out the window of the playground and the forest shrinking beneath us as we climb higher into the clouds, I'd think we were still on the ground. And if all goes my way, it'll be another half a decade before we touch land again.

It's funny how that's exactly what I want, and yet I dread it more than anything.

After a short eternity, I look out the window and *there it is*. A monstrous silhouette behind a shield of dark clouds, hovering ominously miles above the ground.

The Rainloft Academy.

We're back.

Ryn winks at me, a competitive grin spread across her face. "Let's blow this popsicle stand."

I plaster across my face the most genuine smile I can manage at the moment, then I turn back to the window and swallow hard. *This is happening*. I stupidly put off trying to change their minds so now the Rainloft is coming down.

And I have no idea how to stop it.

Chapter Eleven

And that's when I wake up.

In my bed in my cold Rainloft dorm room, in the dark, surrounded by piles of overdue schoolwork and discarded uniform parts. I never left. *It was all a dream.*

Not really. But it very well could've been. Every morning since I got back here, I've had to stop and question myself: *did that actually happen? Or was it all just some crazy dream my brain conjured up?*

Sometimes I can't help but wish that were the case. It would certainly be easier that way. Then, everyone here wouldn't treat me like I'm a bomb about to blow up. Then, I wouldn't have remembered just how great it is to have real friends and I would've been able to carry on with Thomas and Fiona as my only company. Then, I wouldn't have gotten a taste of what life is like outside of the Rainloft's walls and it would've been infinitely easier for me to live out the rest of my days as a charitable prisoner.

But that's not what happened.

I switch on the harsh white lamp on my nightstand and promptly go blind for a few seconds. I muster up the courage to drag myself out of bed and change into the brand-new copy of my uniform that they had to make for me upon my return. Ryn and I both abandoned our old uniforms somewhere in the Starview Mall in favor of Halle Ross clothes that were much more comfortable and objectively far more fashion-forward. The thought makes me inexplicably sad. I know it shouldn't. That was one of many near-death experiences on our little 'vacation' (as my teachers have called it an excessive number of times). I shouldn't want to go back there and relive that day as much as I do.

I smooth out my wrinkled mustard-yellow blazer and consider tying my hair back in its usual ponytail but change my mind. I don't feel like putting in any more than the bare minimum amount of effort today, so I leave it down.

I swing my leather messenger bag over my shoulder and leave the room. As expected, Fiona stands outside my door, leaning back against the wall with her arms crossed in an over-the-top attempt to look cool.

"Finally. You're up," she says around the wad of bubblegum in her mouth. "I've been waiting out here for *years*."

"I highly doubt that," I grumble. When I set off down the mostly-empty Type Three hallway, she trails me. "So where'd you get the gum?"

It's one of the many Rainloft rules: chewing gum is, under no circumstances, allowed. Professor Becker, our Rainloft history teacher, would sentence Fiona to detention for life if she were to catch her, and I think she knows that. She flaps a hand dismissively. "Oh, they started handing it out at lunches," she lies to my face, snapping her gum obnoxiously. "You wouldn't know. You weren't there."

"Ah. Just like the free puppies they started raffling off at dinner?"

"That only lasted a day," Fiona counters, tossing her perfectly-straight blond hair. "You just had to be there. I'd be really jealous if I were you. And super embarrassed that I tried to escape like that. That was really dumb."

I sigh. "Yeah. Maybe it was."

"I'm gonna hand you off to Thomas after breakfast," she says passively. "He'll take you to Combat. I have Rainloft History on the other side of the school, so."

"Okay."

I could say the Rainloft is exactly the same as I left it, but that would be a lie. The school itself is the same— same colorless, lifeless decorating, same uncomfortable tile floors and the inescapable echo that comes with them—but there are a few things that've changed.

For one, I've lost my privilege of going anywhere without an escort. According to my teachers, it's so that I always have someone to keep an eye on me and make sure I don't do anything 'crazy or rash.' Hence, Fiona. She and my second favorite person in the world, Thomas, have been tag-teaming as my personal bodyguards for the past few days. Now, thanks to Avalon, mealtimes are no longer the only parts of my day that I have to deal with them.

We walk in blissful silence for a full minute before Fiona speaks again. "So why didn't you tell me?" she asks casually. "Not that I would have, like, wanted to go with you or anything. But we're, like, friends. Why didn't you tell me you were escaping?"

"I don't know," I say, and she visibly deflates a little.

We round the corner into the giant dining hall where five long tables stand between us and the breakfast line, each of them jam-packed with students in a different uniform color. Before I head to my seat, I do a quick headcount: I spot Ryn at her table, talking with one of the other Type Ones. I check Grayson off my list when I find him in the long breakfast line. And then there's Atlas at the Type Two table.

Once I've assured that none of them are posing an active threat to the school's existence, I follow Fiona to our seats. The seating arrangement is basically the same as it used to be: same people, only shifted over to the farthest end of the table. After our return, Avalon took it upon herself to meticulously redesign the cafeteria layout. Seeing as my table is sandwiched between the Two and Four tables, this way I am, under no circumstances, in the eyeline of Grayson or Atlas. Because according to Avalon's logic, if one of us so much as makes eye contact with another, the entire world is at risk. I understand her need to protect the timeline and all, but this seems a little extreme.

Having Atlas back at the Rainloft has been strange, to say the least. By now, I hardly have any recollection of the years before he escaped—all of my personal memories have been replaced by the hundreds of worn-out, probably-false rumors that've circulated endlessly around the school for the past few years. Seeing him in that jade-green uniform again feels like a two-part dream—after so long you start to forget that the first dream ever happened, but one night when you fall asleep, it randomly picks up where it left off and it's like *oh yeah, this again.*

News of Atlas's great return had reached practically everybody in the school before we even set foot back in the building and sent the entire student body into a frenzied, frantic epidemic of rumor-spreading.

"You're late," Thomas observes by way of greeting as Fiona and I take our usual seats. "Why are you late?"

"I overslept," I tell him.

"Why did you oversleep?"

"Um." I pause. "Because I was tired?"

"Why were you tired?"

"Well, I didn't get to bed until pretty late last night, so—"

"Why didn't you go to bed on time?"

I sigh, finally registering what he's trying to do. "I'm not used to going to bed on school time because I destroyed my sleep schedule over my 'vacation'," I admit flatly.

Thomas sits back in his seat, looking way too proud of himself. "There you have it," he says smugly. "Reason number twenty-seven why escaping the Rainloft is a terrible idea."

Reason number twenty-seven why I wish it weren't against the rules to punch your classmates. I have to bite back the words. By now I know better than to say something like that out loud.

While I can't actually see her, I can feel one of the lunch monitors' eyes boring into the back of my head. So I catch myself, flip my disgruntled, mildly-hostile frown to a terse smile and tell Thomas "Thanks for looking out for me. I appreciate it."

I turn to see the lunch lady walking away, her suspicions adequately extinguished. I let my smile drop again and let Thomas bore me with another lecture on how unwise my choices were until the end of breakfast.

A few hours later, I'm sitting in my Rainloft History classroom and now it's Professor Becker lecturing me rather than one of my own peers. I've been walking around on autopilot all day, letting my feet carry me from class to class, my head somewhere entirely different. This is how every day has felt since my return. Now that I've had a taste of what life is like outside of these walls, I have zero motivation to care about whatever my teachers spend hours droning on about. Everything about the Rainloft just feels so dull and lifeless. And yet, I've made it my number-one priority to protect it from my own friends. Funny how your wants and your goals can totally contradict each other like that.

"… and that's why Headmistress Avalon founded the Academy. I hope you all have found this project to be just as intriguing and enlightening as I have," says Professor Becker in the most bored voice I've ever heard. She pauses. "Well, those of you who were *here* for the project, that is."

I start to feel the red imprint my hand has left on my cheek from slumping against it for so long and catch

Becker's beady eyes fixed on me. It's not until this exact moment when I realize I've been zoned out for the entire class period and haven't registered a single word she's said. *Crap,* I curse myself in the split second before my teacher announces "Miss Winters."

"Yes?" I say weakly.

"Can you tell me the name of the company that designed the Rainloft Academy?"

For a second the only sound is the buzz of the bright fluorescent lights above us while I attempt to rewind my memory, searching for the answer, but it's gone. Then I'm saved by a voice on the opposite side of the room. "It's Willow Tech Construction," Ryn responds for me. "Professor Becker, may I please use the restroom?"

"Fine," Becker glowers, even though Ryn is already out of her seat. Her escort, another Type One girl with white-blonde pigtails, trails after her. "Raise your hand next time, Miss Sharp."

Ryn intentionally takes the long route to the door and subtly taps me on the shoulder as she passes by my desk. I take that to mean I should follow. "I, um, also need to use the restroom," I mumble, then fly out of the classroom before Becker has the chance to stop me.

Ryn is waiting for me in the hallway, her escort standing patiently by. She starts walking as soon as she sees me. "Come on," she mutters as I catch up. "We don't have long before Becker starts to get suspicious."

She cuts across the hallway, and her escort and I follow her into the girls' lavatory. Ryn quickly scans the row of stalls to make sure there's nobody else in here, then whirls to face me. "So here's the deal: I came up with a plan," she says, clapping her hands together, and already I have a sense of impending doom. "Tomorrow night, during dinner, we'll leave the dining hall and head for the control room. All four of us. We'll fight through the guards if we have to, but I think by now we've proven that won't be an issue, and then we'll bring it down. Boom. It's that eas—"

"Wait," I cut her off. My eyes wander to her escort, who's been staring up at me through round blue eyes and I don't think she's blinked once since we left our classroom. I look back at Ryn and raise an eyebrow, hoping the gesture gets across the question I don't want to ask right in front of this girl's face.

"Oh! *Duh,*" says Ryn, smacking herself in the forehead. "June, this is Addison Prior. Second-year. She's my escort, and she's in on it all."

"You can call me Addy," the girl says eagerly. "Or don't. Whatever floats your boat. Oh, I am *so* excited to finally meet you. I'm your *biggest* fan. I just love what you all are doing with the rebellion and everything. It's about time someone stood up to Avalon!"

Those words feel sort of like a slap across the face. Seeing as I'm basically on Avalon's side now. "I agree," I get out, a heavy load of shame settling on my shoulders. "It's about time."

Great. Now I'm a traitor and *a flat-out liar.* I've dug myself a hole that's almost to the point of being too deep to climb out of. It's only getting deeper the longer I push off telling the truth of where my loyalties lie, but right now just doesn't feel like the right time. Professor Becker will be expecting us back in a matter of minutes. I can't just drop a massive truth bomb on Ryn like that and then ditch her to go back to class. That's not something a friend would do, right? But when else am I going to tell her?

"So, are you in?" Ryn asks hopefully.

"I, ah…" In the next three seconds, I mentally calculate all the possible outcomes of every response I can think of, but it comes clear that there is no good way out of this. "Yeah. I'm in."

"Amazing!" Ryn exclaims. She holds out her hand, palm-down, like they do in the movies. "Team, um, Anti-Rainloft, on three."

Her escort, Addison, bounces forward and enthusiastically adds her hand to the stack. Feeling guilty and conflicted as ever, I do the same. Not two seconds after Ryn's counted down and we've thrown our hands in the air, Becker's voice rings out through the hallways. "Oh, you two are in for it now!"

"June, spread the word to Grayson," Ryn mutters hastily. "I usually pass by Atlas in the hallway after this class, so I can talk to him then."

"Got it," I manage. My head is starting to spin from all the lying. I don't get how some people do it so easily.

Addison, on the other hand, looks like she's about to burst from excitement. "I love being a part of something!" she sings. "Oh, June, can I have your autograph?"

That feels like a wound in salt, but I sign her sketch pad anyway, knowing for a fact that she'll regret asking as soon as the truth comes out. If it ever does.

Before I know it we're being corralled back into the Rainloft History classroom by a red-faced Professor Becker. She yells at us for a while and I think she deals out some form of punishment, but I'm too distracted to focus on her stream of reprimands. I have bigger things to worry about. If I don't find a way to change Ryn's mind, then the Rainloft is coming down tomorrow.

Three classes and one epically boring dinner later, I find myself ignoring the tower of homework on my desk in favor of pacing back and forth around my dorm room. I have no other choice but to come up with a way to stop this. I'm the only one who knows Ryn's plan and isn't actively going along with it. And, seeing as my friends still think I'm on their side, I have an advantage compared to someone like Avalon, if she were to try and stop them. Obviously they'd be more likely to listen to their loyal (for now) teammate than the very woman they're fighting against. But how am I supposed to tell the truth without them immediately writing me off as a lying traitor and going through with the plan anyway? After all, I'm not exactly a vital member of the team. Ryn, Grayson and Atlas would easily be able to fight past the guards and Alumni without me. I'm more of an impairment than anything in a fight. Just another person for the ones with helpful powers to keep track of, for them to save when I inevitably wind up in danger. They don't need that. Why wouldn't my friends just ditch me instead of wasting their time on a total backstabber?

My head is a jumbled mess, my thoughts too tangled for me to flesh this all out by myself. I need someone to bounce ideas off of. Usually that *someone* would come in the form of one of my teammates, but since they're the ones I'm conspiring against (as evil as that word makes me feel) I'm completely alone in this. I have nobody on my side.

Well. Maybe not nobody.

Without even bothering to think this through, I leave my room and I'm halfway across the near-deserted school in a matter of seconds. The dim cracks of light that shine out from under closed doors as my the only thing between me and total darkness, I pad down hallway after hallway, keeping my steps as light as possible. Though I'm not quite sure why. If I'm caught by guards, what are they going to do? Take me to the headmistress's office? Seeing as that's exactly the room I'm trying to find now, I'd consider that a favor. Four years as a student here and I still don't know my way around this school.

Even with all the added time it takes me to get there due to the absurd number of wrong turns I make, I reach the ornate double doors to Headmistress Avalon's office completely undetected. Hesitantly, I raise a fist to knock, but before I even make contact with the wood there sounds a muffled "Come in" from inside the room.

I shrug and let myself in. My mother sits at her desk, gray eyes already fastened on me from behind her mask. The low blue lamplight casts sharp shadows across her face and the odd, mismatched furniture scattered around the small room. The walls are covered in haphazard collages of the most random things imaginable—I note multiple portraits of kittens, an old superhero poster, a large oil painting of a dishwasher. Avalon's white wood desk is eerily clear, no evidence to suggest she'd been busy with anything before I got here. Like she's been expecting me.

"I've been expecting you," she says, immediately confirming that theory. She gestures to the chair on the opposite side of her desk. "Have a seat."

I stiffly cross the room and sit down in front of her. I already feel very weird being in here, but I can't quite put my finger on *why*—maybe it's all the unusual decor, or because last time I was in this room I was completely oblivious to Avalon's true identity. Back when I was under the impression that Avalon Lockhart was exactly who she said she was, she fit perfectly inside this bizarre office. After all, there's not a whole lot about our headmistress that screams 'normal'. But knowing that this room's decorator is none other than my mother… I just can't seem to connect the two. The Lucy Winters that I knew would quite possibly faint if she walked into a room that looked like this. She was the single most organized, systematic person I'd ever met. I guess the change of her name warranted a total personality flip to go along with it. It doesn't make sense, but then again, nothing about anything really makes sense right now. I decide this belongs at the very bottom of my list of problems.

"Headmist—er, *Mom*, there's something I have to tell you," I confess, forcing myself to focus on her and not this room's wacko design choices. When she motions for me to continue, I decide there's no going back now and say it. "They're planning on bringing down the Rainloft. My friends are, I mean. They're going to shut off the engine tomorrow night."

I've fully prepared myself to grab the telephone off her desk and dial the medical wing when she inevitably faints due to shock—but that doesn't happen. She just gives a small *hmph* and says "I assumed as much."

"What?" I blurt out. "You knew?"

"Not everything, but I suspected there was some sort of master plan like that in the works," my mother says evenly. All I can do is gape at her, so she elaborates. "If I know the first thing about you and your brother, it's that you're stubborn. Both of you. You would never give up as easily as you did, especially not Atlas. I've been trying consistently for the past two years to bring him back up here, and he's found a way to evade capture every single time. I knew there was no way he'd give in just like that, without any form of fight or fanfare—there was something else afoot. It was a brilliant plan. Both of you are incredibly intelligent. But you got that trait from me."

I nod, taking all of that in. "Okay, so… now we have to stop the three of them from going through with it." For a second she just stares at me. "What?"

"I'm just so glad I have you on my side," says my mother, her tone suspiciously genuine. "It's lonely, you know. Feeling like you're in the wrong all the time, as if the only ones who support your choices are the people required by law to do so. I truly appreciate you trusting me on this, June. It helps more than you might realize to have my daughter on my team."

Those words make me feel both better and much worse about my switch in allegiance. "I'm not… on your side," I say. "Ryn, Grayson and Atlas are all still my friends, and friend trumps person-who-sacrificed-all-our-lives-for-the-sake-of-this-one-silly-timeline. This isn't me going against them; I'm just trying to keep them from making this huge of a mistake. Like any good friend would do."

"I understand," she says, unfazed as ever. "I'm simply glad you've kept your loyalty from tainting your rationality and chosen not to make that mistake along with them."

"Yeah." I can't help hanging my head a little. "So how are we going to stop the others?"

"That *is* the question." Avalon stands up and starts pacing slowly around the back half of the room. "The most logical course of action would be to prevent the three of them from going through with it in the first place, as I can no longer count on my Alumni to fight them off at the control room doors. You four have defied them too many times already, I couldn't risk leaving the entire Academy in their unskilled hands again. Perhaps I could lock your friends inside their dorm rooms, station the entire body of Alumni outside their doors for if they try to break out? I could brainwash them all into joining me… have their combat teachers stage some accidents that render them incapable of fighting—"

"Mom, *no,*" I cut her off because these ideas are getting progressively more morbid as they go on. "You're not going to win them over by brute force. You should just try and talk to them."

She stops pacing and looks at me like I just suggested she change their minds by means of interpretive dance. "Talk to them?"

"Yes, talk to them," I say. The gears are really turning now. "For starters, Ryn wants to bring down the Rainloft as a way to avenge her parents—the ones you killed in the Lebanon Massacre. So apologize to her."

My mother shakes her head. "No, no simple apology could ever make up for what I did. Nothing I could say would possibly be enough."

"Have you ever tried?" I return. "I mean, you're right— words aren't going to fix everything. An apology won't bring Ryn's parents back, but if you mean what you say to her, then that has to count for something."

She nods thoughtfully. "And the others?"

"Grayson won't be difficult," I say, thinking back to our conversation at the cabin. "He didn't agree with me, but he didn't disagree either. I think if there were a way for *me* to talk to him, he wouldn't be too hard to sway."

"You should do that tonight," says Avalon. "Whatever you need to do, I'll instruct the guards to let you two interact. Now, what about your brother?"

"Tell him the truth," I say simply. "Tell Atlas who you really are, explain why you've done all the things you have—that should help."

"He hates me, though," she points out, "and for a perfectly valid reason. Knowing his own mother put him through all that I did will only make matters worse."

"Believe me, the worst thing you could do is keep on lying to him," I advise. "Lay it all out exactly as it is. Focus on gaining his trust or he'll never believe a word you say."

She pauses, then sighs. "Okay. But would you help me? Clearly Atlas trusts you, and if you're with me, I think that would help him. If I call you both down to my office tomorrow, would you be willing to do that?"

My initial response would be a solid *no*—my brother and I are in a good place for the first time in years, but our newfound bond is still fragile and I'd rather not risk losing that again by openly siding with his mortal enemy. But she does have a point. "Fine. But you have to do the explaining. This is your battle, not mine."

"I will," she says with a heavy sigh. Then she turns to look me in the eye. "Thank you for helping me with this. I've never had the greatest… what do you call them… *people skills.*"

So I got that from you. I can't help but grin a little. "You're welcome."

"So, in summary, you'll go to speak with Grayson once you leave here," my mother says. "I'll call Ryn down to my office tomorrow, then you and Atlas later."

"Sounds like a plan."

We're both quiet for a minute after that. The surface of her desk is littered with framed pictures, all turned to face her. I dare to reach out and spin one around. Sure enough, it's an old photo of Atlas and me, maybe seven or eight years old at the time. We're both covered in sand, grinning at the camera, and each of us has one arm slung around the other's shoulders. A perfectly-manicured golfing green blurs in the backdrop.

"Ah! I remember that day," says my mother, clasping her hands together. "There's a bit of a story behind that picture, if I do recall. Your father and I decided to take you kids golfing for the first time, but neither of you had any sort of interest in the sport. All you cared about was the golf cart." She laughs. "You begged us to let you drive it, but we refused, as it didn't belong to us. Then, as soon as our backs were turned…"

"We committed grand theft auto and drove it straight into the sand trap," I finish.

At that, we both start cracking up. "Oh, it was hysterical," my mother says. "In the mere three seconds that we left you two to your own devices, you devised a plan and executed it so, so poorly. The company was furious—it took nearly ten workers to lug that cart out of the sand—but I didn't mind. It was my favorite thing, watching my kids have so much fun together."

I smile. "I take full credit for that idea, by the way," I admit. "I'm just shocked I got Atlas to go along with it."

"I'm not." Her eyes settle on me. "You did everything together. Whenever one of you had an idea—no matter how reckless it was—the other would support it fully without a second thought. As hectic as the past weeks have been, it's been wonderful to see you two reconnect after all these years."

She hangs her head a little. "I suppose it was me who took that away from you in the first place, wasn't it? What a mother I am. First I left you all. Then I stole you from each other. I really did destroy our family, didn't I?"

I nod, because she's not wrong. "Yeah."

"Sometimes I wonder if I made the wrong choice," she confesses, a faraway look in her eyes. "I chose the timeline over my own family, who needed me. I should've—"

"Mom, you didn't have a choice," I remind her. "If you hadn't gone back in time to start the Rainloft, then nobody would have, and the entire world would've been doomed."

She nods. "Yes, you're right," she says, but I can tell she's not convinced.

There are still dozens more pictures on her desk, so I point to one and ask "What's this one?" We spend the next hour reminiscing, recalling the stories behind each individual photo—some are of me and Atlas, some of all four of us, some of just her and my dad, a face I haven't seen in eons. Laughing with my mother is something I haven't done in years, and it takes me back to a time when things were so much simpler. I almost forget just how pressing our current situation is, until the clock on the wall jolts me back into reality and I remember there's still something I have to get done tonight.

"I should go talk to Grayson," I say, still grinning as I rise from my seat. "Before it gets too late."

My mother wishes me good-luck and I leave her office, off to make my second stop of the night. I think of Grayson, trying to figure out what my approach is going to be. It needs to be personal, probably, so I rack my brain, trying to recall some of his interests. I remember how I met him and a masterful plan forms itself in my head as I walk.

When I reach Grayson's dorm room, his lights are still on. I knock briskly then let myself in. Still in full uniform, Grayson sits at the desk, chipping away at his pile of homework like the responsible student I most definitely am not. He spins around as soon as he hears me. "*June?*" His eyes go wide. "What are you—?"

"I need you to come with me," I say, nodding back at the door. To his credit, he follows me without any further questions. Just as my mother promised, the guards let us walk freely through the dark halls, even though this degree of disobedience should earn us at least a year of detention. That doesn't mean I don't catch the side-eyes and disapproving looks the Alumni shoot us as we pass.

I've never actually *been* to the room I'm taking us now, so we end up going in multiple circles around the building before I find the door. I have to hope Grayson doesn't notice. Once we reach what looks sort of like it could be the correct entrance, I pull it open and let us inside.

The Rainloft's training grounds shut down hours ago, but this room still hums with quiet energy—dimmed fluorescents buzzing overhead, steel appliances ticking with leftover heat. Everything is spotless, polished to a gleam, and scented faintly with lemon cleaner.

"The kitchen?" Grayson asks. "Why?"

I spin to face him. "Hear me out," I say. "There's something I have to explain to you, and this is the best way I know how to do it."

I scan the room like a vulture on the hunt and zero in on a salt shaker sitting in a corner. In one fluid motion, I seize the salt, unscrew the cap and dump the entire thing onto the countertop.

I jab a finger at the grainy dune I've created. "This is Lavon," I state. "The entire population—all thirteen gazillion or however many of us there are now."

"Grayson raises an eyebrow. "Okay…?"

Gingerly, I pluck a singular grain of salt from the pile and hold it up to him. "This is the portion of Lavon that's forced to be involved with the Rainloft. Alumni. Our families. Us. Pushed to our limits on the daily, captive, isolated, and permanently changed."

A shadow crosses Grayson's face. Clearly he knows where I'm going with this, but he lets me keep talking. I set aside my one grain of salt, then motion to the remainder of the pile. It looks heartbreakingly untouched. "That's the rest of the world," I say, the words heavy. "Because of our sacrifice, they get to live their lives in peace. We have the opportunity to save *so many people*. Even if it costs us *our* lives, isn't it worth it? In the grand scheme of things, the number of us that have to face the consequences of a crime-free world is *microscopic*." I gesture to the lonely grain of salt and let that image say the rest.

"So what I'm hearing is, you've really changed your mind?" asks Grayson, his brow furrowed. "You think the Rainloft should stay up?"

"Yeah." I sigh. "I do."

I can see him mulling all that over in his head. "You're right," he says finally. "Bringing down the Rainloft is a solution to a problem that only a tiny portion of the population has, but the fallout would impact the entire world."

With one sweep of my hand the entire pile of salt is on the ground. I realize too late how terrible of a choice this is, but the dramatic effect makes it totally worth it.

"I think maybe I've known all along," Grayson admits, tone tinted with guilt. "I've known from the start that we couldn't go and end the Rainloft's existence entirely. That would doom the entire world. I think I just went along with it, since you and Ryn and Atlas are my friends. I knew how much Avalon has hurt you all, so I wanted to be supportive. I didn't really think we'd get this far with it. But now that they're planning on bringing it down *tomorrow*..."

"We have to do something about it," I finish. "Don't worry about that. I've already worked out a plan with Avalon."

"Wait. Avalon?"

"Yeah," I say. "Oh, she's my mother, by the way."

So I spend the next hour explaining and re-explaining how it's even possible that Avalon has been my mother all this time while Grayson and I broom up my salt mess. Once the kitchen has been returned to the state we found it in, it's time for us to leave.

"I liked your salt metaphor," he tells me as we're walking out the kitchen doors. "Very persuasive."

I grin and take a little bow. "What can I say? Cooking analogies are my specialty."

Once I get back to my dorm room, a fraction of the weight has been lifted off my shoulders. *One down, two to go,* I think as I flop onto my bed. Maybe this won't be as difficult as I thought. Ryn and Atlas will be just as easy to win over, the Rainloft will still be afloat once tomorrow is done, and we'll all get to live happily ever after. Right?

I make sure to knock on the wood of my nightstand before I fall asleep.

*   *   *

The next day arrives with an unmistakable sense of foreboding. The first thing I notice when I wake up is that it's raining outside—not just rain but a fully-fledged storm, thunder growling and lightning snapping like crazy. *Come on, sky,* I scold the clouds as I get ready. *You couldn't give me even the slightest hint of sun? A little bit of good luck for this sure-to-be terrible day?*

As I'm walking out the door, it strikes me that I might never see this room again. By the time the school day is done, the Rainloft very well could have hit the ground already. Then it occurs to me how pessimistic I'm being.

So I close my door and walk away without looking back, because I am most definitely going to see that room again. The Rainloft isn't coming down, not today, not ever. Not if I have anything to say about it.

Fiona escorts me down to the dining hall, where I take my daily mental headcount. A little while later, at lunch, I do the same thing. Ryn is eating innocently at the Type One table. Grayson and I exchange a glance between tables—he looks almost as jittery and nervous as I feel, which is somewhat comforting. Atlas is in the lunch line, not doing anything blatantly incriminating, unless you count ordering pineapple pizza. That's a federal offense in my mind.

The next few periods pass without incident. Soon I find myself sitting in what might be my last Rainloft History class—no, scratch that—what is *definitely not going to be my last Rainloft History class ever*, watching fat droplets of rain splatter against the window. Professor Becker's lecture is cut off by the shrill ring of her classroom telephone. We're all silent as she goes to answer it, and suspense builds as the phone call drags on. Once she finally slams the phone back onto its holder thing, her eyes narrow on Ryn from over her rhinestone-edged glasses.

"Miss Sharp," Becker snarls. "You've been summoned to the headmistress's office."

Predictably, all eyes are now on Ryn. "Why?" she asks defensively. "I didn't do anything wrong."

Becker purses her lips. "Hmm. I find that hard to believe. You should go now. Wouldn't want to keep the headmistress waiting."

I cringe when Ryn's chair screeches against the tile floor. She meets my eyes as she passes my desk. I shrug and immediately feel guilty about it.

Becker opens her mouth to continue her lecture, but the bell has the good nature to ring at that very moment. The classroom is empty in seconds. Most are heading straight to their next class, but I let curiosity get the better of me and wander off to Avalon's office instead.

The next bell has rung by the time I get there, meaning the hallways are virtually deserted now. The office door is closed and soundproof enough that I can't clearly make out anything they're saying inside, but that doesn't make a difference to me. It's not like I would eavesdrop if I could. That would be very rude and a huge invasion of privacy. I would never do that.

Now, the individual words they're saying are muffled, but I can definitely still pick up on volume—one minute,

Ryn and my mother are speaking at a normal level, then the next they're borderline shouting. But things de-escalate quickly and their voices are so quiet that I can barely hear anything at all.

The door opens. Ryn walks out, a whole spectrum of emotions playing across her face at once. She freezes when she sees me. "June?"

"Hey," I say naturally, trying to pretend I don't know exactly why Avalon wanted to see her. "What's going on? Are you in trouble or something?"

"No." She looks down, a distinct conflict in her voice. "June, Avalon just *apologized* to me. For what she did to my parents."

"Really?" I ask. When she's quiet for a moment, I ask tentatively, "Well… how do you feel about that? Do you forgive her?"

"What? No," Ryn says decisively. "Of course I don't forgive her. I mean, she sounded genuine, like she really felt bad, so I appreciate that. It's nice to know that she regrets what she did… but an apology doesn't make up for it. Nothing could. I guess it's nice that she tried though."

I nod. "Does that make you have any… I don't know… second thoughts about bringing down the Rainloft? Just grasping at straws here," I add, trying to suppress the hope in my voice.

She opens her mouth to respond, then closes it again. Her eyes narrow at me. "Why?"

"No reason."

She studies me a minute longer while I will myself not to give in and spill my guts to her. "Wait. Did you *know* about this?" she accuses.

"No." I bite my lip. "Yes."

"I knew it! You're a *really* bad liar," she remarks before she sighs, searching my expression. "I don't understand—why?"

I take a deep breath. "Look, there's no easy way to put this, but the Rainloft can't come down."

Her face drops. "What?"

So I tell her everything. How I so ignorantly agreed when she first suggested we bring down the Rainloft, only thinking of myself without bothering to consider what such a drastic change would mean for the rest of the world. How reading those newspapers back at the cabin made me realize just how huge a mistake we'd set ourselves up to make. How Avalon explained to me personally her reasoning behind founding the school, and how I later spilled our whole 'master plan' to her, basically making us teammates. I do omit the tiny little detail about Avalon being my mother, since that would require me to answer a whole lot of questions and I just don't have time to get into that right now. I tell Ryn how it was my idea to have the headmistress apologize for killing her parents.

"She really did mean it, though. Whatever she said," I say earnestly. "She was just afraid to say it before, because she knew no apology could never make up for what she did and apparently didn't see the point in trying."

Ryn nods thoughtfully. "Why didn't you tell me any of this earlier?" she asks. "Instead of, you know, *two hours* before we shut off the engine?"

"I should've," I admit, looking down at my shoes. "I just didn't want you to hate me. I haven't had a friend, a *real* friend, like you in a *long* time. I was too afraid of losing that, I guess."

"What?" Ryn says as if that's the dumbest thing she's ever heard. "June, I could never hate you. If you'd told me not to go through with it earlier, I would've listened. I trust you enough to tell me when I'm making a bad decision."

"Really?" I ask with a glimmer of hope. "So… does that mean you're not going to do it?"

She sighs. "Don't get me wrong—I'm not happy about

it. But if you really think bringing this place down is a bad idea, then I won't."

A massive wave of relief washes over me. "Thank you!"

"I have a feeling I'm not the problem though," she says, somewhat sadly. "Have you talked to Grayson or Atlas about it yet?"

"I got Grayson to agree yesterday using a pile of salt." When she just stares at me, I add, "Don't worry about it. But I still haven't talked to Atlas."

Ryn's eyebrows shoot up. "You haven't told him yet?" she asks. "*Yikes*. You really waited 'till the very last minute."

"I did," I say, the knot of unease in my stomach tightening. "But that shouldn't be a problem, right? He won't be *that* hard to convince."

"Okay. You keep telling yourself that."

I glance at the clock on the wall. Eighth period ends in five minutes, and it'll have to be within the next couple classes that my mother calls me and Atlas down to her office. I can't be absent when she calls my teacher. "We should go to class," I tell Ryn.

"Wait," says Ryn. "It's not too late to change your mind, you know. Are you sure this is what you want? We're going to be stuck in this place *forever*."

"Not necessarily," I shrug. "We could always go on another little vacation. I mean, it was pretty easy to escape last time. What are they going to do if we try it again? Expel us?"

A mischievous smile crosses her face. "Count me in." I thank her again before the bell beckons us to our next classes. I'm practically skipping down the hallway as I make my way to Calculations. *Two down, only one left to go.* Judging by how easy Ryn and Grayson were to sway, with my mother's help, it will be a breeze to win over Atlas. Right?

Everything is going to be fine.

The call doesn't come until dinnertime. Avalon sure is taking her sweet, sweet time to summon my brother and me to her office. Which is incredibly concerning, because if I do recall, Ryn's original plan said that we would infiltrate the control room *during dinner tonight*. I'm sitting in my assigned seat, fidgeting with my bracelet, my eyes on the clock above the dining hall doorway when one of the lunch monitors approaches me.

"Miss Winters, the headmistress needs to speak with you." She doesn't have to tell me twice. I'm up and out of the dining hall so fast I'm sure I leave my chair spinning like a dreidel in my wake. As I pass by the Type Two table, I note that Atlas isn't in his normal seat. I assume it's because he's already headed down to Avalon's office and make for the doors myself.

Unfortunately, my flight doesn't go unnoticed by my escort. "Wait!" Thomas cries after me. "Where are you going?"

"Headmistress Avalon's office. She called me down. You really don't have to follow me, Thomas," I insist. But he does anyway. It's not until we've reached the doors of my mother's office and he's assured that this isn't another escape attempt that he reluctantly leaves my side.

My mother sits at her desk, mask on, exactly as she was the last time I saw her. Across from her are two chairs. Both of them are empty.

"Where's Atlas?" I ask her.

"Oh, I'm not sure. I called him down, though," she replies, clearly not as worried as she probably should be. "We'll give him a few moments. Have a seat."

I lower myself into one of the two chairs across from her, still fidgeting. I can't shake the feeling that something's gone wrong. That there's a reason Atlas isn't here right now. Instinctively, I find the blue indicator light on the wall—the Escapee Alarm, the one that's supposed to start blaring if there's a student posing an immediate threat to the school. For the moment, it's still. I try to take that as a good sign.

"I had a thought," my mother says, rescuing me from my mind. "I'd like to run it by you before I propose it to your brother."

"Sure."

She hesitates. "June, our conversation last night made me think. I'd really love to get closer to you and Atlas. I know I've messed up in the past, repeatedly choosing the timeline over my family. But it doesn't have to be that way anymore. Not once you both know who I am."

"What are you saying?" I ask.

"Well, if it's alright with you," she starts, "I'd like to implement nightly family dinners. It could be just like this—you two could bring your food down to my office, and we would all eat together. And chat. As a normal family would do."

I feel my heart lift. "Really?"

"Yes, really." she smiles. "I know how much you hate it here, yet you've so nobly chosen not to act on that. So, as both a way to make your Rainloft experience slightly more bearable *and* a way to reconnect with my kids, I would love to give this to you. Only if you're okay with it, of course."

"Yes, absolutely, that sounds amazing," I say immediately, my smile threatening to split my face in two. Nightly family dinner. That's something I've missed for so, so long. Of course, it wouldn't be the same as it used to be—due to the obvious absence of my father, plus the clearly less-than-normal circumstances—but that doesn't matter. It would be like a piece of my old life, stitched onto the quilt of the new one that's been created for me. A piece of home in a place that's as far from homey as it gets. Plus, that's one meal less that I'd have to spend with Thomas and Fiona. That's a reason in itself to accept the offer.

Yet there's something that feels off about it. My smile fades. "Mom, it wouldn't be fair," I say. "Atlas and I got lucky. We're the only Rainloft students with a family that came here with us. Nobody else has that. It wouldn't be fair to give us special treatment just because we're your kids."

My mother frowns. "But I just thought, since you two have had a hard time here…"

"Everybody's had a hard time," I tell her. "We're not the only ones who were torn from our lives and stolen from our families the way we were. Believe me, nobody has had it easy here."

"Oh." She's quiet for a second, like this is news to her, though it really shouldn't be. "We don't have to do it, then. It was only an idea."

There's silence for a moment. That silence is promptly shattered by the Escapee Alarm. My gaze snaps up to the blue light on the wall, now flashing wildly with a frantic pattern of screeches to accompany that. Dread crashes over me. I look back to my mother, now on the phone, the visible portion of her face gone ghostly pale.

"It's your brother" is all she has to say.

"Let me handle it," I tell her brusquely as I fly out the door. I set off in the direction of the infamous control room, the hallway flashing bright blue under the light of the alarm.

"Wait! June!" Thomas wails after me. "You're not trying to escape, are you?"

Before I can stop myself I whirl to face him. "Thomas, you need to leave," I snap. "If I don't get to the control room in time, my brother is going to cut off the engine." I pause. "And I'm the only one who can stop him."

He eyes me suspiciously, then points down the corridor where we just came from and says "You're going the wrong way. The control room is on the opposite side of the school."

"Oh." Unfortunately, he's right. For the first time in as long as I've known him, Thomas is actually helpful. "Thanks."

I break into a run in that direction, my heart attacking my rib cage. I don't know exactly where the control room is, but I know it's at the nose of the airship, so I keep going until I reach a narrow hall at the furthermost end of the school.

When the alarm light flashes enough to illuminate the dark hallway, my breath catches in my throat. There are multiple leather-clad Alumni on the ground, every one of them unconscious. I'm forced to step over them to reach the door at the very end of the hall.

I brace myself, then shove it open.

The control room is a semicircle shape. The rounded part of the wall is covered by a large panoramic window showcasing the endless stretch of fluffy clouds below us. The control panel itself is large enough to warrant four different pilots to watch over it—every one of said pilots is lying unconscious on the ground now.

The button that controls the engine is unmistakable—large and bright red, straight out of a comic book. And of course, there in the middle of it all, his hand hovering just centimeters above that button, is Atlas.

Chapter Twelve

"Don't press that button!" I shout.

Atlas freezes but doesn't turn around from the control panel. "June, what are you doing here?" he asks, his voice low.

I'm standing in the doorway right now, breathless from sprinting across the entire school. The familiar rumble of the engine beneath my feet is louder in this room than anywhere else in the building. I take a second to gather my composure before I say, "You can't do this."

"Okay." He turns to face me, hands in the pockets of his jade green blazer. I don't see how he could've possibly known before this moment about my flip in allegiance, but somehow he doesn't seem surprised in the slightest. "Give me one good reason why not."

"Easy," I say. "If you shut off the engine, it will send this airship into a free fall straight to the ground. Not only will the entire school be absolutely obliterated, but there's an *extremely* low chance that everyone makes it out of the crash alive."

I glance out the window. The sheet of clouds below us looks like a fresh blanket of snow or a desert of powdered sugar, and for a second I can imagine that if we fall, we'll land safely on top of them. But that couldn't be any further from the truth.

"There are safe rooms for that," says Atlas simply. "Those rooms were designed to withstand the impact of a crash, for in case something like this ever happened. And as for the school, *that's the whole point!* We need the entire thing to be destroyed. So there's no chance Avalon could just haul us all back up here and start school right back up again."

"Have you ever considered that maybe this isn't all about us?" I ask, notes of desperation creeping into my tone. "Avalon founded this place for a reason. We students are the ones who keep the world intact, and without us, they'd have *nobody* to protect them. Nothing to prevent Lavon from slipping right back into a state of pure chaos, exactly the way it was before the founding."

"But the Rainloft is wrong," Atlas insists. There's an unmistakable tension hidden behind his cool front. "It's inhumane, what they do to us here. No kid should be forced to give up their entire life the way we were. I get that it's for the sake of the world and all that, but it's *not right*."

"Who are we, really, to decide between right and wrong?" I ask him. "Who are we to make that decision for the *entire world*? Yeah, the Rainloft can be cruel—I can't disagree with you there. But in the grand scheme of things, I think our sacrifice is balanced out by the sheer amount of good we bring to Lavon. Point is, there are two sides to everything. Just because we got the short end of the stick doesn't give us the right to ruin it for *everyone* else."

For the first time, I catch a flicker of something different in his eyes. Doubt. Atlas turns back to the control panel, unsure now. Like he's trying to hold on to something that's slipping away. "I could brainwash you," he says. "Make you change your mind."

"But you won't," I return. "That's not who you are."

"You don't know anything about me."

"Yes, I do. I'm your sister and I know you well enough to say, for a *fact*, that you're not the monster everyone thinks you are," I say decisively, taking a step closer to him. "But if you press that button, if you *knowingly* choose to doom the world this way, then I hate to say it but *you will be*. You can't keep letting other people tell you who you are, Atlas. You're my brother. Somewhere, deep down, you're still exactly the same person you were before the Rainloft. And you wouldn't do something like this. I know you wouldn't."

Silence. Nothing but the low drone of the engine and the tension in the air between us. I hold Atlas's gaze until his steely expression falters and he looks down at the ground. "I won't do it."

I barely even realize I've moved. In three strides, I've crossed the distance separating us and pulled my brother in for a hug. "I didn't think so," I murmur into his shoulder.

At first he stiffens, of course, but then all the fight leaves him and he hugs me back. It feels like a thousand-pound weight has been lifted off of my chest. And for the first time in a *long* time, I let myself believe that maybe—just maybe—everything's going to be okay after all.

"This is all my fault."

That doesn't come from me or Atlas. At the sound of the voice, Atlas immediately pulls away, his guard snapping back up again. I force myself to turn around and face the speaker even though I recognize the voice already.

Avalon. She stands in the doorway now, long black dress billowing silently behind her. Her feathered mask is clutched in one hand.

Meaning it's no longer on her face.

My stomach turns to ice. I curse myself for neglecting to mention this—arguably *the most significant detail*—in my explanation to Atlas. The second he sees her, every muscle in his body goes taut. "Mom?"

Our mother's expression melts. She moves across the room and before I have a chance to register what's happening, her arms are wrapped around Atlas. He doesn't resist it but he doesn't hug her back either. It's the strangest thing—he's almost the same height as her now, yet I've never seen him look so small.

"I'm so sorry," she says to Atlas. "I'm so, *so* sorry. For everything."

This is too much for him. At least all at once like this. So I step in, placing a hand on my mother's shoulder and lightly pulling her back. "Mom, what are you doing here?" I ask, searching her eyes. "I told you I would handle this, and I did."

"You did. Thank you for that." Then she shakes her head. "But I was wrong."

"What do you mean? Wrong about what?"

By way of response, she sweeps an arm around the room. Her hand is trembling. "All of this. I was wrong to do this to you. To everyone."

Suddenly I feel sick with unease. "Mom, what are you saying?"

"I'm saying that I never should've founded this place." There's a heavy weight behind her tone. "I never should've put you two through everything that I did. What kind of mother am I? What kind of mother traps her own kids inside of a floating prison and forces them to spend their entire childhoods there?" She looks to Atlas now. "What kind of mother sends droves of brainwashed, violent gunmen after her child following a simple act of rebellion? What kind of mother makes her own kids' lives absolutely miserable for the sake of something as intangible as a timeline?"

"Mom, stop—

"No." She looks between my brother and me through glassy eyes, one hand clutching her heart. "I'm done playing the role of Avalon. I'm done being the destroyer of lives, the dictator that everyone fears. It's high time I acted like the mother you two so deserve. I should've put family first all along." She takes a breath. "It's time for me to end this."

In one fluid motion, she steps up to the control panel and presses the red button.

There's a split second of silence. Then the hum of the engine beneath us begins to wind down, slowly at first. Like a dying breath. The alarm light that had flashed blue just moments ago blooms scarlet across the control room, painting our mother's face the color of blood.

"Emergency descent in progress," a voice crackles over the PA system. "Locate a safe room immediately."

Before I can even begin to grasp the magnitude of what's happening, our mother spins to face us. "There's a safe room down the hall," she says. "We have to go."

She seizes Atlas and me by the wrists and then we're moving. Just as we're leaving the control room, the floor starts to drop out from under me. My stomach jumps into my throat—it's like the feeling you get on the drop of a roller coaster, only one-thousand percent more deadly.

Things go from bad to worse in a matter of seconds. I have no choice but to forget about everything that just happened in the control room and make a hard shift into survival mode. I'm putting my life in my mother's hands by trusting her to guide us to safety. *Don't think, just run,* I tell myself but I can hardly hear my thoughts over the cacophony of screeching metal and deafening howl of wind. The entire hallway sways dangerously like a ship on stormy waters. Every step I take feels wrong, my feet connecting less and less each time they strike the ground. At one point I can pretend I'm floating. But I'm jolted back into reality when gravity snaps back and launches me straight into the wall.

I barely have a chance to register the pain before my mother yanks me back to my feet. And then we're running again. I'm vaguely aware of the stitch in my side, but I force myself to concentrate on the only thing that matters right now: not dying.

Above my head, a light fixture bursts with a *pop*. We're showered in a sizzling hail and I instinctively duck down, but my mother doesn't stop. She doesn't let go of me or Atlas until we've reached a heavy-looking door at the very back of a hallway I've never seen before.

She pulls the door open and pushes the two of us inside. The space is completely empty, its walls made of sturdy-looking metal with a thick railing that wraps around the whole room.

I turn to face my mother, expecting her to follow us inside. But something's wrong. She lingers just outside the door, her face gone ghostly pale. "Mom?" I say, panic rising in my throat. "What are you doing? What's wrong?"

"The pilots," she says. "And the guards. They're still unconscious in the control room. They won't make it to safety in time."

Those words hit me like a punch to the face. I don't even have to ask what she's implying. "Mom, no, you can't go back, you'll die."

"I'll go back," says Atlas, finally snapped out of his shock. "I knocked them out in the first place. I should be the one to go back and wake them up."

Our mother shakes her head softly. She seems oddly at peace with her decision, even though I am anything but. "Mom, please don't—it's too risky." I'm practically begging her now, even though I have this sinking feeling that she's right. Somebody has to go back for the Alumni, and the fact that she has all five of the powers on her side makes her more qualified than either of us.

She leans in to plant a kiss on each of our foreheads—first Atlas, then me. Her hand lingers on my cheek for a split second longer than it should. "I love you both," she says softly.

And then she turns.

Before I can do anything about it, she pulls the door shut. It closes with a hiss of pressure that seals her fate.

I'm left staring at the metal door, at my own warped reflection, too stunned to do anything else. "No, no, no," I murmur, shaking my head.

It doesn't cross my mind that the ship is still crashing until gravity yanks the floor out from under me and I'm sent reeling into the wall. Atlas manages to grab the railing. He catches my arm just in time, keeping me from hitting the metal head-on.

There's a fleeting moment of safety where we both have a solid grip on the railing. I press my back against the wall, my fingers locked around the metal, hoping with all the hope I have left that it'll make a difference when the ship makes impact.

It doesn't.

Without any sort of warning, the room pitches violently in the other direction. I'm ripped from the railing and hurled at full force into the opposite wall. My right shoulder hits first, followed by the side of my head.

Stars explode behind my eyes. Pain blooms across my forehead, blinding and intense. Immediately, I lose all sense of direction as I lie flat on my back, staring up as the features of the room blur. I think someone shouts my name but I can hardly hear it over the ring in my ears. I try to reach out and grab onto the railing, but my hand feels heavy and strange.

I can't fight the black vignette that closes in on my field of vision. All the chaos fades into silence as the world goes dark.

Chapter Thirteen

I wake up to a cacophony of chaos. My eyes snap open and everything hits me at once—smoke is swirling above me, turning the wide-open sky a dreadful shade of gray. I'm lying in a small patch of gravel surrounded by twisted metal. My head is pounding and my ears are ringing and the faint scent of something metallic meets my nostrils— I think it's blood and the thought is terrifying.

Shakily, I push myself into an upright position, sharp pieces of gravel digging into my palms. My mind is foggy and I can hardly form a complete thought. *Hands… legs… nothing broken… good,* I think. Slowly, I get to my feet. There's a dull, throbbing pain in my right temple and I can't help but wince when I touch it. When I pull my hand back, there's blood on my fingers. *Strange,* I think, my mind still too muddled to fully process the extent of my injuries. But then a realization cuts through the haze like a dagger: *my family.*

The last thing I remember before I blacked out was being thrown by gravity into a wall. My brother was in the room too, I think. Fog blocks out most memories I have of what led up to that moment, but there's this lingering sense of dread that tells me maybe I don't want to remember. "Atlas?" I call out.

My worries are extinguished by a distant "Here." I look toward the source of the voice to find what I think used to be the roof of a classroom. Somehow it pancaked cleanly on top of the rest of the wreckage when the ship hit the earth, and now it stands like a metal stage overlooking the area. Atlas stands on top of it with his back turned.

He hardly glances in my direction when I clumsily make my way up there to stand next to him. The color of his once-vibrant green uniform is dulled by a layer of soot and stained by blood from the long gash across his face. Other than that, though, he doesn't seem too badly injured.

I open my mouth to say something, but my words die on my tongue the second I see the view from here. I knew that if the airship crashed, it would be bad. After all, it would be impossible for any vessel even close to the Rainloft's size to land gracefully. But nothing could've prepared me for what I'm looking at now.

Ruin. As far as the eye can see.

It stretches on for miles—the point where the wreckage ends is out of my sight and hidden by smoke. The classrooms I used to spend my days in are all destroyed, desks reduced to nothing but charred blobs of metal, shards of whiteboards scattered across the wreck. It's like someone took a colossal box of scrap metal and tipped it over in the sky.

"What in the world did we do now?" Atlas murmurs. Teachers and students in their colorful uniforms dot the endless expanse of gray, the size of ants from my vantage point. Many of them are up and moving around, making their way toward safety. Many of them are not.

It strikes me just how lucky we are to have made it out of this alive—not to mention relatively unscathed. There must've been a stampede to the safe rooms the second that alarm went off. In the two minutes we had after my mother hit that button, the odds that everybody made it to safety in time are heartbreakingly low.

My mother.

She never made it back to our safe room.

The full force of that statement hits me at once and I'm shoved into action. Before I can begin to process what I'm doing, I've pinpointed the remains of the control room and jumped down from the platform.

"June, what are you—?" Atlas starts, but I'm already running. I fly through the wreckage and dodge the jagged shards of metal jutting out at me in every direction, focused on one thing and one thing only.

"Mom?" I shout out, smoke straining my voice. In the back of my mind I know that there's no chance she survived the crash. The closest safe room to the control panel was the one that Atlas and I were in. And she never came back there after she left.

But still I press on. Alive or not, I have to find her. I owe it to myself. Closure is something I never really got after her disappearance so long ago. I spent every day after wondering if she would ever come back, my hope for her return dying more and more as the time passed by. If she's gone, for real this time, then I need to see it for myself. As much as I know it will kill me, I need to find her and verify that my mother isn't coming back.

Then again, though, maybe she's alive. Maybe she made it to a different safe room or found some other way to survive the impact. It wouldn't be the first time she's managed the impossible.

But as soon as I find her, I know it's too late.

My breath catches at the sight of her body. She's lying on the ground, half covered in shattered glass and bits of scorched metal. For a second—one terrible, cruel second—I think maybe she's just unconscious and my heart lifts.

But then I see the massive shard of glass—probably from the control room's giant window—buried deep inside of her chest. It's placed in a spot that leaves no doubt multiple vital organs have been destroyed, but in case of some off chance that she'll pull through I drop to my knees beside her.

When I check her wrist for a pulse, against all odds I find one. There's a beat of silence. Then her hand snaps up and locks around my wrist.

I sit there, holding my breath as her pale eyes flutter open and find my own. "Mom," I say through a sigh of relief. I glance back at her wound. "Don't worry, we'll find you help, just hang on a minute, you'll be fine…"

I trail off when she shakes her head. It's small, virtually imperceptible and looks like it causes her a whole world of pain, but it's enough to send a whole tsunami of dread crashing down on me.

"Thank you."

Her voice is faint and fraying at the edges—a stark contrast to my own. "Wh—thank me?" I panic. "Why? Why are you thanking me?"

"Because you did it," she says. "You fulfilled the timeline. You… you not only found a way to end the timeline in the way it was intended, but you've righted my great wrong in the process. Thank you for that."

"But that wasn't me, that was *you*. You brought down the Rainloft," I say, talking fast. "You righted that wrong yourself."

In answer, she shakes her head again. "June… listen to me. You helped me achieve my future. Now it's time you start paving your own. It's time you start *living*. Be young. Laugh way too loud. Live… like you were never a part of this nightmare. Live the life *you* want to live and please—*please* don't let my choices hold you down."

In this moment, she's not Avalon. She's not the infamous founder of the Rainloft, the ruthless destroyer of lives. All those emotional layers fall away and now here I am, playing firsthand witness to the death of my mother. The woman who took us out for dessert so often that the bakery staff knew us by name. Who bought me roller skates and was there to clean my wounds every time I fell down. The woman who watched TV with me late into the night and pushed me on the swings and never failed to be there when I needed her the most. It's just her, plain and true.

"Mom, stop it," I say sharply, blinking back tears. "You're not dying. We're *going* to get you help." Still clutching her hand, I spin around to find Atlas standing a few paces away. "What are *you* doing?" I cry. "Don't just stand there, go find help!"

"No." My mother's voice is barely above a whisper now. "That won't be necessary."

"But—"

"I love you, June," she says. "I love you both—so much."

"I love you too," I manage just as her eyelids fall shut.

And then she's gone. She lets out one final breath and then goes still. I stay right there, holding her hand as its warmth fades, tears rolling silently down my cheeks.

I don't know how long I sit there, but it must be a while because at some point Atlas crouches down next to me and lays a hand on my shoulder. "June, she's gone," he says softly.

"I know." I nod and swipe at my eyes with the back of my free hand. It takes every ounce of my will to let go of my mother and let Atlas help me to my feet.

There's a beat of silence before the sound of footsteps crunching on gravel behind me cuts through my cloudiness. Before I have a chance to realize what's happening, Ryn bursts through the wreckage and throws her arms around Atlas and me.

"Oh, thank goodness you're both okay," she gushes. Grayson stands a few feet behind her. Despite everything that just happened, I can't help but feel a rush of relief that they're both alive. *Two fewer people that I'll have to mourn.*

Ryn pulls back. She looks slightly worse for wear, but somehow not at all like she was just in the same catastrophic crash the rest of us were. When she sees my tear-streaked face, her wide smile immediately flips to concern. "Are you okay?"

"I'm fine." I plaster across my face the best smile I can manage at the moment. Which proves to be a pointless waste of effort because Ryn doesn't look convinced in the slightest.

She opens her mouth to say something, but Grayson cuts her off. "Uh, guys?" he says uneasily. "Is this… Avalon?"

I can't bring myself to turn and face my mother's lifeless body again. "Yeah, that's Avalon," I mutter, my eyes on the ground. Ryn's gaze bounces between me and the headmistress, clearly trying to make the dots connect. Thankfully, Atlas does the explaining for me.

"Avalon was… our mom," he says.

"*What*?" Ryn bursts out. "She was your *mom*? Why didn't you tell me before? And—*how?*"

"No clue. I just found out an hour ago."

"That's… wow."

At some point, their conversation starts to fade into the background. It grows strangely muffled, replaced by a dull ringing in my ears. My mind is a mess. I can't process all of this right now. But there's something my mother said before she died that's been replaying itself in my head, over and over again. *You fulfilled the timeline.*

I think back to the conversation I had with her. When she explained everything over ice cream in olden-day Lebanon. She told me that everything she'd done as Avalon—starting the Rainloft, selecting Atlas and me as students—it was all to keep the timeline intact. She told me she'd seen the future, how said timeline was supposed to 'end'. And that was with a catastrophic, world-altering disaster.

This—the fall of the Rainloft—is that disaster. There's no question about it. When she traveled into the future and saw what she claimed looked like 'the end of the world', it was this. But I can't shake the feeling that there's more to it. I rack my brain, trying to grasp all the hazy details of that conversation. There was a reason she was so insistent on making sure my brother and I made it to this specific version of the future. That we ended up here, in the middle of all this.

Then it hits me.

"June?"

The sound of my name jolts me back into reality. At some point while I was lost in thought, I started wandering off from the group without realizing it. When I turn back to face the three of them, they're all staring at me like I'm crazy.

"We have to help," I say decisively. That only seems to confuse them more, so I look to my brother and elaborate. "Atlas, it was Mom's lifelong goal to get us to this exact version of the future. That was so we could help people out of this wreck. She told me she saw us here, on this day, helping out like a beacon of light in a sea of tragedy or whatever. We have to do it. To make all her efforts worthwhile."

I realize too late that probably did nothing to alleviate the confusion, but Atlas nods anyway. "Okay."

"There are first responders, though," Grayson points out. "You don't think they've got it covered?"

"All of *this*?" I ask, sweeping an arm around the endless expanse of ruin. "Plus, we have *powers*. That automatically makes us more qualified than any first responder to help."

"Alright then," says Ryn. "Let's do it."

And so we do. We finally find the point where the rubble fades into a vast green field where rows of fire trucks and ambulances are lined up. Atlas and I start guiding lost survivors in that direction. Ryn uses her powers to free those who are trapped, and Grayson gets the more severely injured out of the wreckage via teleportation. Using my extensive amount of medical knowledge, I help bandage up minor cuts and scrapes while Atlas rounds up paramedics for those who need them the most.

By the time we're all too exhausted to keep going, the sky has gone dark and the smoke has thinned enough for stars to shine through it. The four of us find a spot to sit in the field just outside of the wreck.

I've in no way forgotten about my mom, but I feel better now. Lighter. She's gone, but she finally accomplished the goal she'd spent her whole life chasing. She got to see her efforts pay off before the end. I made that possible. At least for now, the thought of that is enough to put my cares to rest.

Tons of civilians' cars have begun to pour onto the field. Terrified parents step out of their vehicles, horror etched across their faces as they scan the crowds for their kids.

"There are so many," Ryn remarks, her face lit up by distant headlights. "Even in a crash this devastating, all those people still have enough hope to drop everything and come look for their kids. It's so tragic and so beautiful at the same time." She turns to the rest of us. "I think we should play I Spy. Let's play I Spy. Grayson, you go first."

We all look at Grayson expectantly, but he just stares straight ahead. "I see my family."

"Wait, really? You do?" I ask.

He's on his feet in an instant. "Yeah." He turns to wave goodbye to us before breaking into a run toward a group of people I recognize immediately from the pictures around his cabin. As soon as Grayson's family sees him, he disappears into the biggest group hug I've ever seen. I can't help but grin.

"Good for him," says Ryn, her smile fading. "Guess it's just us three now."

I can't speak for Ryn, but one glance at Atlas's expression tells me we're both thinking the same thing: there's probably no one coming for us. I have very little doubt about that. The only family we have left is our father. Neither one of us has seen said father in nearly half a decade, nor do we have any evidence to confirm that he hasn't fallen off the face of the earth in that span of time. We don't have the slightest indication of his whereabouts or current situation. The fact that both of his kids are wanted criminals is just the cherry on top of it all. When you put it that way, I'd say there's not much reason to be optimistic right now.

I watch as Ryn scans the growing mass of people, her eyes never settling in one place for long. "Someone will come. I'm sure of it," I tell her, then immediately wish I could swallow my words. Given what I know of her family situation before the Rainloft, her odds are even worse than my own. I am in no position to make promises like that.

Ryn just shakes her head. "I don't think so," she says, picking at the dried-out blades of grass by her feet. "Before I was taken to the Rainloft, I was staying at my grandparents' house. Now who knows if they're still… or if they'd even *bother*, you know, after—"

She cuts herself off with a sharp gasp. I follow her gaze to an older woman standing by the edge of the crowd, wearing a sweater with a clock stitched into it and an expression that's just as gobsmacked as Ryn's.

"I have to go," Ryn breathes. Before I can begin to process that sentence, she's gone. The woman meets her halfway, running at a shocking speed for an old lady. Ryn throws her arms around her grandmother, her grandma hugs her tight and that's the last thing I see before they disappear into the crowd.

I let myself be happy for her for a minute, then sigh, turning to Atlas. "Maybe he just hasn't gotten here yet," I shrug, infusing my tone with as much optimism as I can muster up. "He might live, like, halfway across the country now."

"You never know," he agrees. We're quiet as we search for familiar faces in the sea of people, both our optimism dimming as minutes drag by.

Then Atlas freezes. "June."

"What?"

I spot him just before Atlas points him out and instantly stop breathing. Standing there, the headlights of his old SUV silhouetting him like a spotlight, his familiar blue eyes wide with disbelief, is our father.

I reach him first. Atlas is only half a step behind. Our dad catches us both in one embrace. It's rib-crushing and bear-like and kind of terrible—and it's what makes me believe, for real this time, that everything's going to be okay after all.

Things aren't going back to the way they were. I know that much. Nothing will be the same as it was during or even before the Rainloft's existence. But still, for the first time, I don't need to see the future to know that everything's going to be alright.

And that's more than enough for me.

Acknowledgements

Special Thanks:

Brace yourself, because this acknowledgements section is about to be longer than the story itself.

Calling the process of writing this book 'a journey' doesn't even begin to describe it. I started writing it way back when I was thirteen, just starting the eighth grade, and now I'm almost sixteen and the book is *finally* done. This was easily the hardest, most complicated story I've written yet. There were multiple occasions along the way when I was ready to hit *delete* on the entire document and/or chuck my computer across the room. There were also times where I decided to put the story down forever, only to come back to it a few months later and realize, *wait, I actually want to finish this.* And I'm glad I did, because as grueling as the whole process was, I now have my sixth book to show for my efforts. I definitely didn't do it all alone, though. I'll stop rambling now and get to actually thanking people.

First of all, a huge thanks to Grandpa, obviously. It always felt like you cared about this book just as much as I did, and I loved having someone so invested in the story to bounce ideas off of. Thanks to Mom and Dad for taking the time out of your busy schedules to read over the book and help me with the formatting/technical details of it all. I really appreciate the work you put into my books, as tedious and uninteresting as it can be. Special thanks to my wonderful sister Addie for requesting access to my document because she wanted to 'read it,' then proceeding to highlight the entire thing and drop a comment on it saying "I don't like this book." I truly appreciate you. Thanks to all my friends for providing much-needed distractions from this book and thanks to the rest of my family for always supporting me. That includes my lovely dogs Sam, Bartlet and Arlo, plus our food-obsessed cats Simon and I guess maybe even Celeste.

Final Manuscript Line and Copy Edits: Jessica Smithers, Jason Smithers

Cover Art: Cover art created using AI-assisted design tools. Concept and final edits by Jason Smithers and Maci Smithers

Cover Design and Type: Amanda Tuttle

ABOUT THE AUTHOR

Maci is a six-time self-published author. At the age of eight, she told her parents she wanted to write and illustrate a book. Her parents explained that if she learned to do every part of the process, including storyboarding, writing, illustrating, page layout, and choosing fonts, alongside her dad, they would help her self-publish it. Within just a few months, she completed her first picture book, *Maci and Addie's Fairy Adventure*, followed by her second, *The Portal*.

During the challenging year that was 2020, when most kids were faced with adversity, ten-year-old Maci harnessed her creative spirit and a bit of boredom to complete her first novella, *Ally Lancaster & The Enchanted Fortress*, marking her third literary endeavor. Two years later, at age twelve, she finished its sequel, *Ally Lancaster & The Gemstone Sirens*. While wrapping up that project, she began exploring an idea for a middle-grade time travel mystery that became her third novella, *The Stone of the Past*.

Her sixth and newest book, *The Rainloft Academy*, marks her debut young adult novel, a thrilling story about a girl discovering the hidden truth behind a school for gifted students and the mysterious disappearance of her brother.